Short Stories
for Long Days

Short Stories
for Long Days

S.A. Horwitz

This is a work of fiction. Names, characters, places and incidents either are
the product of the author's imagination or are used fictitiously, and any
resemblance to any actual persons, living or dead, events, or locales is entirely
coincidental.

This book was printed in the United States of America.

To order additional copies of this book, contact:
Xlibris Corporation
1-888-795-4274
www.Xlibris.com
Orders@Xlibris.com
20925

Contents

TO HAVE A CHILD

Ed was known as a young man in a hurry. He had only been in the office for three years and he was already more than halfway up the corporate ladder. This particular afternoon he was not in a hurry. It was six o'clock, he was the last to leave the office, and he moved slowly. Visiting hours at the hospital were not over until eight o'clock and he didn't like to get there until the crowd had left. Ellen was in a private room with a private nurse so he could visit any time. He was depressed about Ellen's problem, and he hated to eat in a restaurant alone which is what he had been doing since her hospitalization.

Ellen wasn't ill, she had had surgery. Ed memorized what it was: panhysterectomy and bilateral salpingo-oophorectomy. That meant her uterus, tubes, and ovaries were removed. Ed and Ellen had just been married a year. She was young and beautiful and obsessed with love for Ed. They had both wanted children but before she could become pregnant she began to bleed from fibroids. Nothing medical could adequately control it so surgery had to be done. The surgeon said he would ordinarily leave her ovaries in but because her mother had died of an ovarian cancer he asked her what she would prefer. Ellen elected to have them removed and relieve herself at least from that worry.

Ed didn't like looking forward to a life without children and had been considering his options. Before the surgery he had suggested to Ellen that if she kept her ovaries they could have in vitro fertilization and a surrogate mother to carry the baby. Ellen didn't like that idea, and anyway was afraid of cancer. Now the ovaries were gone and so was any chance of Ellen having a child.

Ellen's three to eleven nurse was a pleasant, cheerful, good-looking young woman in her mid-twenties, a few years younger than Ellen. She was doing her best to keep Ellen comfortable and occupied to minimize the inevitable depression. This was the evening of the third post-operative day. Ellen got walked in the morning and again in the afternoon, then had a nap. She and Sandy, her nurse, were watching television when Ed walked in. He walked over to Ellen and kissed her, saw what they were watching and said, "Don't turn it off. I'll watch the end of the program with you and then we'll talk."

Talk they did. Ellen said she had slept so much during the day she wasn't sleepy and kept Ed until it was time for the third shift of nurses to come on. Sandy went out to give her report and Ellen said, "Ed, could you give Sandy a lift home. Her car is laid up and she will have to take a cab. This is Friday, you don't have to get up early tomorrow."

"Sure," said Ed, "if you want me to. I hope she doesn't live out in the country someplace."

Sandy didn't live out in the country but by the time they got to her apartment it was midnight. On the way in they had talked about Ellen and her depression. Ed acknowledged he was depressed too. Ever since college he had been planning to have a wife, a home, a family, and a dog. He now had the wife, the home, and the dog.

Without a family and without the prospect of one he felt incomplete.

"Sandy," he said as they pulled up to her place, "I think you got yourself into a tough case."

Sandy put her hand on Ed's. "It will work out," she said, "would you like to come up for a cup of coffee before you go home?"

"Yes, I would like that. I've had a long day and I'm tired. It will keep me awake for the drive home."

In the apartment Sandy went into the kitchen to make the coffee. Ed sat down in a big comfortable chair and promptly fell asleep. Sandy went into her bedroom took off her uniform then decided to get all undressed and into her nightgown and robe. When she came out, Ed was still asleep. She woke him up and they went into the kitchen for the coffee. Ed wanted to know something about her.

"Not much to tell," she said, "I'd like a family too, but I have no husband and I broke up with my boyfriend. I guess maybe we have something in common."

"You'll have no problem. You'll find a man who wants a family. So far, I see no solution to my problem."

"Ellen told me something about you. You're a bright man, you'll work something out."

"I hope so. Thanks for the coffee, I'm sure I'll stay awake long enough to get home. Will I see you tomorrow?"

"Yes, I'll be working tomorrow."

"Will you have your car back?"

"No, not until sometime next week."

"I'm taking next week off from work. If you don't get your car back I'll be glad to drive you home."

"Thanks, I appreciate that."

Ed took Sandy home the next five nights, stopping in her apartment each night for coffee. They talked a lot and

Ed looked forward to those evenings. The fifth night, Wednesday, while they were having their coffee Sandy said, "Ed, I'm not working tomorrow, I've got a substitute for Ellen. She really doesn't need me now, she'll be going home in a day or two. I'd like to make dinner for you here before you go to the hospital. Will you come?"

"I'd love to. I'm long overdue for a home cooked meal."

Ed came with a bottle of wine. When the meal was over they each had had just one glass. Ed was getting ready to go back to the hospital when Sandy said, "Ed, will you come back after the hospital? We really should finish the wine."

"I will, thank you. That will be much better than going home to an empty house."

Ed came back to the apartment before eleven. "Ellen looked tired, I thought she needed her sleep."

"Yes, depression is fatiguing. You must know, Ed."

"I do, Sandy, and I don't know how to get out of it."

"For starters, let's finish the wine."

They finished the wine and both were feeling relaxed. Ed was quiet, wondered whether he should tell Sandy he was attracted to her.

"You're so quiet. What are you thinking, Ed?" Sandy inquired.

"I'm thinking you're a damn attractive woman and I haven't had any sex in a long time. Don't be frightened. I don't make passes, not physically anyway. Have you got yourself a new boyfriend?"

"Not yet. You're the only boyfriend I've got now."

"I'm flattered that you call me your boyfriend."

"I wish you were really my boyfriend. I wish you weren't married. I'm getting awfully fond of you—I think I must be getting drunk."

She got up and walked over to Ed, sat on his lap, and gave him a long erotic kiss. "Let's go to bed," she said, "your blood alcohol is too high to drive home anyway."

"I don't know," said Ed, "I've never cheated on Ellen before."

"She won't mind, considering her indisposition. Besides, if you don't tell her she's not going to know."

He began to unbutton her blouse. "Sandy, you knew damn well I couldn't resist you."

That was the beginning.

With her post-op condition and her depression, Ellen was not up for sex for three months. During that time Ed and Sandy had an ongoing sexual relationship whenever Sandy's schedule permitted and Ed could find an excuse to get away from work or home. Ellen was too involved with her depression to notice.

Ellen had her last appointment with her doctor on a Friday. After dinner that night she said to Ed, "My doctor told me I was depressed and would stay depressed until I talked to you about what's on my mind. He wants me to call him in two weeks and if I'm not coming out of it he wants to refer me to a psychiatrist."

"All right, Ellen, tell me."

"I'm depressed because I'm sterile and I know you want a family. Oh, Ed, what are we going to do?"

"I don't know. I've been doing a lot of thinking about it. Have you considered adoption?"

"I've thought about it. If that's what you want, I'd go along with it."

"I'd prefer my own, but I think that's the next best."

"You can have your own. I'll give you a divorce if you want it."

"Oh, Ellen, then what will you do?"

"I'll kill myself."

Ed got up and went to Ellen. He kissed her and embraced her and said, "Ellen, if you did that, it would kill me too. I love you, Ellen, much more than I would love a family." He went on, "Ellen, I'll do whatever you want. You'll have to decide about adoption. Either way it will be okay with me. I just want you, and I want you to be happy."

"Thank you, Ed. I feel better. The doctor said I could have sex now and I would like that, how about it?"

"It's been a long time, Ellen, I thought you'd never get back to it."

The next day Ed said he had to finish up some work at the office and went directly to Sandy's apartment. He had decided this was the time to end the affair.

Sandy let him in and before he could open his mouth said, "Ed, I'm glad you came. I've got big news for you." She closed the door. "I'm pregnant!"

"My god," said Ed. He walked into the living room and sat down without taking off his coat. "I thought I had the big news today, but I think you topped me."

"What's your news?"

"I was going to tell you our affair is over. Ellen is back in my bed and I'm going to stay with her. She said she was willing to give me a divorce so I could have my own child and when I asked her what she would do then, she said she would kill herself, and I believe she would. I couldn't live with that."

"It's all right, Ed, I'll have an abortion."

"Wait a minute. That's my child. I couldn't live with that either."

"Ed, be sensible. You can't have it both ways."

"I'd like to. I'd like to have you, Ellen, and the baby.

"Ed, I've had a chance to think about this and you haven't.

I'll tell you what I've decided and then you can think

about it for a day or two, no more than that. I've decided I don't want this baby unless you marry me. I've made an appointment to have an abortion in three days."

"Does it have to be that soon."

"Yes. I can't have it hanging over my head; the sooner the better."

Ed slowly took off his coat. "If you'll give me a drink and a half hour maybe we can come to a decision," he said.

"What will it be?"

"Bourbon on the rocks for me, nothing for you. If the decision is to keep the baby it's no alcohol, drugs, or bad health habits for you. I'm glad you don't smoke."

Ed took ten minutes to finish half his drink. Neither Sandy nor he had said a word. He spoke first, "Sandy, would you be willing to come home with me so you, Ellen, and I can talk about this together?"

"I think that would be a mistake. Ellen has already indicated what she would do: give you a divorce and kill herself. She may decide just to kill herself and save the trouble of a divorce."

"This sounds like you've decided you have no choice but must have an abortion."

"I only decided that after you told me you planned to stay with Ellen."

"You already had the appointment."

"That was just in case. I can always cancel it."

"Sandy, I have a crazy idea. Tell me if you'll go for it. Would you be willing to share me with Ellen?"

"Ed, I'm not going to be your mistress and give birth to your bastard."

"Would you be my wife and let Ellen be my mistress?"

"Would Ellen go for that?"

"If you would I think she might. We could ask her."

"If I were in Ellen's place and you told me about an affair you had had with me and then presented this proposition, I would want to kill you and me. That's no good, Ed. Look, if

I hadn't gotten pregnant this would all have been so simple. We would end the affair, Ellen would never know, and we would all live happily ever after."

"I wouldn't be happy, would you?"

"I guess not for awhile, but I'd get over it, and so would you."

"I don't know. You haven't answered my question."

"What question?"

"Would you be willing to marry me if Ellen were to be my mistress? Yes or no."

"Yes."

"Even if we all lived in the same house? Yes or no."

"Yes."

"All right. I'll talk to her. If you don't hear from me, go ahead with the abortion and send me the bills." Ed got up and went on, "Well, 'if 'twere be done, 'tis better it be done quickly.' That's how I remember it, I'm sure Will said it better."

"Wait a minute, Ed, you're no Shakespeare. It might be better if I spoke to Ellen."

"Do you mean that?"

"Of course I mean it."

"Do you want me there?"

"Hell, no."

"When will you do this?"

"Now. You go on to your office. I'll call her and ask her if I can come over. Stay in your office and wait for a call from me or Ellen before you come home."

"All right. Good luck!"

Ellen was surprised and pleased to hear from Sandy. She hugged and kissed her when she arrived, and Sandy returned the affectionate greeting.

They spent fifteen minutes in small talk and then Sandy said, "Ellen, I'm in trouble and it involves you. We have to make some decisions."

Ellen didn't answer. Sandy went on, "You had asked Ed to take me home. He did, every night while you were in the hospital. We became friends, and, slowly, more than friends. Today, on his way to the office, he stopped at my apartment and told me our affair was over. I told him I was pregnant."

"Are you?"

"Yes."

"You did it deliberately."

"Yes."

"Now you want me to give him up so you can marry him."

"That's up to you. I told him I would have an abortion. I have an appointment in three days."

"Fine. Keep it." Ellen stood up. My guess is you seduced him into the affair, misled him about birth control, and now want to marry him. You think you can get away with it because you know how badly he wants a child. Well, I'm not going to give him up."

Sandy remained seated. She said, "You're right on all counts, Ellen, and you have good reason to be angry, but don't make a bad situation worse. Sit down and let's talk about the consequences of what you decide."

Ellen sat down again and said, "Okay, I'm listening."

Sandy went on, "Ed told me two things: he didn't want to lose you, and he didn't want to lose the baby I'm carrying."

"Looks to me like he's going to have to make the choice."

"That's what I told him but he suggested a way out. I told him I would be willing if you would. He said he would talk to you about it but I suggested it would be better if I did. If you don't agree I will have the abortion and that will be the end of it. I won't see Ed again.

The way out that he suggested was that we share him. We will all live together in this or another house. You will give him a divorce and I will marry him so the baby will have his name as well as his genes. We will both share his bed.

"Before you say, 'No', let me warn you that if I have an abortion Ed will blame you for killing his child. He may not ever mention it but it will never leave his mind and he will never forgive you."

Ellen said, "I have to think. Do you want a cup of tea?"

"Thank you. I feel I could stand a martini but as long as I'm pregnant I'm off alcohol. Tea will be fine."

Ellen came back with a tray: cookies and tea. She poured two cups and handed one to Sandy and then passed her the cookies. "That five minutes gave me time to cool down a little," she said, "You know, Sandy, the worst part of this whole business is that I liked you. Even now I can't hate you. Ed is no infant, he has equal responsibility. It's not all your fault."

Sandy said nothing. Ellen went on, "My initial impulse was to tell you to have the abortion and get out of my life and Eds, but I think you're right about Ed. He would never forgive me." She drank some tea and ate a cookie then continued, "I can't agree to you coming into this house to be the lady of the house. If I give Ed a divorce the house will be mine and you will be wife number two, I will be number one and Ed and I will share the master bedroom."

Sandy said, "You will have the house and Ed; what will I have?"

"You will have his name and his child."

"That's not enough. If I can't share him the deal's off."

"How much of a share do you want? I won't give up the master bedroom."

"I'm willing to leave that to Ed so long as you don't retaliate, verbally or otherwise, when he comes into my bed."

"I don't know, Sandy, I don't think this will work. I don't think I could tolerate that arrangement. Maybe you better just go ahead and have the abortion. Be noble. Tell him you had a miscarriage."

Neither woman said anything. They finished their tea.

"Is that your final word?" Sandy asked.

"Yes. I'll take my chances with Ed's feelings. We'll both have some forgiving to do."

The women stood up and neither spoke again until Sandy

was leaving when she said, "Ellen, Ed's at the office waiting to hear from you before he comes home. Will you call him?"

"Of course. Good-bye. I hope not to see you again."

"Good-bye, Ellen."

Right after she closed the door Ellen called Ed. He answered the phone immediately.

"Hello, Ed," Ellen said, "Sandy has just left. You can come home now."

"Do you want to tell me anything now?"

"No."

"I'll be home as soon as I can."

"Don't speed. This is not an emergency."

"Okay, good-bye."

Ed let himself in and found Ellen sitting in the dark. "Is it all right if I turn on a light?" he asked.

"Sure."

He turned on the light and took a long look at Ellen. "I'm sorry about this, Ellen. I assume Sandy told you the whole story." He continued looking at her. "I would like you to stand up so I can take you in my arms and kiss you."

"I think I better stay sitting, Ed, if I stood up I would just feel like a rag to you. I'm in a state of shock."

Ed sat down. "Ellen, if I had it to do over I would do it differently but none of us can go back. What have you decided to do?"

"I told Sandy to get an abortion and get out of my life."

"Did she tell you I wanted the child?"

"Yes."

"Did she tell you what my plan was?"

"Yes."

"You want her to kill my child?"

"It's not a child. You couldn't even see it without a microscope."

"It will be a child, and it will be mine."

"Are you sure?"

"What do you mean?"

"I can think of several possibilities: first, you have no proof she's pregnant in the first place; second, if she is pregnant you have no way of knowing whether she may miscarry; and third if she is pregnant and doesn't miscarry you don't know whether it will be your child or some other man's. All you really know is that she wants to marry you."

"Suppose I check with the doctor to make sure she's pregnant and after the baby is born check to confirm I'm the father, will you then be willing to take the chance she won't miscarry?"

"Check with the doctor, then we'll talk about it."

"Okay, how about coming out for dinner with me? I still love you, you know."

"All right. I'll go with you."

The following day Ed called Sandy and told her about his conversation with Ellen. Sandy gave him the name of the doctor and invited him to come along when she had the abortion. Ed called the doctor but could get no information over the phone. He called back Sandy and she invited him to come to her apartment and she would call the doctor's office and he could listen in. He said he would call her back and then phoned Ellen. He told her what had happened and then said, "Ellen, what do you want me to do?"

"I think we ought to take her up on her offer."

"We?"

"Yes, I want to go with you."

"That's a good idea. I'll call her back and let you know what the arrangements are."

He called back in a few minutes. "Sandy said that would be fine but we'll have to be at her apartment by 4:30 or we won't be able to get the doctor's office."

"I'll meet you there at 4:15. Give me her address."

Ed got there first but waited in his car until he saw Ellen getting out of the cab. He got out of his car and joined her. "Ellen," he said, "you have no idea how much I admire you for this. There are aspects of yourself you've never shown me before."

"There may be more you haven't seen."

Sandy greeted them in a friendly way and ushered them in. She dialed the doctor's office and Ed and Ellen picked up the extension in the bedroom. Sandy identified herself and suggested that the receptionist get out her chart and then let her speak with a nurse. When a nurse finally got on the phone Sandy told her she had been in the office a few days before and had been told she was pregnant. She said she would like that report sent to her. The nurse looked at her chart and said, "You have an appointment in two days. Would it be all right to give you the report when you come in, or are you cancelling that appointment?" "I didn't call to cancel it. Could you read me the report again over the phone. I just want to be sure."

The nurse read the report: a positive test for pregnancy.

"Thanks very much," said Sandy, "I guess that will be enough. I'll pick up the report when I come in."

The phones were hung up. Ellen and Ed came out of the bedroom. No one said anything until Ed spoke up. "I'm feeling uncomfortable about this whole business. Would either of you object to discussing it with me, after all I'm involved and I haven't had a chance to talk it over with both of you together."

"I object," said Ellen, "Sandy and I have thoroughly explored it. We have reached a decision and I don't want to reopen the subject."

Ed said, "Ellen, you told me you would talk about it after we made sure Sandy was pregnant."

"I said you and I would talk about it. I didn't include Sandy," Ellen replied.

"Are you afraid?" asked Sandy.

"Yes," Ellen replied, "I'm afraid you and I could never get along. I don't trust you and I never will."

"You have no reason not to trust me," said Sandy, "You're angry because Ed and I had an affair and because I'm pregnant with Ed's child. You're not afraid because you don't trust me; you're afraid because you think I'll take Ed away from you."

"I don't trust you because you admitted you seduced Ed and then lied to him about your taking birth control pills so you could get pregnant," Ellen replied.

"I just wanted to give him the child he so desperately wants, and you can't give him. Are you going to deny him that, Ellen?" Sandy asked.

Ellen sat down. "It appears we've reopened the subject," she said.

Sandy continued, "I'm not going to take Ed away from you, I don't think I can. I offered to share him and let him determine the shares, and I agreed to your tough terms. Ellen, it would work out. You and I can be good friends; we were in the hospital."

Ed turned to Ellen. "Ellen, what were your 'tough terms'?" he asked.

Ellen answered, "I told Sandy that if I gave you a divorce, the house we live in would belong to me. You and I would share the master bedroom. Sandy, although she would be married to you, would in fact be wife number two. I would be wife number one and the boss in the house. In return I would make no objection, explicitly or implicitly, to the times you chose to spend in her bed."

"That sounds like you worked out a deal. What happened?" Ed asked.

"Ellen changed her mind," Sandy replied, "I'm still willing."

"Ellen, what changed your mind?" Ed asked.

"I didn't think it would work," Ellen said, "I thought we would all end up unhappy."

"I don't think we would be unhappy, I know I wouldn't, and Sandy is willing to give it a try," Ed said.

"I don't want to do it," Ellen said, "it's a crazy idea and to me it spells trouble."

They were all quiet a few minutes then Sandy spoke, "I invited Ed to come with me to the abortion. Now I'm asking you to come too. Do you have the guts to do it?"

"You want me to feel responsible for the abortion. It's not my responsibility. That's between you and Ed," Ellen replied.

"I don't want to be responsible for it," Ed said, "I don't want the abortion."

"I don't want to be responsible either," Sandy said, "I certainly don't want the abortion. It seems to me it is your responsibility, Ellen, you're the only one who wants it."

"If I wanted you to jump off the Brooklyn Bridge and you did, whose responsibility would that be?" asked Ellen.

"Ed," said Sandy, "I'm going to cancel that appointment. Neither you nor I want it and I think Ellen is right; it is our responsibility."

"Ellen, would you be willing to try the plan you worked out with Sandy?" Ed asked.

"If I said, 'No.', what would you do, Ed?" Ellen asked.

"I don't know what I would do," Ed answered, "don't say, 'No', Ellen."

"I'll have to think about it some more," Ellen said, "there's no hurry now, the abortion is cancelled. Let's go home, Ed."

It was a major effort for Ed but he didn't bring up the subject again. It felt it was wiser to let Ellen think about it without pressure from him. She knew where he stood, he thought, she'll come to a decision. He resolved to say nothing for a month but he didn't have to wait that long. Three days after the meeting with Sandy Ellen brought it up after dinner.

"I spoke to Sandy today on the phone," she said.

"Oh?" said Ed.

"I invited her to come live with us on a trial basis."

"That's a wonderful idea. What did she say?"

"She wanted to know if we were planning a divorce. I told her that was something we could talk about later. She wanted to know when she could move in. I told her in three months. She said that was too far away. I told her she was most likely to have a miscarriage in the first three months and I wanted to wait so we wouldn't have to disrupt our lives unnecessarily. She didn't like it but I told her those were my terms, there was no hurry, and she could think about it."

"Don't you think a miscarriage is a pretty unlikely occurrence?"

"It's not unusual."

The next day Sandy called Ed at the office and left word to call her back. He did just before he left for the day.

Sandy said, "I suppose Ellen told you she called me yesterday. What do you think about her idea?"

"I think it's great, and I think you ought to take her up on it."

"And wait three months? She's stalling on the divorce. I think we're going to have trouble, and meanwhile I'm getting more pregnant. It won't be too long after that before an abortion can be ill advised. Ed, tell her three months is too long."

"I don't think that's wise, Sandy. If I start putting pressure on her for any reason she's very likely to reject the whole idea. Be patient. Moving in with us is a giant step. It's a great opportunity, don't blow it."

"All right, Ed, when are you going to see me?"

"I'm not, Sandy, until you move in, that is unless you clear it with Ellen."

"'Clear it with Ellen'?! Why do I have to do that?"

"Because until you move in I'm not going to do anything to upset her, and I don't think you should either."

"Damn it, Ed, I'm beginning to feel like a surrogate mother. You want Ellen and a baby, you don't want me."

"Sandy, don't feel that way. Once you're my wife everything will change. If you don't want to clear it with Ellen, I will."

"You do that and let me know tomorrow. Good-bye."

Ed did bring up the subject with Ellen and she was adamant: he was not to see Sandy until she moved in. Sandy was unhappy and angry about this but went along, compensated somewhat by talking on the phone with Ed daily and by receiving little gifts from him several times a week.

Sandy did not miscarry and in exactly three months moved in with Ellen and Ed. In accordance with the house rule that Ed made the decision where to sleep, he chose to sleep with Sandy four nights the first week she was with them. Ellen kept her promise that she would show no evidence she was aware of the nights Sandy and Ed were together.

In a month the women had fallen into a routine of sharing the household duties. They were wary of each other but their relationship was warming up. At Sandy's insistent urging Ed got a lawyer to handle the divorce. Ellen said she saw no need for a lawyer yet and did not get one for herself. Another month went by and Sandy was becoming concerned and impatient. Ed's lawyer told him that unless Ellen was willing, a divorce would be difficult on the grounds that Ed could present. Sandy wasn't satisfied and went to the lawyer with Ed and was told the same thing. Sandy then confronted

Ellen and wanted to know when she was going to implement what she had promised about a divorce. Ellen told her to come back in a month and she would talk about it.

The month passed. Sandy was now more than seven months pregnant and Ellen had taken advantage of the time by becoming socially active in the executive suite of Ed's office. She was well liked, especially by the men and particularly by the big boss, whom she had taken pains to cultivate.

The evening after the month had passed when the three were together Sandy said, "Ellen, the month is up. It's time to talk divorce."

"All right," Ellen said, "what do you want to know?"

"I want to know when you're going to the lawyer to make arrangements," Sandy replied.

"Sometime after the baby comes," Ellen said.

"That's not the way I understood the arrangements we made," Sandy said.

"What did you understand?, Ellen asked.

"I understood you and Ed would get a divorce and I assumed it would have been immedidately," Sandy replied.

"That was your assumption, not mine," said Ellen, "apparently Ed didn't tell you what my conditions were so I'll tell you. They were first, to make sure you were pregnant, second, to make sure you carried through the pregnancy successfully, and third, to make sure Ed is the father. So far only the first requirement has been fulfilled."

"When all the requirements are fulfilled will you then agree to a divorce?" Sandy asked.

"Then we'll talk about it," said Ellen, "who knows, by that time you may not want to marry Ed, or he you."

"Ellen," said Sandy, "now that it's too late I know I've made a terrible mistake; I've ignored the first rule in any contest: never underestimate your opponent. I never thought you could be this clever. If this were a chess game, Ellen, I'd resign now. What are your plans?"

"That depends on events," said Ellen, "we'll have to wait and see."

As the date for the delivery of the baby approached, Ed noted a change in the relationship between the two women; they now seemed genuinely friendly to each other. He was pleased about that.

About two weeks before the date he asked about plans for the baby's arrival at home. Sandy told him both Ellen and she were superstitious about that. All the plans had been made but would not be implemented until the baby was ready to come home. Sandy said to him, "Please don't talk about it anymore. Everything has been taken care of."

And so it had.

A baby boy was born, seven pounds ten ounces, resembling his mother. Mother and baby did fine.

The day Sandy was to leave the hospital Ed took the afternoon off and after lunch went to pick her up. When he arrived on the floor the nurse told him a man had picked her up midmorning but there was a letter for him. He thanked her, took the letter and went to the visitors' lounge to read it:

"Dear Ed,

When you read this letter I will have gone. You had wanted to end our affair and now it is. Don't try to find me. I will only be in the city a few days and then will be far away.

I don't know whether you are the father of my son. The other man who might be has been after me since he learned two months ago that I was going to have a baby and figured it might be his. Ed, the baby is secondary to him. He wants me. He doesn't care what I do with the baby. Without a blood test he will accept it as his but if I want to give it to you for adoption that's okay too. I'm not going to give permission for a blood test. The man who wants me gets the baby.

If the baby resembles you I suppose I'll have to think of you, otherwise I hope to forget.

> Good-by Ed, give my love to Ellen,
> Sandy.

Ed read the letter three times, folded it, and put it away. He would show it to Ellen and wondered how she would react. Would she feel as devastated as he?

Ed let himself into his home and called, "Ellen". There was no answer. He looked around for baby paraphernalia but there was none. On the dresser in the master bedroom there was a note. He picked it up and read:

"Dear Ed,

I've been thinking about this for two months, that's when I got a very interesting proposition from Jeff, your company's 'Big Boss'. Two weeks ago I decided to take him up on it and he was delighted. He wants me, Ed, not a baby.

I decided today was the day to leave. You can come home with Sandy and your son and have a proper family. I'm leaving you my address where your lawyer can contact me. If you're reasonable there will be no problem with the divorce.

Give my love to Sandy,

> Goodbye,
> Ellen.

COPING
WITH GENIUS

They had a lot in common. They were young, just starting college, strictly limited funds, no place to live. They stood together looking at the bulletin board where apartments to rent were listed. He had a street map in his hand which he examined periodically to check on where a listed apartment was located.

SHE: *(A petite girl with a pretty face and a trim figure)* There's nothing new here. I checked them all out yesterday. There are two good ones but they're both too big and too expensive for me. If you got somebody you want to room with try this one. *She pointed to one.*

HE: *(A big guy with a handsome clean-shaven face and a well developed body)* I don't have anyone to room with and I don't have much money. I think I may have to end up in a rooming house—Are you a freshman too?

SHE: Yeh, what are you signed up for?

HE: Engineering, how about you?
SHE: Engineering.
HE: Engineering?
SHE: Engineering. Something wrong with that?
HE: No, no. You just didn't look like an engineer to me.
SHE: Yeh. *eyeing him up and down* Do you smoke?
HE: *Figuring out what's coming and sizing her up* No. Do you?
SHE: No. Do you cook?
HE: A little. Do you?
SHE: I'm a terrific cook, but I'm not much on housecleaning.
HE: I'm a terrific housekeeper.
SHE: Can you afford a hundred dollars a month?
HE: If I don't buy a meal ticket I could—if I can get food stamps.
SHE: Would you like to take a look at that apartment with me?
HE: Sure. Can we walk it?
SHE: You don't have a car?
HE: No, I got shoes.
SHE: Okay, we can go in my car.—Are you sure you can afford this? How are we going to arrange about the food?
HE: Don't worry about the food. We'll each be responsible for our own. I probably eat twice as much as you, maybe three times.
SHE: Okay, let's go. My name's Angie.
HE: Mine's Jeff.

They got in her car, a four year old Honda Civic and found the apartment. It was not great but was within easy walking distance of the university. It had two bedrooms but only one bath. The furniture was beat up dormitory style. There was a small living room/dining room, a small but adequate kitchen, no laundry.

ANGIE: This is nothin' great.

JEFF: Did you check out any of the others you thought might need a roommate?

ANGIE: Yeh, I checked them all out. I think this is the best we can do in an apartment. I didn't check out the rooming houses, but that would be the last resort for me. What do you think, Jeff?

JEFF: Well, I can walk to school. I'll have to check and see whether I can get food stamps. I don't think I can swing it otherwise.

ANGIE: You should be able to get a part time job. Are you a decent student? Could you manage a part time job and still get the studying done?

JEFF: I'd rather not work, at least the first semester. I'm here on a scholarship and I have to maintain at least a B average to keep it.

ANGIE: Wow, you must be a brain! Hey, I like that in a roommate, especially if he's taking the same courses I am. Look, if you help me with the studying, I'll do all the cookin'. That should give you some time to work part time if you have to. C'mon, Jeff, we can manage it.

JEFF: You really want this place, don't you?

ANGIE: I think it's the best we can do this year. And I like the idea of a brain for a roommate.

By the end of the first semester Angie had decided Jeff was not just a brain, he was a damn genius. He already knew so much and she so little she gave up the idea of engineering and switched her course to psychology, maybe she could get some insight into the workings of genius. Jeff performed like a genius in engineering but a moron in social relationships. After the first month he got a job with the college in one of the engineering labs so the money situation eased for him. In the apartment everything was on a strictly professional basis. The finances and the housekeeping chores were equitably divided as arranged by Jeff with Angie's approval. Angie was agreeable to everything he proposed. She decided early on that he was the guy she wanted and she was determined to get him. She felt he was going to be an outstanding success in his field and become if not wealthy at least very comfortable financially. He was very quiet, rarely began a conversation unless related to something having to do with the apartment, and resisted any inquiries into his private life before coming to college. He was considerate of her and gentle. He was a neat person and the apartment was always clean. Housekeeping was his job, cooking was hers. He seemed to spend all his spare time either in the library or the lab. He was a morning person: went to bed by ten and usually up by four to study in his room. He never made a pass at her.

At the end of the first semester there was a break in classes. Jeff stayed on to work in the lab, Angie went home. She came back a day early and walked in on Jeff unannounced. He was studying at the dining room table and seemed genuinely glad to see her.

JEFF: (*Looking up and smiling when he saw her*) Hi, Angie. (*He pushed his chair back.*)
ANGIE: Hi, Jeff, boy, am I glad to see you! (*She giggled and rushed over to him and kissed him plunk on the mouth.*)
JEFF: (*Surprised*) Hey, what was that all about?
ANGIE: That was all about a kiss.
JEFF: I recognized what it was.
ANGIE: Good for you. Did you like it?
JEFF: Well, (*Thinking*) yes, I did.—Did you have a good time on your break?
ANGIE: No, that's why I came back a day early. (*She leaned down and kissed him again as before. He didn't say anything, just looked at her.*) Well, you said you liked it.

JEFF: Yes, I do.
ANGIE: I've got lots more available if you're interested.
JEFF: *(He stood up)* I'm interested.

Angie was sitting on the patio by herself. "That was thirty years ago.", she thought, "It doesn't seem possible. It's just a dream. Jeff's patent that became lucrative, like winning the lottery; two sons born, growing up, becoming men and independent; Jeff's other patents; his travels as consultant; his many talks at scientific meetings; his honorary degrees— all dreams.

"Everything has changed in those thirty years—everything but Jeff's behavior. He's still a very private person living in a strange world of his own that few people can understand or enter. He still seems to come back to the world of ordinary people reluctantly. He has to be led in and shown the way. I've been doing this for thirty years and he's still not able or willing to find the way in himself. He's happy in his own world that I cannot enter. Yet when he's really with me I believe he loves me. His first love is his work but at least I think I come second, which is probably the most that I can expect.

"The problem is he's not really with me very often. Besides being a genius he's a damn workaholic. I've been unable to get him away on a vacation. He says he doesn't need one; instead of feeling relaxed he would be tense, thinking of all the things in the lab he would rather be doing than whatever is done on vacations. That's about all he could say at one time. On another occasion he said he thought the only people who needed vacations were those who worked because they had to make a living. They didn't enjoy what they were doing and got no lasting satisfaction from their job. These are the ones who hate going into work and love getting out of work. He said it's just the opposite with him so he doesn't need a vacation. He doesn't say so but I think he doesn't understand why I would need a vacation from what I'm doing, which I think he considers is one long vacation.

"I find I'm feeling lonely. It's not a good feeling. The boys are gone and Jeff was never here. I don't like the prospect of spending the rest of my life this way. But what are my options? I know I can't change him so if there are going to be any changes I'm going to have to make them.

"I'm beginning to feel like a battered wife. Poor Jeff, if I ever mentioned this to him he would be so devastated he would retreat into his own safe world and never come out.— I wonder if the spouses of other geniuses have this problem. Maybe I could put out a call on the internet. We could form a support group for spouses of geniuses.—Well, so much for innocent fantasy.

"My only real option is to leave him. I would be a wealthy divorcee. I'm still young enough, unencombered, and reasonably attractive for my age. With this combination and money the chances are good that I could get another man.— But somehow, I don't know whether I could do it. I love the guy I got.—I guess some battered wives stay with their husbands because they love them in spite of the beatings. There may be something masochistic about it. Maybe I'm a little masochistic myself.—It must be the good moments that keep us all in bondage. Jeff is kind and gentle and considerate. I believe I am the person he loves the best but his world doesn't have any people in it. He has to come into my world to meet me and he doesn't come often enough. If I stay with him I'll have long periods of lonliness for the rest of my life. Of course if I leave him there is no guarantee that will end; it could even be worse.

"There is another option: a compromise. I could immerse myself in an avocation and spend as much time in that world as he does in his. I'm not sure I'm up to spending the time and effort necessary to prepare myself for a career that would be gratifying for me. The only one that I might consider would be one in counseling. That would require at least another two years of full time schooling, I don't know if I could handle that. Yet if I were to leave him that's probably what I would do. I would plunge into the work to keep myself occupied. That would replace all the social activities I have now with the women at the club: the bridge games, the golf, the tennis, the luncheons, the swimming pool; and the rare club activities I can drag Jeff to. As I think about the life I'm leading it really isn't very productive. Sure I do some volunteer charity work that may do a little good but certainly not enough to give me any deep feeling of satisfaction. Sure I run the house by hiring and firing the help and tellling them what to do but none of that is necessary. I could hire somebody to do that. I enjoy the club activities at the moment but when they're over I'm not left with any good feelings of accomplishment. Maybe my feeling of emptiness doesn't all come from loneliness, maybe some of it is because I have no feeling of accomplishment.

"I think maybe I could be a good counselor.—Okay, somebody comes to me with just the problems I have, how would I treat her? Let me think about that.—I would say, 'You said you didn't think you could handle going back to school under your present conditions and yet thought you could do it if you were divorced. How do you explain that?' She would say, 'A divorce would free up all my time. I would be independent, go where I pleased anyplace in the country to the university I wanted and then settle anyplace I pleased to practice my profession the way I wanted to. I couldn't do that staying married. I would be constrained by Jeff's life.'

ME: Could you free up your time now, if you wanted to?
SHE: I suppose I could.—Yes, I could.
ME: Is there a university close by you could attend?

SHE:	Yes, there is one I could probably attend.
ME:	Would Jeff object to you doing this?
SHE:	No, he would encourage me.
ME:	What are the disadvantages of doing it?
SHE:	I wouldn't feel free.
ME:	Are there any other disadvantages?
SHE:	Not really
ME:	What have you considered the risks of freedom?
SHE:	Just one, loneliness.
ME:	Have you ever been lonely?
SHE:	I'm lonely sometimes now. It's a form of torture but it's only a temporary feeling. If I take my freedom the loneliness may be prolonged.
ME:	Is loneliness the only risk?
SHE:	I guess it depends on how you define loneliness. As part of it I include missing Jeff: the man himself and the sex.
ME:	It appears that you have to decide whether feeling free is worth the price of loneliness. Have you thought about the traumatic effects of divorce itself?
SHE:	Yes, but I can't estimate how traumatic it would be. I know Jeff would not contest it and will be generous in regard to the financial settlement. The boys are grown up. I expect they will think I'm foolish and may even try to dissuade me but they won't be traumatized.
ME:	What about Jeff? How do you think he would react?
SHE:	I think he would be shocked. I think he has never considered the possibility that I may not be perfectly happy in the marriage.
ME:	That sounds like there has been some breakdown in communication.
SHE:	I can't communicate with Jeff, he doesn't talk.
ME:	If you ask him a direct question, won't he answer?
SHE:	Yes, he'll answer in as few words as possible.
ME:	Will he respond to a statement?

SHE: Yes, he'll respond with a grunt or a couple of words that are directly to the point. I think he is concerned with the conservation of energy. If a grunt will do he will not waste energy in talk.

ME: It may be worthwhile to make the statement to him that you are unhappy. You may get a few words directly to the point. I expect you will get the usual answer which is a question: what are you unhappy about? Do you have an answer to that?

SHE: Yes, and I know what will happen. He will encourage me to make a career for myself but will see no reason why we must be divorced for me to accomplish this.

ME: When we talked about the stress of divorce, you considered the effect on the boys and mentioned Jeff very briefly. You said he would be in shock when you told him. What do you think would be the longer term effects?

SHE: It's strange to say after all these years of marriage, but I don't know Jeff well enough to even guess the answer to that question.

ME: Okay, now we get to you. How do you think you're going to handle the stress?

SHE: I don't know. I know there are going to be losses. I'm going to lose my beautiful home and estate, my carefree life, my household help, my gardeners, my chauffeur, and my husband. I recognize I will do some grieving.

ME: And you said you would be lonely. Where will your support come from? Your sons are not likely to be sympathetic. Do you have friends who will support you or do you plan to take off to some distant place where you have no friends?

SHE: I do have some friends in other places but I can't lean on them for support. The answer is I don't know where support will come from. I guess I felt I could support myself.

ME: You will be grieving, you will be lonely, you will have no support. That sounds like a prescription for a depression.

SHE: So what can I do?

ME: You might consider talking it over with Jeff. You might be surprised.—Now, look at the time. I better go see how Mary is doing with dinner."

ONE OF THE FEW

The first time I met him he was already my brother-in-law. This was in the summer of 1946. My sister, three years younger than I, was a registered nurse. She and I both enlisted in the Army Air Force about the same time in 1942. She went to Enland with a hospital unit attached to an airfield. I went to the Pacific as Flight Surgeon to a squadron. We both got discharged in early 1946 at about the same time. I came home with wings, ribbons, and malaria; she came home with Peter.

Peter was a handsome young Englishman. Winston Churchill said, "Never have so many owed so much to so few." Peter was one of the few, a fighter pilot in the RAF. My sister met him at one of those joint affairs where the English and the Americans got together. I might say that my sister, Helen, has all the good looks in my family. The photographs taken at their wedding show a very attractive couple.

Well, my sister wouldn't marry Peter if he stayed in the military so he got out. He had not been trained to be anything but a fighter pilot and he had no prospects for earning a living in England so it didn't take much persuading from

Helen to convince him that America would be the better place to make his life. After all her father had a very successful insurance business and a place there could certainly be found for him. He made a very good appearance and his English accent didn't hurt either. Besides, her only brother was a doctor with no interest in the business so some day Peter would be in a position to take it over.

In retrospect Helen admitted to me that in England she had had stars in her eyes that prevented her from seeing Peter might have some problems. When I first met him he presented as a very neat, well groomed, quiet, handsome young man with an English accent that went along with his appearance. The quiet part was the dominant feature. He spoke only in answer to a question and made the answers as brief as possible without being rude. He seemed to be the opposite of what might be expected from a salesman. I wondered what my father could do with him in the business. My father told me after he had spent several sessions with Peter that he didn't know what to do with him either. They had explored all the different aspects of the business, Peter was not enthusiastic about any of them but was willing to try anything my father suggested. It was finally decided that he might do best as a salesman for life insurance so my father sent him off to take a training course given by the life insurance company my father dealt with. He did not mention that Peter was his son-in-law. He got back a letter from the company suggesting my father not hire him. In effect, Peter had flunked the course.

My father spoke to me. He said I was the doctor, couldm't I do something with Peter?

"You were a Flight Surgeon, you must know something about the problems of pilots. Please talk to him and see if you can help him."

I said, "Okay, let me have the letter you got from the company."

I took the letter and called Peter. I told him my father

would like me to talk with him and I suggested he come to my office the following morning. He readily agreed without asking any questions and we set a time.

He was precisely on time. We got settled and I said, "Peter, my father got this letter about you and I think you should read it."

He took the letter, read it without showing any emotion, and handed it back to me without saying a word.

"What do you think about it, Peter?"

"I think every thing in the letter is correct."

"You don't think my father should hire you?:"

"That's right. I'd be a terrible insurance salesman."

"You're glad my father got that letter?

"Yes, I am. I tried to tell your father I would not be good in his business, but he wouldn't listen."

"Have you been thinking about what you would like to do?"

"I've been thinking a lot." He apparently had no more to say.

"Have you ever done anything that you really enjoyed?", I asked.

"Oh, yes. I enjoyed being a fighter pilot. That was my whole life. If my number had come up, I wouldn't have minded at all. It would have been part of the game."

I could see he was thinking so I said nothing. We were both quiet for several minutes. I was determined that he would speak first and he finally did, "Well, my number didn't come up and the game ended. I felt abandoned."

He was silent again and this time I spoke, "What about Helen?"

"Helen was in love with me. She was sure she could help me, and I could see no future. I felt I had no choice so I agreed to marry her."

"She old me you gave up a military career for her."

"To join the regular air force would not have been a good deal for me. I had a temporary rank of major; my rank

39

would be reduced to lieutenant and I might not even be put on flying status. The military would be a last resort for me. I wanted to keep my rank and my status and they wouldn't agree."

He was quiet again and so was I.

Finally, he resumed, "Basically, I'm still just a dumb, reckless kid and I don't know if I'll ever grow up. I had my moment of glory and that's more than most people have in their lifetime. I can't expect any more glory but I want to hang on to my freedom . . . . Helen wants to start a family but I'm not up for that."

Another long pause then he continued, "I suppose I might as well tell you now what I plan to do. I don't want you to tell Helen, I'll do that . . . . I'm going to take off. First, I'll arrange a divorce which will not be difficult; there's nothing to divide.

"There are lots of wars going on all over the world; I'll choose one and pick the side that appeals to me. I'll offer my services while my credentials are still good. My moment of glory has spoiled me for anything else. The only thing I'm good for is to fight, and I don't think I'll ever be at a loss to find a war to fight in.

"Helen will be devastated for awhile but better now than later. You will have to explain to her that sometimes rescuers end up victims."

Peter got up and so did I.

I said, "I'll do that, Peter."

THE GURU

I was among the early ones onto the plane. I found my row and took my seat next to the window. I put my carry-on under my seat, buckled on my seat belt, and looked out my window to watch the baggage being loaded.

The other two seats in my row stayed empty so long I thought I might be alone. After everyone else had been settled a lone man strolled down the aisle and stopped at my row. He slipped off the backpack he had been wearing, took a yellow pad of paper out of it and slung the pack into the overhead compartment.

I watched him do this. I guessed he was in his mid-fifties. He was dressed like a vagabond: faded yellow T shirt, baggy tan slacks rolled up to the mid-calf, and sandals on bare feet. He had a heavy beard and mustache crudely trimmed, long stringy brown hair with a bushy ponytail held together by a big rubber band. He settled into the aisle seat, kicked off his sandals, and buckled his seat belt. He turned and looked at me. "Hello", he said, "I'm Guru Ganguly."

"Hello, I'm Tom Hall", I replied.

"It appears that we two are going to share this row." He

spoke softly and precisely, not at all consonant with his appearance. He continued, "Would you like to converse? We will be together many hours."

ME: I think that may be interesting—and instructive for me
HIM: And, I'm sure, for me too.
ME: May I ask you a question?
HIM: Of course, but I may choose not to answer it.
ME: Is 'Guru' your name or a title?
HIM: Both.

There followed a brief period of silence while we continued looking at each other.

ME: Would you care to elaborate on that statement?
HIM: It's my name and it is also my title
ME: How did you get the title?
HIM: Same way I got the name. It was bestowed upon me.
ME: By whom? I assume your parents gave you your name. Did they also give you the title?
HIM: It's foolish and sometimes dangerous to make assumptions.
ME: I agree.

I was getting impatient but not quite ready to give up the game. I said no more and decided to leave the ball in his court. We continued looking at each other, both of us remaining silent. The plane was being pushed backwords. I turned my head to look out the window.

HIM: Is our conversation over?

I turned away from the window to look at him.

ME: I don't know. I was waiting for you to answer or say you don't want to answer that question.

HIM: Are you angry?

ME: No, just curious. I understand you may not wish to answer those questions.

HIM: Is your curiousty just about my name?

ME: No. Originally, I was curious about your appearance but now that you've told me you're a guru I can understand that. Now I'm curious why a guru would be traveling in a plane. I had the idea that gurus were settled in one place. Either my idea is wrong or your being here is just a temporary displacement.

HIM: What is your conception of a guru?

ME: To me a guru is a charismatic man who presents himself as both a philosopher and a psychotherapist. I don't know how a guru attains the designation. I don't know of any guru schools or examinations or licenses. I suppose after a period of time his followers bestow the title. I have the impression some of his followers form a close circle around him and become his disciples.

HIM: Have you ever listened to a guru?

ME: If you're one you'll be the first I've ever seen.

HIM: Don't you believe me?

ME: Why should I? Would you like me to assume you're telling the truth? You said it's foolish and sometimes dangerous to make assumptions, and I agreed.

The plane was taxying to the runway

HIM: That's good. I'll answer your question. I bestowed both my name and my title on myself. I did it before I had enough followers to do it for me.

ME: And do you have enough now?

HIM: Oh yes, more than enough; in London, Paris, Amsterdam, Vienna, Rome, and Florence.

The plane was on the runway now, turned and ready for takeoff. The motors were revving up.

ME: Pardon me, I like to watch the takeoff.

I turned to look out the window as the plane took off and rapidly climbed. After a couple of minutes I turned back to him.

ME: Please excuse the interruption. Watching the takeoff and landing are the best part of the flight for me.—I was about to ask how you got your followers.
HIM: My agents got them. I have one in each city.
ME: How did you get the agents?
HIM: With money. Is there another way?
ME: You must be well capitalized.
HIM: Not really. I only needed capital the first time. After that my followers always generated more than enough.
ME: You must be very good. Do you have any special qualifications?
HIM: I'm a well trained psychiatrist and practiced many years including some in academe. I gave up a professorship to become a guru.
ME: That's a fascinating story. Sounds like you had a mid-life crisis.
HIM: Something like that. I found my life too static. I like to travel and I thought this would be a good way to do it. I was right.
ME: You're not married.
HIM: No, just a woman companion in each city I practice my profession. I try to limit my work to a week or ten days in each city, depending on how the hall is filled. I stay longer just for rest and relaxation depending on my mood and my woman.

I've done lots of traveling. Once on a sabbatical I was in India and spent some time with two different gurus. I

44

decided then I could be as good a guru as they. I continue to travel extensively. Over the course of years I've covered the world pretty well. Where I don't practice I travel more vagabond than luxury style. It really suits me better . . . . I'm going to meditate now, will you excuse me?

He sat straight up and closed his eyes. I looked at him and decided to close mine too.

HEREDITY

I have no heredity . . . well, I guess that's not exactly true, it's just that I don't know what my heredity is. You see, I'm an adoptee, and that's not easy to be. If you think it's not tough just go to the internet and search, "adoptee". You'll find about ten thousand references. There are all sorts of organizations, non-profit and profit, to help adoptees find their birth family and visa-versa, and to legislate for better laws. I know. I've been trying for the past year to find my biological parents using the internet.

I have no complaints about my life with my adoptive parents. They have treated me as though I were their own natural child and I treat them as though they were my natural parents. But deep down I know and I think they know that's not really how it is. I don't have their genes. I have no trouble talking to them openly. I've told them I feel a part of me is missing, I'm not a whole person. They're understanding and are helping me in my search although I think they have some reservations about the wisdom of it.

My mother has told me all she knows. Everything was done through her doctor. She had been unable to get pregnant and then because of uncontrolled bleeding her womb had to be removed. She was devastated and her doctor was very sympathetic. He said he would be delivering a young unmarried girl who would be unable to take care of the baby and wanted to have it adopted. He suggested my adoptive mother take it. He arranged that my adoptive mother would take it right after it was born, the natural mother would never see it. This was the way both women wanted it though they never met each other and didn't know names. The sex of the child was not known before birth and the natural mother never did know nor wanted to. The only thing my adoptive parents knew about my natural father was that he was a young man who had gone away to college and didn't know he had fathered a child.

Well, that was hardly enough to restore any of my missing parts. As my summer vacation was approaching I thought I would spend it doing some of my own detective work. I couldn't afford having some professional company search it out for me, besides I thought I could do a better job myself. I planned to start with the doctor who delivered me.

> Dear Dr. Schiff,
>
> I am Daniel Taylor. Exactly twenty years ago you delivered me and handed me to my adoptive mother, Ethyl Taylor.
>
> In the fall I will go into my third year at Columbia University as a premedical student. I intend to spend this summer in an attempt to find my birth parents. For the past year I've been working at it through the internet with no success. I will continue using the internet but have little hope of any luck with it. My mother gave me your name and although you have changed your address and are a half a continent away I was fortunate in finding you. I am hoping you remember both of my mothers and may even have some records.

I'm sure you are aware that adoptees have problems related to their ignorance about their birth parents and can use some help.

I hope you will answer this letter. I will be grateful for any information you can give me.

Sincerely,

Dear Mr. Taylor

I was pleasantly surprised to receive your letter. When my patients move away I rarely hear from them again. Your parents moved away about a year after you were born and I had no further contact with them.

So far as your biological parents are concerned I have bad news for you. I've been retired now for eight years and no longer store my old records. I had to keep them for seven years and then was free to destroy them. What I told your mother and father before they decided to adopt you they probably remember better than I do. However, there may be some things about your birth mother they may not know. I remember her well, probably because she was a beautiful young woman and very frightened and upset. She was just nineteen years old and nothing had gone right for her according to the story she told me. I had no way of knowing how truthful she was and suspected she did not give me her right name. In any event she had not considered an early abortion which her parents wanted and would have simplified her life. She was determined to carry the pregnancy to term to give her child a life even though she couldn't provide it. She told me she had been having an affair with your father from their high school graduation dance through the summer. In the fall he had gone away to college not knowing she was pregnant. She waited for him to write but he didn't so she wrote him off. She had never met your father's parents and refused to talk about her own. After I delivered you she left town and I have not heard from her since.

The only good news I can write you is that since I am retired I have the time to write a letter like this so if there is something else you think I can help you with don't hesitate to write.

Sincerely,

Dear Dr. Schiff,

Thank you for responding to my letter. I'm sorry you could not give me more information but I'm happy you didn't shut me off.

I have two questions. Do you think the hospital would have any additional information and do you think it would be worthwhile for me to come and check around the neighborhood where she lived to see if I could get any information from anyone who may have known her?

Sincerely,

Dear Mr. Taylor,

I'm afraid the hospital records would be of no help to you. She gave your father's name as "John Doe", and gave a motel as her address. I knew she came from out of town and she would not tell me where she had been living before. To my knowledge she came alone.

I think it would be useless for you to come here. Unless you strike it lucky on the internet I see no way you can track her down.

You might consider some counseling to help you adjust.

Sincerely,

Dear Dr. Schiff,

Thank you for the information and suggestions. I'm not ready to give up. I will continue advertising on the' internet and am making inquiries about professional searchers.

I don't know how a counselor will be able to help me. What specifically could one do?

Sincerely,

Dear Mr. Taylor,

I think you are among the most fortunate of adoptees. You wrote me that you've had a wonderful life with your adoptive parents.

To some extent I've investigated the internet and my impression has been that the adoptees most anxious to find their birth parents are those who have had an unfortunate experience growing up with their adoptive parents.

The only reasonably good survey of adoptee reunion with birth families that I know about showed that less than fifty percent resulted in a satisfactory relationship and only thirty-five percent in a close one.

In your case you already have important information. You know your mother was young and healthy with a strong sense of what for her was morally right. She broke off a relationship with her parents for your sake and she refused to let your father know she was pregnant because she didn't want you to be unwanted. She was a strong, determined woman. She was attractive and I expect that she eventually married and probably now has a family of her own. There is a good chance her husband does not know about you. Your mother may not even be willing to acknowledge you. Of course you can fantasize many other scenarios, some of them bad. If she's alive and looking for you. you will find her on the net.

You know your father was ambitious and intelligent enough to go to college. That's not much but it's enough.

From what you wrote me it's apparent that you have good genes. I doubt you want to exchange them for anyone else's unkown.

Mr. Taylor, you must be careful what you wish and work for, there may be unanticipated consequences. I suggest you stop your search and if your mother is interested let her do the searching.

Sincerely,

HARRY'S STORY

I suppose I should feel guilty about what I did, but I don't. I'm not much for "shoulds" anyway. I know people say Anita put me through law school and moved me to Chicago and then after we were all settled there I dumped her for another woman.

You have to know the whole story before you can pass judgment on what I did, so I'll start from the beginning. I met Anita in college. We liked each other from the first so it developed into a romance. The last two years of college we were living together. She graduated with a B.S. in nursing and I with a B.S. in engineering. She had no problem getting a position in a hospital, while I had no opportunity for a position anywhere. It was obvious that this was no time for a career in engineering, even PH.D.s in engineering couldn't get a job. I decided a double degree is what I needed, and set my goal for law. I figured there would be a niche for a lawyer with an engineering degree. I applied and got accepted to a law school half a continent away. Anita wanted to get married and come with me but I couldn't see taking on the responsibility. It was going to be tough enough to get that diploma without the handicap of a wife. Anita said it would be no handicap; on the contrary it would be a help. She knew I would have a problem with finances but she would be an adequate breadwinner and in addition I would be covered on her health insurance if I were her husband. She was confident she could get a position in a hospital wherever we lived. Finally, I told her she could come with me and if she got a position we would get married.

Well, that's how it turned out. We went, she got a position, and we were married. Those were tough years. Law school did not come easy for me. I struggled but I was determined to get that diploma. Anita was a tremendous help to me. She gave me great support, kept me at the books, and actually helped with the studying. She's smart, probably smarter than I am, and would have done better in law school than I did. Her income was enough for us to live decently without my earning a damn cent. She became an operating room nurse which brought in additional income but sometimes led to odd hours of work. One of the outstanding surgeons liked her work and had her assigned to him so if he had an emergency operation in the middle of the night off she would go. We were both too busy doing our own thing to have her sometimes erratic hours bother us.

Finally, the end of my long rough voyage was in sight. I had taken my last exam and passed it. There was a week before graduation and I could relax. I had some free time to help Anita so I began to do the grocery shopping. One day she was getting ready to go to work and I was going to shop but I couldn't find the grocery list. She told me to go look for it in her handbag. I looked but couldn't find it, but then women's handbags are mysterious places for me. She told me to look in **all** the compartments, that it was there someplace. I looked in all the compartments, dug through all the mysteries, finally found the list, put everything back the way I had found it, said good-bye to her, and went shopping. Of course for me doing the shopping was a bigger problem than even finding the shopping list. You can imagine what a big help I was to Anita.

Graduation wasn't the end of examinations for me. I still had the state bar exams to take and studying for them would be as much of a struggle as all the exams in law school. Once more Anita was a tremendous help to me. I freely admit I may not have been able to do it without her, I had sent resumes to several law firms where I thought my double degree could be helpful. As it turned out I was doubly lucky. I passed the state bar exams and I was offered a position in the patent department of an excellent law firm in Chicago, three hundred miles away. I also had got an offer from a law firm in the university city where we were living, although I didn't think that position was up to the one in Chicago. When I interviewed in Chicago I met a young woman, Fran, who was also being interviewed. We became acquainted and spent a few days there together. When I got the offer from there I called her. She said she had also been given an offer and planned to accept it. I told Anita I wanted to take the Chicago offer. As I had expected, she was reluctant to leave the hospital where she was working, but she agreed to quit and come with me to look for a place to live.

We went to Chicago, I went to work, Anita found a place to live and moved us. She worked like a beaver. Meanwhile, I was becoming better acquainted with Fran. She had been married in college but it hadn't worked out and she got a divorce after two years. We liked each other and had a lot in common. We worked late one night, and after we had finished our work made love on the couch in the library. That began an ongoing affair. It was not long before I knew Fran would be a better wife for me than Anita.

Anita got our new place all settled and began checking the hospitals to see which could give her the best offer. She said she didn't expect to get a position as good as the one she had had in the university city. I asked her if she would like to go back there, and if she could get her old job back. She said she would love to and knew the surgeon would take her back because he told her so before she left.

I told her I was going to divorce her and she could go back without looking for a job in Chicago. She was astounded and angry. She accused me of having another woman and said she would get a lawyer and make sure I would pay to support her for the rest of her life. I told her I didn't think that was likely to happen because I knew she had been having an affair with the hospital's chief surgeon and didn't think she would want to drag him through a messy divorce proceeding. She didn't deny it, just asked me how I knew. I said maybe I had had a private detective.

I didn't tell her I had deduced it after finding a condom in her handbag.

IRMA'S BED, BATH, AND BREAKFAST

Talk 'bout wimmin, let me tell ya 'bout Irma. You guys is jus' like me: drive all tha time, meet lots o' wimmin, don't 'member none of 'em, 'cept mebbe one er two things 'bout 'em, an' then don't 'member wich faces went wit wich asses, an' cain't nivir git tha names strate iffin ya 'member 'em atall Well, iffin yure ivir lukky 'nuff to meet Irma, thass one helluva wommin ya ain't nivir gonna firgit.

One time ah wuz drivin' fur a guy what got sick, cuntry wher ah nivir bin afore. It ment two nites on tha road. Tha fust nite ah et dinner wit a guy drivin tha same rute in tha opsit drekshun, it wuz his sekkin nite out. We et togetter and wuz havin a few beers wen he sez to me, "Ah bin sizin ya up, ah'd say ya kwaleefy."

"Kwaleefy fur what?" ah sez.

"Fur Irma's Bed, Bath, and Brefist," he sez.

"Yeh?" ah sez, "What do ah git fur kwaleefin', a free fuck?"

"No," he sez, "iffin ya git thet ya pays fur it."

"Whuts so grate 'bout thet?" ah sez, "iffin ah pay ah kin git it frum eny hore."

"She ain't no ord'nary hore," he sez, "ya git 'er fur the hole fuckin' nite, an' ya ain't nivir hed it so gud. It's like fuckin' a goddam queen in 'er own palace; an' ya ain't nivir hed such a brefist as Irma'll giv ya—but iffin ya ain't intristid, firgit it."

"Ah ain't sed ah ain't intristid," ah sez, "tell me mor."

"She's a gorjus wommin, got 'er own place a coppel miles off tha road ya'll be drivin' an' 'bout a day frum 'ere," he sez, "Ah'll giv ya drekshuns. She takes only one guy a nite— five nites a week—thass providin' summun cums an' she likes 'im. She takes 'em only iffin a guy she's hed sends 'em. Iffin ya go ya gotta tell 'er ah sent ya. Ma name fur 'er is, 'Bernie Brown'. Ahm aweways, 'Bernie' an' ma las' name aweways starts wit a, 'B'. I like it short, colors is gud: 'Brown, Blue, Black.' Fur Irma ahm, 'Brown'. Ya tell 'er, 'Bernie Brown sen me'. She'll let ya in, ah think she liked me."

"What's 'er place like," I sez.

"Like no place ya ivir seed," he sez, "real hi class, like ya feel ya caint sit on tha furn'shur without yure clos jus' com' frum tha cleaner."

"How much all this gonna cost?" ah sez, "Ahm gittin' 'spishus sumpin ain't kosher."

"Thet depends," he sez, "on wether she likes ya an' wether ya take a rumm or go wit 'er in 'er rumm."

"Thet ain't gud 'nuff," ah sez, "wha's tha mos' ah gotta pay?"

"The mos'? Mebbe two hunnert," he sez.

"Thass a dam 'spensiv hore," I sez.

"Ah ain't sed it's gonna cost thet," he sez, "ah sed thet wud be the mos'."

"Wuz jus' ya two in thet house?" ah ast.

"Yeh, jus' us two," he sez.

"Hell," ah sez, "iffin ya tol' 'er ya ain't payin' what wud she do?"

"Ya don' pay ya don' git tha key to yure rig or yure lisens," he sez.

"Ya giv 'er yure key?" ah ast.

"She keeps yure key an' yure lisens 'till ya settel up, an' she got records o' evathin'. To evirbuddy but the guys what wuz sent she runs a 'spektabl place. She's eevin got 'er name in sum book wit four stars. Iffin the guy what inspekted 'er bin sent like ya, he wudda hadda giv' 'er five stars," he sed.

"Okay, Bernie Brown," ah sez, "mebbe ah'll luk 'er up."

"Won mor thing," he sez, "ya better go rite after ya eat, an' iffin ya git in ya better git tha sleep ya need rite off. Wonst yure wit 'er ya ain't gonna git ta sleep agin."

Ah sez, "Okay," an' he giv' me the drekshuns. 'Er place is on a country road an' tha nearist house to 'ers is 'bout a quater mile. He sez ah cain't miss it, they's a big sign out front sez, "Welcome to Irma's Bed, Bath, & Breakfast".

Ah went ta bed thet nite figgerin' ah'd spend the nex' nite in Irma's bed an' bath.

The nex' mornin' the wether turn'd bad an' kep' gittin' worse wit' hevvy wind an' sokkin rain. Enny sane guy wudda quit a hunnert mile short o' Irma's, but guys wha' drive rigs like mine ain't known fur bein' sane. Ah kep' goin' thinkin' 'bout Irma an' pitshurin' how she mite luk: drest, half drest, an nekkid. Ah wuz runnin' late, no time fur dinner so I stopt an' pikked up sum vittels an' et drivin'. Ah got ta Irma's an' it wuz rainin' hevvy. Ah pulled ma rig inta 'er big parkin' space back o' tha house. It wuz em'ty 'cept fur a Ford Escort. Ah figgird Irma wuz hom aloan. Ah got out near 'er back porch, grabbed ma bag, an' run fur it. Ah din't see no bell so ah banged on the dore. Ah hed to bang four ta five times but finely tha dore open'd an' thar studd tha purtiest damm wommin ah iver seed. Thar wernt no part of 'er din't luk gud. She lukt so gud ah mos' firgot how tired ah wuz. Ah follerd 'er inta a lited hallway war she turn'd an' tuk a gud luk at me.

"Lukken fur a place to stay?" she ast.

"Yep, iffin ya got one," ah sez.

"How didja git here?" she ast, "Ah ain't eggzactly on the main drag."

"Bernie sent me, he giv' me gud drekshuns," ah sez.

"Bernie who?" she ast.

"Bernie Brown," ah sez, "he wuz wit' ya two nites ago."

"O, thet Bernie," she sez, "he din't lose no time rekomendin' me. Nex' time ya see 'im tell 'im thanks fur me. Did he tell ya what it cost 'im?"

"No, he jus' sed he cudint complain," ah sez, "ya gotta place?"

"Yeh, ah gotta place fur ya," she sez.

"How much?" I ast.

"'Spensive, let me show ya afur ya yell 'bout it," she sez, "take off yure shoes here, ah don' wancher trakkin up ma house."

Ah tuk off ma shoes an' follerd 'er tru a kichin what shined an' up tha stairs ta a big rumm wit two dubbel beds an' its own big batrumm. Each lookt betteran any otel ah ivir bin in.

"Verry nice," ah sez, "how much?"

"Fur this an' an 'all ya kin eat' brefist one hunnert dollars," she sez.

"It may be wurth it," ah sez, "but ah ain't got thet much money. Sorry ah tuk up yure time, ahll be movin' on."

"Movin' on," she sez, "on a nite like this?"

"Hey, ah don' wanna," ah sez, "but ah got no choice, ah don' hev thet much money."

"How cum?," she sez, "ah thot ya guys carried wads o' money."

"Yeh, ah hed it but I los' it inna crap game," ah sez.

"How much ya got?" she ast.

"Sixty fi' dollars," ah sez, "how 'bout givin' me the rumm an' skippin' the brefist?"

"Ah guess ah better," she sez, "ah cain't send ya out agin in this wether an' ya luk tired 'nuff to fall asleep talkin' ta me."

"Ahm tired awright," ah sez, "but afur ah go to bed kin ah see t'other rumm, Bernie tol me 'bout it."

"Shur," she sez.

In the rumm we wuz in ther wuz a door in tha middel o' one wall. She opened it an' ther' wuz 'nother door back to back wit it, she opened thet one inta a rumm big 'nuff fur beds fur two futball teems. In tha middel wuz a king size bed up onna platform an' ther wuz furn'shur like ya see in tha movies fur sum fancy place. Tha batrumm wuz big 'nuff fur a swimmin' pule an' hed mor difrunt siz tubs than ah nu whut ta do wit.

"Wow," ah sez, "how much is this?"

"This is my rumm," she sez, "if ya wanna share it wit' me it'll cost ya two hunnert dollars."

"Ya mean ya comes wit' the rumm?" ah sez.

"Thass rite," she sez.

"Wen do ah hafta chek out," ah ast.

"'levin aclok, after brefist," she sez.

"Iffin ah hed tha bred fur this rumm," ah sed, "ah'd skip brefist an' stay wit ya till 'levin. Luk, ah'll keep ma door open. Ifen ya wanna share my rumm ah won't charge ya nothin'."

"Thanks," she sez, "ah'll see ya in tha mornin'. When yure redi fur brefist nok on ma dore. Iffin ah don' ansir cum down stares."

"Wate a minit," ah sez, "caint we work sumpin out 'bout payin?"

"What ya got in mine?" she ast.

"Rite now all ah got in mine," ah sez, "is takin a shour and goin ta sleep, but when ah wak up ah may hev sumpin else in mine."

"Okay," she sez, "when ya wak up iffin ya fine a way to pay cum on in, ma door will be opin too."

Ah tuk a shour an' jus' 'bout maid it ta bed afor ah fell asleep. It musta bin 'bout ate aclok.

It musta bin a littel pas' won when ah got wuk up by sumbuddy gittin' inta bed wit me. It dint tak me long to figgir it wuz Irma nekkid. Ah nivir sleep wit nuttin on maself.

"'Lo, Jack," she wispurred, an' went rite ta work on me. In 'bout ten seconds she sed, "Well, ah guess yure awak now". She jumpt outta bed and stude lookin down on me. She wuz ezy ta see cause lite wuz comin' from 'er rumm—an' she lookt mitey gud ta me. "Ya figgerd a way ta pay yit?" she ast.

"No," ah sez.

"Well, keep workin' on it," she sez, "iffin ya think o' sumthin ah'll be nex dore, but 'member ya cum thru thet dore it's gonna cost ya a hunnert bucks."

She went back in 'er rumm leevin tha dores open so I cud see 'er nekkid on 'er bed. A lite on 'er bed wuz on so she wuz like inna spotlite. Ah figgerd she wuz 'spectin' me to run rite in affir she got me hot reel quick, but I wuz gittin mad fur 'er waking me lik thet. Ah got up an' started fur 'er rumm an' she wuz watchin' me. When ah got ta tha dores ah closed mine an' lockt it. Ah went bak ta sleep, ah wuz still tired, an' ah felt gud thinkin' how she felt wen ah clost tha dore.

'Bout three aclok ah wuk up by maself. Ah figgird thet wuz 'nuff sleep and begin thinkin' 'bout Irma. Ah got up and opent ma dore ta 'er rumm, 'ers wuz still opent. She wuz asleep atop er' bed wit' nuttin' on. Ah nokt on 'er dore 'till she wuk up.

"Whaddaya want?" she sed haf asleep.

"Ah wancha ta waik up," ah sez, "ya wok me up an' ahm jus' returnin' tha favir, an' ah wancha ta no ma dore is open case ya wanna visit me agin.

She din't say nuttin an' ah went bak ta bed thinkin' she'd

be in afore long—an' she wuz. Ah wuz jus' droppin' off ta sleep agin wen ah felt 'er gittin' inta bed wit me. She rite away begun workin' on me. It din't tak long an' she begun ta jump outta bed agin but this time ah grabbed 'er.

"Don' do thet, Jack," she sez.

"Wy not?" ah sez.

"Cause ya kin get inta big trubbel," she sez, "ah no evry cop in tha county. This is jus' for play, nuttin' mor, git it?"

Ah let 'er go.

"Ya want mor, ya gotta pay," she sez.

"Ah got no mor money," ah sez.

"How ya gonna eat afta ya leve 'ere?" she ast.

"Ah'll use ma creddit card," ah sez.

"Wy din't ya tell me ya gotta creddit card?" she sez, "ah take creddit cards. Now iffin ya want me ya kin hav me an' use yure creddit card." She started bak ta 'er rumm.

"Wate," ah yelled, "c'mon bak, "we'll start 'ere an' go to yure bed later."

Fur tha nex' for er five owers we wuz goin' frum one bed ta tuther. 'bout ate aclok ah lookt outta tha windo. Tha tempashur hed dropt an' everthin wuz ice. Frum T-V we learnt all majur hiways wuz clost. Ah cawld ma boss an' tol 'im ah wuz stuk an' wud call 'im wen ah cud git goin' agin. Ah ast Irma iffin ah cud stay an' she cud giv me dinner too. Ah sed she cud put it all on ma creddit card. She rolled over on top o' me and sed, "Sure, sport, wy not."

All tol ah spent thutty six owers wit Irma an' we wuz wit itch udder evry minit includin' tha battubs. All thet time wit a wommin wit no clos on wuz a new 'spearience fur me. Try it sumtime an' yull git to no eech udder purty dam gud. Irma an' me did an' we hit it off real gud. After we wuz lokt in by tha ice Irma got real frenly, an' ah think she begun ta injoy tha party same as me. We evin tol' each udder 'bout arselves. Irma wuz planin' on maryin' a real rich man an' wuz tryin' ta deeside 'tween a fansee cruse or a fansee reezort ta meet a guy. She figgird she'd say she wuz the widder o' a rich ranshur. Thet wuz allmos tru 'cept 'er huzbin warn't rich an' warn't no ranshur. He hed a littel farm an' a littel trakter which run 'im over an' kilt 'im tha sekin yare they wuz maryed. Ah tol Irma she hedda larn ta talk better iffin she wuz gonna pull it off. Rite thin she begun tawkin' like a real laydee. She sed she cud fit her tawkin ta the peepul she wuz wit. She sed in kollig she wuz inta playaktin. How 'bout thet, a hore wat went ta kollig.

Well, tha wether hed to cleer an' ah hed to git movin. Irma giv me a speshul brefist an' a bag a' fud ta taik wit me. Ah giv 'er ma creddit card an' she giv it bak ta me.

"Firgit it," she sez, "ah do a strikkly cash bizniss. Ya don' oh me nuttin."

Ah tuk all tha money ah hed an' giv it ta 'er. It cum to sevintee dollers an' thutty sens. Ah sed, "here, tak whut ah got."

She sed, "No, sport, ya don' oh me nuttin'. Ya giv me a gud time, ah injoid it."

Ah tuk ma money bak an' sed, "Irma, ah got sumpin fur ya in ma rig." Ah wint an' got a littel pakig ah hed inna hidin' plase in ma cab an' giv it ta 'er.

"Open it," ah sez. She opent it an' 'er ize got big. She lukt it over an' kept lukkin' an' turnin' it. Ah stud watchin' 'er an' finely set down she wuz takin' so long. She din't say nuttin. Finely she wuz dun an' set down. Ah cud tell she wuz eggcited. She lukt at me real hard. "ya don' wanna giv me this," she sed, "ya don' no nuttin' 'bout whut it's wurt. Wear dija git it?"

"It wuz giv ta me," ah sed, "an ole injun drivin' a pick-up got stuck an' ah stopt ta hep 'im. He wuz a purty gud makanik hisself but he warn't gittin nowairs. Ah spent mor time wit 'im than ah shudda but tha dam truk riled me an' ah got stubbern 'bout fixin' it. Ah musta bin a cuppel owers wit 'im, usin' ma tules, an' ah giv' 'im one o' ma spar parts. Ah got tha thing goin' an' he wanted ta pay me but ah tol 'im, "No." it wuz a pressant ah wuz givin' 'im.

He sed, "All rite, an' ah will giv ya a pressant." He tuk this offin 'is neck an' giv it ta me. He sed he made it hisself.

Irma lukt at me. "Jack," she sed, "Ah no injun joolry an' ah ain't nivir seed nuttin gud as this, even inna muzeem. A faymus injun artis maid this an' sined it. Thet ole injun musta bin tha artis. E's ded now, ya musta hed this a cuppela years."

"Yeh," ah sez, "ah wuz waitin' ta giv it ta summun speshul. Irma, ya giv me a pressant, now ahm givin' ya won. Ah ain't intristid in wut it's wurth, it's yurn. Ah'll nivir firgit ya, Irma, an' now mebbe ya'll 'member me.

Thass the las ah seed Irma. Ah nivir don thet run agin. Mebbe sumday ah'll go bak jus ta see 'er, but ah 'spect she's got 'erself sum rich guy an' ain't thar no more—an' mebbe thass gud, it cuddint be tha saim enniways.

WHAT KIND OF FAMILY

Some people might characterize the family as dysfunctional, others would disagree. I knew it well. I'll tell you about it and you can make up your own mind.

The family consisted of a husband, a wife, a son, and a daughter; the son was two years older than the daughter. It was the perfect nuclear family except there was no dog. I knew the family through the husband, the titular head of the family. I met him in college when neither of us had any money. We worked our way through school as automobile mechanics, we both loved fooling around with cars. I did it just as a hobby but he ended up with it as a career. I became a clinical psychologist just making a reasonable living, and he became wealthy as the owner of an automobile dealership. Fortunately, our relationship didn't depend on money and we remained good buddies.

Over the years as he went from mechanic to garage owner to used car dealer to a franchised new car dealer and from a bachelor to a married man to the head of a family I watched his progress. He got married right after he was able to get his own garage. By that time he was thirty years old, his wife was twenty. He took the responsibilities of ownership and marriage very seriously. He believed strongly that the man should provide the living and the wife make the home and raise the children. To confirm his feelings he soon made his wife pregnant and their son was born a year after the marriage.

I will call my friend, "Jack" and his wife, "June", the son will be "Roy" and when the daughter arrives she will be "Ruth". If they had a dog they would call it "Rover"

In the first ten years of their marriage Jack was tending to the development of his business and June to the development of Roy and Ruth. By the end of that time the natures of the business and the children were established.

From the beginning Jack had it in his mind, so he told me, to groom Roy to take over the business. June had other ideas. She told me she thought the business and the making of money was Jack's first priority, that she was second, and that the children were third and fourth respectively. She said this was not the philosophy she wanted her children to have and when Jack left the children's early years to her care she made sure they would have different standards.

Well, when Jack thought it was time to take Roy under his wing and teach him the business, Roy wasn't interested. After college, with his mother's encouragement, he went on to Law School. Jack then told me he thought Ruth might marry someone he could groom for the business. She married a poet school teacher who refused to even consider the business.

Shortly after Ruth's wedding June invited me over for dinner. After dinner we were having a cordial when Jack said, "I don't know what the hell to do. I have a wonderful business and neither of my kids wants it. If I sell it I'll have nothing to do, it's all I know. I don't think I'll ever be able to get a partner I would be happy with. If I keep it, it will consume all my time and I'll have no time for June." He turned to June, "And June, honestly, that will be worse for me. June, what would you like me to do?"

June was quiet for a moment then asked, "Would what I want make any difference?"

"June, I promise you that I will do whatever you want, and we have a witness to that promise."

June didn't hesitate. It was as if she had been anticipating the question.

"All right, Jack, what I want is for you to make me an equal partner in the business."

THE WIDOWED MOTHER

It had never been in Mary's life plan to become a widow when she was just sixty years old and she was angry at Clarence for leaving her contrary to her plans. But then her plans had never factored in that he was twelve years her senior.

During their life together Clarence had never done anything that she hadn't approved of, and now, unannounced, he had abruptly left her. She had not been aware that he had had any serious health problems, but he had always been the quiet one, never volunteered any information. Perhaps his profession had something to do with that, a philosopher who was Emeritus Professor of Philosophy at the university. He wrote books and gave papers. Mary thought he spent a lot of time in the clouds with his philosophical thoughts. He frequently worked at his desk after Mary went to bed and occasionally Mary would find him asleep there when she got up the next morning. This particular morning when she found him he was in a sleep eternal.

Everything had been going so well until that morning. When his age mandated his retirement, and they had to give up their house on campus. she decided to move to the suburbs. They bought a little house with a little land. She fixed up the house and had a little garden. With their son nearby everything was just as she had planned.

Their son; he was the only child, the one term pregnancy from five. Mary thought five pregnancies were enough for her and would not try again. Mary could never understand why or how it happened but it was apparent that Clarence was the influential parent where their son, Harold, was concerned. He was a bright child, in school a quick study, a favorite of the teachers, valedictorian of his high school class. Early on he had an interest in science. In school he took honors courses in math and physics. He probably could have had an acceptance in any college he chose to attend but he went to the university where his father taught because he got his tuition free as a faculty member's son and because he could live at home. Expense was a major consideration. He graduated with honors and stayed right at the university to get a double PhD, mathematics and physics. His PhD thesis was outstanding. It was published in a major scientific journal and it made a name for him in the field of physics he had chosen. He had stayed at the university as a post-doctoral fellow and wrote several other articles. He gave a paper at a scientific meeting that attracted scientists from all over the world. As the result ot that paper he received offers of a position in several research facilities here and abroad. Before he could make a decision where to go after his fellowship his father died. Harold had been close to his father throughout his college and postgraduate years. He was like Clarence in many ways: quiet, introverted, completely absorbed in his work, frequently with his head in the stars, socially unsophisticated and uninterested in social events and pursuits, and timid about a personal relationship with a woman. About two years before he died Clarence took Harold aside, told him that the odds were overwhelming that he would die before Mary, and he would be greatly relieved if Harold promised he would take care of his widowed mother. Harold promised.

Now his mother was a widow and Harold felt compelled to remain close by so he accepted the university's offer to remain in the physic's department as a faculty member. He knew he was a hot commodity and made the proviso that he would be given a place on campus where he could live. The university wanted him badly enough that they gave him the title of Research Professor that carried with it the privilege of having a house on campus. In return the university got a share in any patents that might result of work that Harold was doing.

Alice was the fourth girl in her family, and there were no more children. She was born and brought up in a modest home in a mid middle-class neighborhood not too far from the university. Her three older sisters grew up to be beautiful bubble-heads. Alice was not beautiful but her head was well supplied with brains. Her father was a foreman in the huge local factory. His formal education had stopped after high school but he was an avid reader, especially in engineering subjects. At work he submitted numerous suggestions for improvements on the machines he worked on. Many were adopted and he was amply rewarded for each one adopted. Eventually he was moved from machine to machine specifically to get his suggestions for improving the operation. He was making a good income and was happy in his work. Alice's mother had been a grammar school teacher before her marriage but gave up teaching when she became pregnant the first time. She devoted herself to making a home and bringing up her daughters.

Alice was the only child to express a desire to go to college and was mightily encouraged by both her parents. She did extremely well on her pre-college math exam and was offered a scholarship at the university. She took a BS in mathematics with a minor in physics. She decided to take a year off after graduation before going on to a graduate degree and applied for a position in the physics department at the university. She got a position where Harold was working as a post-doc fellow.

Alice was not assertively beautiful like her sisters but was quietly attractive so that a single man looking for a date might readily approach her. Harold was a single man but was not looking for a date, and though he would avoid talking to one of Alice's sisters he would not avoid talking to her. Nor did he when about two months after she began working there she timidly approached him late one morning and asked if he would help her with an equation she had been working on. He was surprised when she asked, and she was surprised when he graciously put aside what he was working on and helped her. She was tremendously impressed and decided immediately she wanted to know him better. It was getting on towards noon and there was still more work to be done on the equation. She asked him if he planned to have lunch in the cafeteria. He said he did and she asked if it would be okay for her to have lunch with him so they could finish working on the problem. He liked the idea.

And that's the way it began.

That Sunday morning when Mary called Harold to tell him his father had died Alice was in the apartment with him. She frequently spent weekends with him. Mary knew it and never objected or raised questions. She had met Alice on numerous occasions and liked her; she expected Alice and Harold would eventually get married. So Alice went with Harold that morning to Mary's house to give some moral support to the sudden widow.

When this happened Harold had not yet decided where to go when his fellowship ended. He expected that wherever he ended up Alice would be with him as his wife so she would have a lot to say about any decision he made. They had discussed this on more than one occasion. Driving over to Mary's house that morning Alice had unhappy thoughts. She realized Clarance's death could disrupt all her plans for the future. Of course she was right.

Events moved very quickly after that day. It was not long after that Harold signed the agreement with the University. He stayed on in his apartment because the promised house on campus was not yet ready. Alice pushed him to get married immediately but he felt the responsibility for his mother militated against a precipitous marriage; he just wasn't ready to get married at this difficult time.

Mary was delighted when she learned Harold was staying with the university and what the terms of the arrangement were. She said immediately that there was no reason to keep her house in the suburb, that she would move in with Harold and keep house for him. So it was that Mary moved back to the campus where she had lived so many years with Clarence, and she took over the little house where she and Harold lived.

To assuage Alice's disappointment and anger Harold turned over his apartment to her so she could move out of her parents' home and have a place of her own. Alice took the apartment but was not happy about it and was determined to change the situation. Harold was the man she wanted but realized Mary wanted him too and so far Mary was winning the contest. To Alice the problem was simple, how to move Mary out of the picture. She considered all the options she could think of but didn't come up with anything practical and safe. She finally decided there was no such solution and settled on a plan that required she take a chance. It took her six months to achieve the goal she had set but finally she was successful. Harold would spend some weekends in the apartment with her and on one of these weekends she made her announcement. They had been making love one Sunday morning and were still in bed when she said, "Harold, I saw the doctor last week."

Harold was shocked and concerned. "Alice, what's the trouble? I had no idea you were having a problelm."

"*We're* having a problem. I'm pregnant."

"Oh, my god. What are you going to do?"

"*Harold!!* What are *we* going to do. This is your problem as much as mine."

"It is?"

"Yes, it is!!. You're the father of this baby."

Harold was quiet, thinking, "I'm a father? When Alice says that, in no way will she have an abortion. She wants to force me into marrying her. Now what will Mary say?" Finally he said to Alice, "Y:ou sprung this on me and I haven't had time to think about it. You've been thinking about it for a while, what do you want to do?"

"I want us to get married—soon!"

"Well, we're to go to Mary's for cocktails and dinner tonight and you can tell her then."

"That sounds good to me. I've been wondering how she will react."

"We'll soon find out."

They got to Mary's late afternoon, and as usual Mary had everything ready.

A half hour after they arrived they were seated in the living room having a drink and canapes and Alice decided this was the time. "Mary," she said, "I have some news to tell you"

"Good," said Mary, "I love to hear news."

"Well, I hope you'll love this. I'm pregnant."

"Pregnant!!," she yelled. She jumped up, ran over to Alice, kissed her and gave her a big hug. Then she took her drink away. "Alice, no alcohol while you're pregnant! I'll get you a soft drink, what would you like?"

"You're right about the alcohol, Mary. You go back and sit down. We'll talk a little bit then I'll get myself something more suitable to drink."

Mary went back to her chair. "Oh, I'm so excited, Alice. That's wonderful news." She paused a moment then, "Are you two married?"

Harold answered, "No, we're not, Mom."

"Well," said Mary, "you can't wait very long." She turned to Alice. "Have you thought what kind of a wedding you'd like?"

"I don't want a wedding. I want to go off next weekend and get married."

"Oh dear," said Mary, "What do your parents say about that?"

"They don't say anything, they don't know I'm going to get married."

"Do you plan to tell them?"

"Oh, I'll tell them after it becomes evident that I'm pregnant."

Mary was quiet a moment then spoke up, "Alice, I think your parents will be terribly upset if you do that. You must have a very good reason."

"Mary, I have three older sisters, each had a great big wedding that costs my parents what was for them a fortune. I don't want to do that and if I tell them I'm going to get married they will insist I have a wedding at least as big as my sisters had. Their weddings took months of planning and I don't have the luxury of that time. I don't like big weddings and I'm disturbed at the thought of my parents spending a large sum of money on me for something I don't even want.

I won't have it, Mary. If you can think of some way I could tell my parents that without upsetting them I'd be glad to know it."

"You don't want your parents or me at your wedding?'

"That's right. I consider it a legal ceremony not a wedding"

"Oh dear," said Mary again. She turned to Harold. "Harold, you're the professor, come up with something."

Harold had been listening quietly while the two women were talking. He didn't answer Mary immediately, so she spoke again, *"Harold!!"*

"Okay, Mom, I heard the order. I was just thinking how to accomplish it. You know I'm a scientist and that's how I think. I send a message straight and to the point. I do not feel responsible for how it's received. I would advise Alice to tell her parents the whole truth; that she's pregnant, that she plans to get married soon, and that she will not have a wedding."

The women were silent. Mary was the first to speak, "I agree with the message, Harold, but not with your attitude, I think it's very important how the message is delivered. I do feel some responsibility for how it's received." She paused. "I think the best way to do it would be to invite them over for dinner to hear some news our children want to tell us. I think if I demonstrate my approval for what Alice wants to do they may be less upset." She turned to Alice. "What do you think, Alice?"

"I think it's a fine idea, but it will have to be some day this week."

"You're right. I'll make all the arrangements. Now there's something else to consider. Alice, I'd like you to move in here when you come back from your wedding. Harold has nice accommodations with plenty of room for his wife."

Alice was prepared for this. She didn't like the idea but couldn't come up with a practical alternative. "All right, Mary, we'll work out the details later."

The week went quickly. The dinner with Alice's folks took place Wednesday evening and went better than Alice had anticipated, mainly because Mary in effect took over, using her role as hostess to full advantage. Alice's folks were shocked and chagrined but considering their situation as guests of the mother of their soon to be son-in-law, they felt unable to raise any vehement objections. Besides, they were very happy to have Harold as a son-in-law. When they got home and talked about it they decided it was much more important to have a good relationship with Harold and Mary than to have a fuss about the wedding decision. They decided the money that had been set aside for a wedding would be added to what they would have given as a wedding gift. On Thursday Alice and Harold went to City Hall and were married. On Friday after work they took off to a little resort not too far away to spend a weekend honeymoon there. Saturday evening after dinner they returned to their suite just to talk. Alice brought up the subject, "Hal, what are your feelings about moving in with your mother?"

"Your feelings are more important."

"I don't like it. I don't like living in what Mary considers is her home. I want a place of our own. Two women in one house is an invitation to trouble."

"What would you like to do?"

"What I would like and what can be done easily are not the same. I would like to take over that house on campus and move Mary into our apartment."

Harold thought for a moment. "That's the logical and sensible thing to do," he said, "Are you going to tell Mary?"

"I think that's your job. She's your mother."

"I can't do that, besides so far as I'm concerned I think having her with us may be a big help. She will be a full time caretaker, both cook and cleaning woman."

Alice hesitated, then, "Okay, you can't do it. Do you object if I do it?"

"No, I don't object. I just hope you can do it without losing her friendship. If you get to the point where you need some help I'll support you."

"Good. I won't do anything right away but if she starts supervising my pregnancy I don't know how long I'll be able to take it."

"That's fine. I'll be giving it some thought too. Meanwhile we'll keep the apartment."

"All right. I feel better about it."

After the honeymoon weekend Alice moved her clothes in with Hal. Mary quickly demonstrated she was more than a full time caretaker, she ran the home; made out the menu, did the shopping, told Alice what to eat and how much, told Alice how to exercise and how long, told Alice how much rest to get and when to go to bed. Throughout that first week Alice was getting more and more frustrated and angry. On Thursday she decided her emotional state was bad for her pregnancy and on Friday she saw an opportunity and seized it. She came home from work about five o'clock but Hal was not with her.

Mary asked, "What time do you think Harold will be home for dinner?"

"I don't know. He's deep into a project."

"Well, I'll give him a call in his office."

"He's not in his office, he's at the apartment."

"I thought he was working on a project."

"He's working on it in the apartment. He has a whole massive computer set-up there and when things get very intense he works there to avoid interruptions at work."

"I didn't know that. He could bring his computer here."

"No, Mary, his equipment takes a lot of space. There's no room for it here."

"Oh," said Mary. She punched in the apartment number and spoke to Hal. When she had hung up, Alice spoke up, "Mary, we've been guests in your house for a week, I think that's long enough. Hal and I will move into the apartment.where he does so much of his work. It will be easier for both of us and I'll be able to be with him.

"Alice, leave it to me. I'll find a place for his computer stuff right here."

"No, Mary, I've given this a lot of thought, it won't do. This is a nice little house and perfect for you. We're moving."

"It's evident you're determined. Just remember, if you change your mind you're always welcome back. I admit I love it here. It's like when I lived here with Clarence."

"I'm sure, and I hope you're able to stay here as long as you want."

"What do you mean? Why shouldn't I?"

"Mary, you know the university considers this a very special place. You live on Professor's Row. When the university finds the professor is not living here it may not be willing to let you stay." Alice paused. "That's a chance we'll just have to take."

Mary was silent, then "Harold will be home soon. I'll get dinner ready."

When Hal came home he told Mary he would be ready for dinner in five minutes and disappeared into his room. Alice followed him in and told him of her conversation with Mary.

At dinner Mary brought it up. "Harold, Alice told me you plan to move into the apartment."

"That's right, Mom."

"Why didn't you tell me, Harold?"

"Alice told you, that's the same thing. Is this a problem for you?"

"Yes. I'd like you to stay here."

"Didn't Alice tell you why that's not a good idea?"

"Yes, but I think I could find a place for your computer equipment here."

"Mom, there's no place here for both my computer stuff and for Alice and me."

"I'd like to come over to your apartment and look at it."

"Fine. Alice can bring you over tomorrow. I'll be working all day on a project I've started. After dinner tonight I'll be going back there." He turned to Alice. "Don't wait up for me tonight, I may be very late or I may sleep there and come back for breakfast."

Everyone ate quietly for a moment until Mary spoke up, "Harold, when do you plan to move?"

"The first chance I have some free time. It won't take more than a couple of hours, it's just clothes."

"Not this weekend, I hope."

"Okay, not this weekend."

The next day Hal went to the apartment early, Alice and Mary came a couple of hours later. Mary looked at the computer array carefully and took some measurements with a tape measure, writing down the figures. She spent another forty minutes looking over the entire apartment. All through the inspection she made no comments. Back home she made some measurements in every room of the house but still no comments. The rest of the day she was unusually quiet and retired early.

At their Sunday dinner the next day Mary addressed Hal, "Harold, I don't like it but I'm reconciled to the move, However, I've decided it will not be as you planned. When the move takes place, you will move your stuff here and I will move myself to the apartment. That's final. There's no need for further discussion." She paused, "Just give me a few days notice so I can pack my stuff." She paused again. "Now, Alice, finish your carrots, the baby needs them."

THE NEIGHBORS

When I opened the front door this tall well dressed young man was standing there. He showed me his identification, a detective from the police department. He wanted to talk to me about our neighbors. I told him my husband was not home and he said he had already interviewed Tom at the police station at the time he brought the pictures in. I invited him in and we sat down in the living room. He said he would like me first to tell him what I knew about the Masons, our neighbors. After I told him what I knew he said he might ask me some questions. I gave him permission to record our conversation so he set up his recorder.

We moved into the neighborhood five years ago right after my husband retired from an active law practice. The Masons were already well established here although Max had retired only a couple of years ago. They were very cordial and we soon became good friends. Max is a few years older than Tom and sort of took him under his wing. He had been in the construction business and was a tremendous help in all the maintenance work a home requires. Millie Mason and I became fast friends, we were about the same age.

We are all bridge players and we had a regular bridge game once a week. The first time we played it was the Masons against the Bradleys but in the middle of the game Max and Millie had a tremendous row over how Millie bid and played her cards. Ever after that it was Max and I against Tom and Millie. Both Max and Millie were pleasant, good-hearted people but had explosive tempers on short fuses.

The day this all happened it was their turn to host the game. At the appointed time Tom and I went over. Tom had his new digital camera with him because he wanted to show it to Max. The door was open so we walked in and called out. The bridge table was set up in the usual place along with the chairs. After we called out a second time without an answer, Tom walked into the kitchen. I heard him say, "Oh, my god!" He yelled out to me not to come into the kitchen but to call 911 and tell them to send an ambulance for two unconsciousness people. By the time I finished calling I could see the flashes from Tom's camera. He was taking a pile of pictures. I yelled if it were okay to come in and by the tone of his negative reply I knew I better stay out. When the ambulance came I sent the attendants into the kitchen I heard talking and one of them on the cell phone talking to the police. They came out first with Millie on a litter; she was motionless. They put her into the ambulance and came back for Max. I heard Max yelling and after awhile they came out with him strapped onto a litter. He was wild, struggling against the restraints. Tom told me to go with the ambulance, he was going to stay and wait for the police.

The detective asked me if they had any children. The only child I knew of was a grown son with whom they had had no contact for seven years. Millie told me he had been living at home for two years after graduating from high school. He was bright enough but didn't want to go to college yet. He just hung out with a bunch of guys and got into drugs. Finally, Max got fed up and gave him an ultimatum. A few days after the ultimatum the boy was gone with his clothes, Max's best luggage, whatever cash he could find around, and the art works and jewelry he could get his hands on. The police recovered the art works and jewelry from a pawn shop. Millie said she and Max had written off the boy, don't know whether he's dead or alive.

Tom became very friendly with the detective and was kept up to date on everything that was happening. The detective was impressed and appreciative of the pictures Tom had taken and treated him as sort of a colleague. What Tom had found in the kitchen was Millie and Max stretched out on the floor unconscious with blood in their matted hair and dried blood on their faces. Between them on the floor was a very heavy frying pan.

Millie had a fractured skull and severe brain damage. She never regained consciousness and died after two days. Max did not have a fractured skull and did not suffer severe brain damage. He was diagnosed as a brain concussion. However, he had no memory of anything that had happened from the time he had had dinner until he was in his room in the hospital.

The investigation showed that the blood on the bottom of the frying pan was both Millie's and Max's, and the finger prints on the pan belonged to both. Outside of the kitchen nothing in the house was disturbed and there was no sign of a forced entrance. The first and continuing impression of the detective was that there had been a domstic argument, that Millie had bopped Max on the head, that he had grabbed the pan from her and bopped her on the head, a little too forcefully. This theory was reinforced by an accumulation of Max's finger prints on the end of the pan where he may have grabbed it from Millie. The only problem with the theory was Max's behavior when the ambulance attendants picked him up. They found the behavior typical of accident victims who had had short periods of unconsciousness. They thought it highly unlilkely it could be feigned. Thinking about that, the detective asked Max before he was discharged from the hospital whether he had ever had a concussion before. Max told him he had after having been hit on head at a construction site. He had no memory of how he behaved then.and couldn't remember anyone telling him how he behaved. On further questioning, Max said he had worked years at construction sites and had seen many men hit on the head. He said he had seen all kinds of concussions; the ones with a severe injury were unconscious, when the injury was not that severe consciousness would be recovered quite promptly and the man might complain of headache or dizziness or sometimes would be confused and be combative if someone was trying to help him.

The detective was convinced Max was very clever and could have simulated a concussion if he wanted to. Tom didn't agree and felt there was no motive to feign. The detective thought there probably was very little time between the fight and when we called out to them. Max would not want his neighbors to know what happened, and perhaps he was a little dizzy. The detective thought Max remembered everything that happened and feigned loss of memory.

Tom said there was a possibility that their son had paid them a visit. The detective thought that was a pretty remote chance. Tom said if Max was accused of killing Millie he would defend him pro bono and was confident of getting an acquittal.

The detective agreed there was not enough evidence for a prosecution and thought the case would never be solved.

OFFICE INTRIGUE

I think the service went very well. Daddy's colleagues spoke glowingly about him as they knew him in the office and many of them told short stories of his many little and not so little kindnesses to help them out of tough spots. Vic, my older brother by three years, told three little stories about how Daddy helped him as he was growing up. In the same vein I told three stories about how wonderful a father he was, especially how he was acting as both father and mother after my mother died when I was thirteen years old. My father remarried two years after my mother had died. My stepmother took over with great understanding and we developed a very affectionate relationship.

However, I told nothing about what happened after I became an adult. That's a story I'll tell now.

Daddy was the proverbial "ball of fire" when it came to his profession. After college he went for an MBA. By the time he finished that he thought he would be more successful as a lawyer so he went to law school and became a lawyer. He got a position as an associate in a small but prestigious firm. After two years he wanted to be made a partner but the firm wouldn't hear of it. Their asssociates were expected to spend rarely four but usually five years as associates before being considered for partnership. Daddy told them if they didn't know his worth after two years they wouldn't know it after five. He left, took three of the best of the other associates with him, and set up his own firm. The four were the partners and Daddy was the managing partner. They were all good lawyers and Daddy managed well. The firm expanded and opened up several branches. This was the situation when I was ending my second year at college, majoring in psychology. One day Daddy asked me if I had made any plans for the future. I told him I wasn't sure what I wanted to do. He asked if I had ever considered the law. I told him it was one of my options. He offered me a summer internship in his office so I could get some idea if whether I might like it as a career. I jumped at the chance, not the least benefit was the chance to be close to Daddy. In the office he was involved mainly in contracts, big stuff, like between labor unions and the management of large companies. He was on the side of the companies.

I spent the summer there but I wasn't working with Daddy. I was attracted to the partner who did the litigation and spent the major part of my time learning about trial work. There was plenty of psychology involved in that. I also got a taste of tax work, estate planning, criminal work, and divorce problems both financial and custodial. By the end of the summer I knew my career would be in the law.

I went to law school and interned at the office for the three summers before I graduated. At my last internship, between my junior and senior years, I met Frank, a new associate who came that spring right after his graduation. He was a quiet, unattached bachelor. He was a CPA who decided after a year of accounting that he didn't want to spend the rest of his life doing that. He went to law school and graduated at the time the firm was looking for someone to do tax and estate work. Frank was hired. I was attracted to him and spent that summer doing tax and estate work. Before I graduated Daddy asked me what I wanted to do. I told him I would like to become an associate in his office and be assigned to tax and estate work. My graduation present was an apartment of my own close to the office. That wasn't entirely altruistic; I think Daddy wanted me on my own and out of the house so he and my stepmother could have their privacy. Anyway, I liked it fine and furnished it on Daddy's credit card before I started work on July 1st.

Working with Frank was enjoyable and educational. He's very bright and knowledgeable. The year he had spent as an associate was a learning experience he took full advantage of. I could see he was becoming the fair haired boy of the firm. He already had several clients of his own and was on the way to get more. He had eyes for me but didn't want to establish any sort of a relationship before he made a pitch to become a partner. If he were successful he was afraid it would be attributed to the influence of the boss's daughter. He made his pitch and it was turned down. Before he made it he had decided if he didn't get it he would leave and form his own company. His quiet demeanor camouflaged an aggressive personality.

He offered three other associates in the office a partnership in the company he planned. He didn't ask me and when I volunteered he turned me down. He told me I could take over his job after he left. He had a long meeting with the associates he had asked to join him. In the end they all turned him down. He decided to go it alones. His contract with the firm ended 12/31 and I stayed with him until then, that was for three months.

At Christmas time there was a party for all members of the firm. It was a great party and with an open bar I had more drinks than I thought was safe to drive with. I asked Frank who had not been drinking if he would take me home. He obliged and when we got there I asked him in. We ended in bed in mutually desired sex. We were back in the office for his final week. He had already rented and furnished an office and was ready to go the day after he terminated here. The day he left he shook hands with me the same as he did with everyone else and said he would be in touch with me.

I continued to work in the same division but spent more time with the chief. He was primarily a tax man but did estate work. He was not at ease with the wealthy widows who came in for help with their estates and shunted them over to me. I did well with them and by three months I began getting new clients by referral from my old ones. It was into April by then and for the first time I heard from Frank. He called me one evening at home and said he would like to take me out to dinner. We made a date. I had had no social life since he left and I was ready.

He took me to an excellent restaurant. We talked about what we had been doing. I told him what was happening with me and asked how he was getting along. He said his practice had begun to grow. He had two in help now and realized he was going to need an associate. He asked me if I wanted the job. I asked him what he was offering and how long it would take before I could become his partner. He asked me what I wanted. I told him I would have to think about it. He took me home, I asked him in, and we eventually went to bed together.

He took me out to dinner again the following week and wanted to know if I had made up my mind. I told him I had not and suggested he hire a paralegal while I was mulling if over. I told him I would like to see his apartment so he took me there. We made love and I stayed the whole night. I made breakfast the next morning and then he took me home. I invited him for dinner the next week at my place. This time he stayed all night and was in no hurry to leave after breakfast. We made love again that morning and I fixed lunch. He said he was interviewing paralegals.

It became a routine I looked forward to, spending Saturday nights and Sunday mornings together. I kept delaying my decision about joining his firm. Finally on the seventh weekend he said he couldn't wait any longer; on the next Monday he would begin looking for an associate. I told him he had beat me to the gun; I had planned to tell him before lunch while we were still in bed . . . I told him I had decided I wanted to be his partner.

"My partner", he said, "right off the bat?"

"That's right; not just in the firm but at home too."

He looked at me a moment then suddenly sat up in bed.

"Are you proposing to me?"

"Yes, I am. I'm proposing marriage. You probably never noticed, but these past six weeks I never had to postpone our love making because of a period. Frank, I'm pregnant and it's your baby."

"My god, Alice, I'm not ready to get married."

"You're not interested in having children?"

"I'm not ready for it."

"That doesn't answer the question."

"I really haven't given it any thought."

"Well, think about it now. You've got until I get out of bed to make lunch. Frank, if you don't want a family I'll get an abortion, and I won't see you again if I can help it."

He lay down again and said nothing. I assumed he was debating the pros and cons. After about ten minutes of silence he said, "Alice, let me tell you what I've been thinking and feeling. I feel angry that you put me in this box yet I recognize you left it open so I can get out if I wish. I always anticipated that someday I would get married and eventually have children. I never wanted to get old without them, and hopefully grandchildren. I never anticipated being faced with making a decision this early, or for that matter faced with marriage so abruptly."

He paused a moment then continued, "I think I may be in love with you because I don't want to lose you. I accept that you're pregnant, but there's a way to go before you have a baby; there's no guarantee that you will be able to carry through the pregnancy. I suggest we wait three months and if the pregnancy is progressing normally I'll marry you. If you miscarry we'll continue as we're doing."

"No. I won't wait that long to get married. I will agree to get married quietly without announcing it. If I miscarry we can get an annulment and that will be the end of it."

"What about this partnership deal? You'll want to be an equal partner at home, what about in the firm?"

"In the firm I'll agree to be a junior partner in the beginning."

"What about your present position? You have a contract, will you be allowed to break it?"

"I don't know, I'll talk to them about it."

"My office can't wait for you more than two weeks . . . . How will your father react to this?"

"I'll find out after I tell him."

"When will you tell him?"

"If you agree, tomorrow right after we get married."

"I have an appointment in the morning but if you make all the arrangements I can make it at noon."

"I'll see you at the courthouse at noon. Now I'll get up and make lunch—after I kiss you."

Everything worked out as planned. We got married by some authorized clerk in the Marriage License Bureau. Frank had to go back to his office after the ceremony and I went to see Daddy.

Daddy listened quietly while I told him the whole story then he called Frank and told him he would like to see him after work today. They arranged a meeting in Daddy's office at 5:00. I said I wanted to be there. Daddy said okay and told me to keep everything confidential for now. I went back to work.

I got to Daddy's office before Frank. When Frank arrived, right on time, Daddy stood up as Frank came over to him and said, "How do you do, Sir." Daddy said, "Hello, Frank, sit down and don't call me 'Sir', call me 'Rex', you're part of the family now." Frank looked shocked and remained standing. Daddy continued, "Sit down, Frank, and we'll talk about what to do." Frank sat down next to me. Daddy went on, "I understand your becoming part of the family is as much a surprise for you as it is for me. Have you given any thought about how to manage two separate law firms in one family?"

Frank said, "No, Sir, I haven't" Daddy looked at him and Frank corrected himself, "No, Rex, I haven't."

"Well, for the past couple of hours I have", said Daddy, "Would you agree that two competing firms in one family is a poor arrangement?"

"Yes, I agree to that", Frank said.

"My thought", said Daddy, "is that the best solution is for the two firms to join. Do you have any thoughts about that?"

"As I consider it now", said Frank, "I have several thoughts. I like the idea of a firm of my own. I've only been at a few months and I'm doing well. Alice probably told you I'm looking for an associate and have offered her the job. I think when a little firm joins a big firm the little firm gets absorbed. I don't want to be absorbed."

"I'm not surprised at that", said Daddy. "Would you consider heading a division for two or three years and taking over the whole firm after that?"

"That's an enticing proposition. Can it be done?"

"That depends on you—and Alice."

Frank turned to me. "What do you think, Alice?"

"Take it, Frank", I said, "the details can be worked out." And they were.

None of this was mentioned at the Memorial Service.

When Frank's firm was absorbed Daddy suggested it would be better for me to move into the litigation division. I enjoyed the work during one of my internships and the man

I had worked under was now the head. He needed help and said he would be glad to have me. Frank was noncommittal. We had not changed our living arrangements.

Three months after our marriage ceremony nothing happened regarding the pregnancy. I wasn't pregnant. Daddy asked me if I wanted to have a big wedding. I told him my relationship to Frank had changed since the firm merger and I was arranging an annulment.

Daddy asked, "Does that mean he is no longer a member of the family?"

"That's right", I said.

The first year after the merger Frank was doing okay in his department and I was doing fabulously well in mine, taking over more of the big cases successfully. I was made a partner.

The second year Frank continued to do well. After the annulment our love affair faded away so I didn't see much of him anymore. My career was booming. I won a mega case and became well known in the firm.

The third year it was time for a new head of the firm to be chosen. Daddy asked me if I wanted it and I said, "Of course I want it, I've been working toward it since I joined the firm."

"There's a lot of me in you", he said, "of course all the partners will have a say in it and Frank has indicated he's interested. However, I'll do what I can for you."

Well, I won.

Frank resigned and started his own firm again. I haven't seen him since.

I didn't mention any of this at Daddy's Memorial Service, but it does say something about the kind of a father he was, and the kind of a daughter I am.

OLD ACQUAINTANCE

As soon as I saw him I recognized him. I scanned a whole roomful of men sitting and waiting. My eyes flew over his face and immediately returned. "That's John Boyle," I said to myself, "I haven't seen that son-of-a-bitch for thirty years but I'll never forget the bastard." Of course he had changed since he was eighteen years old: jowls had appeared, skin had sagged, face had become red, hair had thinned, shoulders had stooped a bit, fat had replaced muscle. But the big frame was still there as were the main identifying facial features. No question, it was John Boyle all right. I made eye contact with him and was sure he recognized me.

Steve had brought me out of my office to look at this group of men who had applied for the job advertised in the paper. There were sixty chairs in the room and all were occupied. There were many more men lined up outside the room.

"Mr. Stern," he complained, "What am I going to do with this mob? You wanted me to pick out the three best for you so you could interview them this afternoon—that can't be done."

I told Steve to pass out the list of requirements to everyone and to give application blanks to those who considered themselves qualified. The applications were to be filled out and left. The ones we wanted to interview would be notified to return. If John Boyle filled out an application I wanted to interview him regardless of his qualifications; Steve could still pick out his three best.

It took Steve two days to look over the applications and check the references of those who looked promising. He came into my office with four folders. "I've got my three numbered in the order of my priority," he said, "the other one is John Boyle's."

"Boyle is not one of your choices," I said.

"That's right."

"What's the problem?"

"I checked his references."

"And—"

"There were no accusations but I figure he's an alcoholic."

I arranged time for the interviews and put Boyle last. They were all to report to the outer office at a given time but would be called in by name for interviews with Steve and me. I told Steve I would interview Boyle alone.

The last of Steve's choices left. My secretary would not send Boyle in until I asked her over the intercom. Steve and I discussed the three men we had interviewed, and agreed on the one we preferred. All were told they would be called the next day. The ones not selected would have their names kept on file. It took Steve and me about twenty minutes while Boyle waited in the outer office.

After Steve left I told my secretary over the intercom to tell Mr. Boyle I would see him as soon as I had finished some urgent business. I spent the next twenty minutes recalling some of the more unpleasant encounters I had had with John Boyle during my high school years. When I had recalled enough to ignite my old angry feelings I went over a few scenarios of how I would handle to the best advantage this unexpected gift from Lady Luck. Going over the scenarios took another twenty minutes, delicious for me and I hoped agonizing for Boyle.

Finally, without deciding on a scenario, I switched on my intercom and told my secretary to send Boyle in. He opened the door and came a few steps into the room. I was seated at my big desk and busied myself with some papers without acknowledging his presence. After a couple of minutes, while he stood there, I looked up. He was standing holding a portfolio, obviously nervous, his face deeply flushed. I wondered whether it was always that color or just at times he was nervous or heavy with alcohol.

"Hello," I said, "close the door and come in and sit down." I pointed to a chair close to my desk.

Without saying anything he turned and closed the door and sat down in the chair I had indicated.

"John," I said, "you know who I am."

"Sure, I recognized you as soon as I saw you."

"I thought you did, do you remember my name?"

"Sure, you're Sammy."

"I used to be Sammy, now I'm Mr. Stern."

"You've come up in the world."

"You put in an application for this job after you had recognized me, you must want it badly."

"I do."

"Bad enough to accept me as your boss?"

"That doesn't worry me."

"You must remember high school as well as I do. You made my high school years a series of frustrating, embarrassing, miserable experiences. For some reason I never could fathom I figured you must have resented me, and I certainly hated you. I finally figured you thought I was a lot smarter than you even though you were big and I was small. I thought that perhaps somewhere in your Neanderthal brain you equated big physial size with a big brain and felt with your size you should be the smart one. From that premise I thought it might not be too difficult for you to suspect I stole your big brain. That was one of my favorite fancies, for besides hating you I considered your I.Q. to fall somewhere between moron and imbecile."

I continued, "You took special delight in bullying me. You were no match for me verbally but I was no match for you physically, an obvious fact which you repeatedly demonstrated. The incident I remember most vividly relates to our junior prom. You had no intention of going, a formal affair was too expensive and too refined for your taste. You would rather spend your money on beer and you couldn't conceive of yourself wearing a tuxedo. For a few weeks before the prom you were razzing me about it and the day before it reached a climax. You grabbed me outside the school and deliberately picked a fight with me. You told me you would give me something to wear with my tux, and you did—a juicy black eye. Do you remember that, John?"

"No, I don't."

"You wouldn't, and even if you did you wouldn't acknowledge it. I remember it well. Do you still want to work for me?"

"I wouldn't be here if I didn't."

"What makes you think I wouldn't make your life as miserable as you made mine?"

"I'll take that chance. I remember you were the good kid who played fair. I don't think you've changed."

I opened Steve's folder on him. "You haven't worked in six months, what happened?"

"I had a good job with the agency but it was bought out and I was replaced with a relative of the boss."

"Were all the salesmen replaced?"

"No, some remained. I had the best record but I didn't get along with the new boss."

"What was the trouble?"

"He was rigid about a whole list of chicken shit rules. I don't work by rules. I work in the way that's efficient for me—and it shows in my sales. He insisted that if I work for him I follow the rules or quit. I wouldn't do either so he finally fired me."

"If you were such a hot salesman you must have a long list of loyal customers."

"That I do. I have it with me, do you want to see it?"

"Not yet. How is it that for six months you haven't been able to get work? Have you tried the other agencies?"

"I can only work for agencies that sell luxury cars. My list is no good for cheap cars. I've tried every suitable agency in the area, including this one. No one has been hiring. You know that from the number applying for this job."

"What about other areas?"

"I can't leave this area. My wife has a good job here, that's what we've been living on.—You knew my wife, Alice Wright.

"Alice Wright?! she married you? My god, how did she ever end up with a bum like you?—I had a crush on Alice once, she was a nice girl and pretty. I remember she had a reformer's zeal. I pictured her as joining the Salvation Army. Maybe she thought she could reform you."

"I'm not a bum, Mr. Stern. I was young and foolish once but so were a lot of us. I'm not young anymore and I like to think not foolish. Alice had nothing to do with my getting older but she had a lot to do with my getting smarter. She's a lot brighter than I am; she's got a masters in social work and I never even went to college."

"Does Alice know I'm the boss here?"

"Yes, I told her."

"What did she say?"

"She thought it was a great break for me. She thought

you would give me the job. She remembered you well and said she had had a secret crush on you."

"Did she know how you treated me?"

"Sure, she called me a typical bully and attributed it to my dysfunctional family and my self-hatred. She said it was a sociopathological attempt to bolster my self-esteem. She said I was to be pitied not condemned, and she could help me. And she did. She knows I'm not a bully anymore.—You probable guessed I memorized her analysis of me."

"You're right.—What does she say about your drinking?"

"Why do you ask that?"

"Because you look like alcoholics I've known. You do drink, don't you?"

"Sure, I'm a social drinker, I've had to be. I've made many a sale over a drink."

"What does Alice say about your 'social drinking'? Does she approve?"

"She knows it's helpful in my business."

"Does she think you drink too much?"

"Well, she thinks I do but she has some pretty rigid ideas about drinking."

"Has she called you an alcoholic?"

"She thinks anybody who has more than one drink is an alcoholic."

"So she thinks you're one?"

"She says she doesn't know if I am."

This line of questioning was making John increasingly nervous. He was twitching in his chair and I expected him to jump up any second.

"Do these questions make you nervous?" I asked.

"I don't like them. I don't see what they have to do with my job. What counts is how many cars I sell not how many drinks I have."

"Okay, John, let's see what's in your portfolio."

He opened it with evident relief and took out a huge notebook.

"These are my customers," he said and handed it to me.

I spent more than five minutes looking at it carefully. Each customer had a page or sometimes two listing vital information about him: how he made his living, his estimated income, his home and it's assessed value, his family with all available information including ages of children and grandchildren, how many cars he had, what type and what year of purchase, what features he was particularly interested in and what he disliked. There was a section on cars: when sold and to whom, and a section listing customers whose cars were two years old, and a complete index.

"This is exceptionally well done," I said and handed it back to him.

"It was Alice's idea and she helped me with it," he said.

I thought the help was probably putting the whole thing together from idea to completion.

"Do you have anything else in there?" I asked.

"Yes, Alice put it in and thought I should show it to you." He pulled out a copy of his income tax form from the previous year. "She wanted me to show you my net income from my sales. That's the bottom line for the kind of salesman I am."

I looked at the form; his sales were impressive.

"That's very good," I said, "do you have anything else to show me?"

"No, that's it."

"There's one more thing, John, I would like to talk to Alice. Please have her call me."

"Why do you want to talk to Alice, don't you trust me?"

"I have no reason to trust you. Let's just list Alice as another reference."

"I don't think that's necessary."

"I do. If I don't hear from Alice tomorrow I'll assume you're no longer interested in the job.—That's all, John, I'll be in touch with you a couple of days after I speak with Alice."

He got up but was clearly troubled and annoyed.

"Well, what are my chances, Mr. Stern?" he asked.

"I won't know until after I've spoken with Alice. Good-day, John."

The next morning Alice called me from her office in a state run clinic. I told her I would like to take her to lunch to some quiet place where we could talk and asked her if she could stretch out her lunch hour. She said that would be no problem and we arranged to meet at a restaurant I suggested, one not to far from her office.

When my cab pulled up I saw her there waiting in front of the restaurant. There was no trouble recognizing her; she was pretty as ever and had kept her trim figure. She was dressed simply and in good taste. I paid the driver, got out, and immediately went to her. She was smiling broadly.

"My god, Alice, you look good!" I said, and on impulse hugged her and kissed her cheek.

She giggled and returned the hug and kiss. "You look pretty good too," she said with a big smile.

We had cocktails and a long pleasant lunch. We confessed we each had a crush on the other in high school and brought each other up to date on our lives with particular attention to our marriages. Mine had ended in divorce after six years. It took my wife that long to acknowledge her orientation was homosexual. I was in love with her when we married and she was as much in love with me as she could be. As the years of our marriage slowly passed my love cooled as I realized something wasn't right in our relationship. The divorce was friendly and we're still on friendly terms, enough so that she will still spend an occasional night with me. My wife had two miscarriages while we were married and was not pregnant again.

Alice's marriage was different. She was married in her midtwenties shortly after graduate school. John had been pursuing her for three years until finally she thought she saw something hidden in him that was of value, something she thought she could bring out.

"Have you been successful?" I asked.

"Only partially," she said, "because of the appearance of two major problems that I did not anticipate: the first was that he was proved sterile. After three years of my trying to become pregnant I insisted that he be examined. It proved counterproductive. He was sterile and nothing could be done about it. This crushed what little self-esteem I had managed to build up in him. I was back to square one. Over the next several years I worked hard with him and had some success. He began to function better in business and seemed more content with himself. However, in the last six or seven years I began to realize that although I had won some battles I was losing the war. The enemy had a new powerful ally, alcohol."

"What are you doing about that?"

"I'm stymied. I, or anyone else, can do nothing about it until he recognizes it's a problem."

After she said that she was quiet. Tears came, she wiped her eyes and blew her nose.

"Is it that bad?" I asked, feeling sorry and tender all at once.

"I'm sorry I told you that," she said, "now you won't give him the job."

"Maybe something can be worked out," I said, "together maybe we can do something."

"Sam, you're still the nice guy I knew and had a crush on. You've brought all my old feelings back. Are you going to give John the job?"

"There will have to be contingencies. I would like to talk to you about that. When will you have time again?"

"John knows I'm having lunch with you today but he won't want me to see you again. He's suspicious and jealous."

"It's too late to work on it now. What do you propose?"

"I can take an afternoon off if you can."

I could, so we arranged to meet after lunch in two days, the next question was where.

"How about your office," she asked.

"I prefer not," I said, "my staff will be too nosy about this. Would you consider coming to my apartment?"

"I would if you asked me, I trust you, Sam. Besides I have a brown belt in karate and I'm well along on a black belt."

"You don't need any belts to take care of me, Alice. I'm not the forceful type when it comes to women."

"Fine," she said, it's settled."

My apartment bell rang right at the appointed hour. When I opened the door and saw her standing there I knew I was smitten.

I had worked out a plan but I needed Alice's help. I would give John the job providing he spent a month at an alcohol rehabilitation facility and thereafter remained strictly alcohol free. I told Alice if her state health insurance didn't cover the cost I would loan him the money, interest free, and deduct it from his pay monthly. Alice would be needed to persuade him to do it. I knew there was such a facility upstate but suggested she research several and pick one. The only stipulation was that it be at a distance and preferably one that permitted no visiting. We discussed several scenarios as to how to get him to agree and finally decided on a strategy. By that time it was getting late and Alice had to leave. By a lot of effort I made no passes, verbal or physical.

I arranged to see John in my office the following day and meanwhile had told Steve to hire the man we had agreed upon.

When I saw John he did not appear as nervous but seemed suspicious on the verge of anger.

"John," I said, "you know I saw Alice. What did she tell you of the meeting?"

"She told you thought you could work something out. I don't know what has to be worked out. You hire me or you don't."

"John, I'll hire you with a contingency. Alice didn't tell

me this but I've decided you're an alcoholic and I don't hire alcoholics. The contingency is that you will see a qualified psychiatrist to have the diagnosis confirmed. If it is confirmed you will attend an approved inpatient rehabilitation center for one month and thereafter remain on the wagon for as long as you work for me. I will fire you immediately if I find you have fallen off the wagon. If you wish you can skip the psychiatrist and go to the center directly. When you return you will have a job here."

"If I do this, who's going to pay for it?"

"Do you have health insurance?"

"I'm on Alice's state policy."

"All right. If it doesn't cover I'll loan you the money, interest free, and take it from your salary over a period of months."

"I'm not an alcoholic."

"If the psychiatrist agrees with you, I'll hire you without a contingency clause."

"I'm not an alcoholic."

"John, do you have any questions? I think I've made everything clear."

"You have."

"I suggest you go home and talk it over with Alice. Let me know if you plan to do it. That's all, John, good-day."

He got up with a deeper flush, said good-bye, and left.

I sat at my desk and smiled.

For over two weeks I heard nothing. I debated whether to call Alice but decided to wait a little longer. Late on a Friday afternoon a call finally came, and it was from Alice.

"John asked me to call you," she said, "he left by plane this afternoon and will stay a month."

"Wonderful," I said, "you've won a great victory, Alice. May I take you to dinner tonight to celebrate?"

"Oh, I'd love that."

I picked her up outside her apartment building. She looked wonderful and was all smiles. I was instantly ready to help her commit adultery. We started off for a restaurant about half way between our apartments.

"How did you pull it off," I asked, "did you get some help from a psychiatrist?"

"Two," she said, "my insurance company won't pay for alcohol rehabilitation without a referral from a psychiatrist confirmed by a second opinion."

"How did you get him to a psychiatrist in the first place?"

"I told him if he didn't see one I would leave him."

"Did you mean it?"

"Yes."

"Alice, would you have said that if you hadn't had lunch with me and hadn't come to my apartment?"

"No. You provided the opportunity."

I could have pushed further but decided that was enough. I'm a soft sell. We had a wonderful dinner and I found myself more and more attracted to her.

As we finished dinner she looked at me and said, "Sam, I would like to invite you to my apartment but that building is like your office: the people there are too nosy."

"Would you like to come to my place?" I asked, "We could have a cordial and listen to some music or watch one of my tapes. I have a big collection."

"I would love that. Your apartment is nicer than mine anyway. I saw you had a big collection and noted an opera section. Do you think we could watch an opera?"

We did watch an opera. I picked a short one, "Pagliacci", because the hour was getting late when we started. It wasn't over until just after midnight. I turned off the VCR. "I better get you home, it's late," I said.

"I don't want to go back to my apartment, Sam, may I stay here tonight?" she said.

I was astounded and my mouth must have dropped open.

"Sam," she said, "close your mouth. If you don't want me here you can take me home."

She stood up. I went over to her and we embraced.

"Alice," I said, "I want you like I want to breathe. I just wasn't sure you wanted me."

She stayed that night and never did go back to her apartment except to pick up her clothes, the food she had had in her refrigerator, and the mail on every day it was delivered. The next several weeks were something like a honeymoon. We both worked our regular jobs but our main activity outside of work was making love.

It was getting close to the time John was due back. One Saturday morning we were lying in bed after making love and I was feeling especially tender towards her.

I said, "Alice, what do you plan to do about John?"

"I plan to go back to him," she said.

"Are you serious?!" I shouted.

"Don't shout. Of course I'm serious."

"And what about us?"

"I'll treasure the memory."

"You'll treasure the memory! Hey, memories aren't good enough for me. I don't want a memory of you, I want you."

"Sam, John needs me. I can't desert him now."

I lay back and thought about that for a minute. Suddenly, it all became clear. I thought, "this must be what an epiphany feels like

I said, "John needs you, do you need John?"

"I don't need him," she said, "but I can't desert him."

"I don't believe that," I said, "I think you do need him. I think you need him to be an alcoholic. When he gets back he will have been off alcohol long enough to have been through any withdrawal symptoms he may have had. If you go back with him, Alice, he will be back on alcohol within a month. You will say he went back despite all your efforts to keep him off, but the truth will be that you subtly led him back. You will deny that even to yourself just as you deny his being an alcoholic serves a need you have. You two have grown dependent upon each other, you're living in a symbiotic relationship. He will come back with a degree of independence, and I hope this time with me has given you a degree of independence. If you go back with him you'll both become dependent again. Symbiosis might be a satisfactory life style for you except that alcoholism has its own problems, social and physical. Don't go back to him, Alice. Give yourself and John a chance to be independent, and give John a chance to stay healthy."

"That was a good try, Sam," Alice said, "I believe you really love me, but I don't agree with a word you said. How do you qualify to be an expert on alcoholism and the relationship I have with John?"

"I had a sister-in-law who was an alcoholic," I said, "I liked her and tried everything I could to save the marriage. I read everything about alcoholism I could get my hands on. I learned a lot but couldn't save the marriage. My brother hung on for two years then divorced her. He married again and is happy."

"Yes," she said, "and I believe you and I would be happy together, but if I left John I wouldn't be able to live with myself."

"What are you going to tell him about us?"

"Nothing."

We had made great plans for that last weekend and it had gotten off to a bad start. I was upset and Alice acted as though nothing had changed.

Finally she said, "Sam, let's forget all about John and enjoy each other this weekend just as we had planned. I love you and I'll show that to you every way I can."

She grabbed me and kissed me but I backed away. "I'll go along with everything you want, with one condition," I said, "Are you willing?"

"What's the condition?"

"That if John falls off the wagon you will leave him and come back to me. I swear I will do nothing to entice him off but he gets no second chance. Agreed?"

"I don't know. When it comes to John I don't know if I can trust you. In the beginning I wondered if you were making a play for me to punish John."

"I admit when I saw John in my office applying for a job all the old feelings of anger came back. I was given the opportunity to bring him to justice and I planned to take full advantage of it. I equated it to a war crimes trial. All that has changed now. Sometimes life has its own way of meting out justice. Someone wrote, 'the mills of the gods grind slowly, but they grind exceeding fine'. John has suffered enough. It's time to end the punishment."

"And you think it will be ended if I leave him? How can you think so ill of me and still love me?"

"Alice, I don't think ill of you. You are as much a victim as he is."

"I don't know why I love you, you have such convoluted thoughts."

"Alice, do you agree to my condition?"

"I can't refuse him another chance if he falls off."

"Then he'll be falling off the rest of his life. Get dressed, pack up your clothes and the stuff in the refrigerator, I'm taking you back to your apartment."

"Do you mean it?"

"I have no choice. You won't agree to my condition and I won't change it. I'm not a masochist, I won't torture myself. I agree with Shakespeare, 'If 'twere done 'tis better to be done quickly', or something like that."

"I don't want to go, Sam. Give me this weekend and a chance to think it over." She rolled over to me, put her arms around me and kissed me again. I couldn't refuse her. I was seduced.

The weekend passed. Thoughts of John were on the back burner.

The last week went as the others had. I did not bring up the matter of John again and neither did Alice. I was adjusting my attitude to accept the idea that the affair would just be a pleasant memory. "That might be the best way," I thought, "it would not be the first affair that turned into a memory."

I took Alice back to her apartment the day before John got back. She asked me not to call her but said she would call me if she got into trouble.

John came back sober and I gave him a job. He turned out to be a good salesman.

About six weeks after he started work Steve came to me and said he wanted me to know something before I found out myself. He said John was drinking again, but he didn't want me to fire him. He was already one of his top salesmen. He had not gotten into any trouble and Steve didn't think he would. His past record did not indicate any trouble before he came to work for us. I said okay but told Steve to keep a close eye on him.

It had been over four months since I took Alice back to her place when she called me at my apartment one evening.

"Sam, this is Alice," she said, "would it be all right if I came over and stayed with you for awhile?"

"Are you in trouble?" I asked.

"No," she said, "I just decided you were right. I don't want to play games anymore.

"Do you want me to come for you?" I asked.

"I'll be waiting outside," she said.

The next day I fired John.

BIRTHDAY PARTY

Dear Diary,

My eighteenthe birthday is coming fast and I can see there's going to be a problem, maybe two problems. The first problem is that my folks want to give me a big party, and Jon wants to give me a party too on the same night. The second problem is the kind of a party Jon wants to give me. We have been doing some real heavy petting but I haven't let it go all the way; I'm still a virgin. Jon thought my eighteenth birthday would be the time to go all the way. I told him I don't know about that—and I don't.

Don't get me wrong. I've got strong feelings about making love, and they're all positive. I like the idea of a man and me undressing each other until we're both naked, and bringing our bodies close together: standing up, or with him on a chair and me straddling him, or with both of us in bed with him on top of me or me on top of him. The idea of taking a bath or a shower together seems pretty good to me too.

So it's not that I don't like the idea of sex; it's just that I'm not sure I want Jon to be the first. Sure, I did some heavy petting with him but I have with other fellows too. That's just experimenting, like testing out different techniques different fellows use. Some are better than others. Jon is okay, some others have turned me on more, and some less. Sometimes I think it just happens to be the mood I'm in at the time and maybe that's more important than the man.

I think I'd feel better about it if I could be sure that losing my cherry would just be an event in itself but I don't think Jon would look at it that way. The way he talks it seems he thinks this would be the start of an ongoing relationship. I don't think I want that. Jon is not the guy I would ever want to marry. I'm not anywhere near to getting married anyway. Another thing, I sure don't want to get pregnant. If I'm going to have it with Jon I'll make damn sure he's wearing a condom.

So what am I going to do? Am I going to wait to get laid until some guy I would like to marry comes along?—I think that's going to be too long to wait.

And why isn't Jon the guy I would want to marry? I don't know. He just doesn't strike me as the kind of guy I could depend on to take care of me. He's a dreamer. He's got some talent as an artist and he writes well. He talks about writing and illustrating his own books. He's bright enough and plans to go to state college next year and major in English. If he goes on and gets advanced degrees it seems to me the best he can look forward to is a teaching job somewhere. It doesn't sound to me like he's going to be a great breadwinner.

He's a big handsome guy, he's very considerate and gentle, and he's nuts about me—maybe too nuts.

That makes me worry a little. He'll do anything I ask him. It makes me think maybe I'll be the one wearing the pants in the family. I'd want a voice in the decisions, but I don't want to be the only voice. I don't know, he just doesn't seem to be decisive enough.

Him being the first to lay me would probably be a good experience because I know he wouldn't hurt me, I'm just afraid that after that he'd feel like he had some sort of claim on me. I think he might get all shook up if I then went out with someone else. He'd figure everytime I went out I'd be getting laid. I wonder about that myself. Maybe once it happened I'd figure, "what the hell, why not? There's nothing to lose."

My cousin, Irene, will be coming to the party my folks give me. All the family living close by will be there. Irene is a year older than me, she's finishing her first year in college and I'll bet she's not a virgin. I'll talk to her about it. I'm sure she'll have some ideas; she's got ideas about everything.

Dear Diary,

Today I told Jon I couldn't party with him on my birthday. If he wants to give me a party it will have to be after my birthday. It will be better that way anyway. When I'm eighteen years old I'm an independent adult. I make my own decisions. I'm the one responsible for me; my folks no longer have that responsibility. Of course that doesn't mean they don't have a say. They're still supporting me and that's a big stick they're holding. They don't have to support me if they don't want to. They can set limits to my behavior by threatening to withdraw support. Anyway, I don't want to fight with my folks.

As it turns out my birthday falls on a Friday, and Dad wants to celebrate it on that day. He wants just

the family there which means Jon is not invited.
Anyway, that leaves Saturday night free, so Saturday
will be the night I celebrate with Jon.—I still haven't
decided how far I'll go that night. When I told him
he would have to give me a party after my birthday,
we petted a while. I asked him if he was a virgin. I
guess the question caught him by surprise because
he was flustered but he admitted, apologetically, that
he was. I don't know whether I like that or not.

Dear Diary,

Tonight was my birthday party. It was a great party
especially because mom and dad gave me a car of my
own. It's second hand but in great shape. It was mom's
and she's getting a new one. It's late now but I'm so
jazzed up I can't sleep. Irene was there of course
and she'll come over tomorrow for lunch so we can
have a chance to talk. We really didn't have a chance
tonight. Irene knows Jon because she met him last
year at school one time when he and I were walking
together. I think his looks impressed her because
later she told me she thought he was quite a hunk.
Won't she be surprised when she finds he's a virgin
hunk!

Dear Diary,

What a day this has been! I slept until lunch.
Irene came over and had it with me. After lunch we
had a nice private talk. Just as I thought, Irene is not
a virgin. She said she hasn't had a lot of experience
but has had sex with three different men. That
sounds like a lot to me but she doesn't think so. She
said her first experience was during the summer
before she went to college. She said it was not a
satisfactory experience because the guy was a virgin
too. She said if she were to do it over she would

make sure the guy had had some experience. Then I told Irene about Jon: what he wanted to do and that he was a virgin too. While I was talking to her Jon called. He said he had just registered into a motel and was calling me from there. He said he had two splits of champagne on ice to celebrate the occasion. He wanted me to come right over. He said for me to tell my folks he was going to take me to dinner and then maybe to a movie, and that I wouldn't be home until late. I told him I would either call him back or come there. I asked Irene what she thought I should do. We discussed all the options. We agreed it wouldn't be right to tell the guy I couldn't make it and just let him sit there by himself with two splits of champagne. I could go but not let him lay me, or I could go and go along with his plans. Based on her experience she thought it would be a mistake for two virgins to struggle through the sex act. She thought the chances are it would not be a satisfactory experience for either of us. I thought if I went we would end up attempting it, especially after champagne. Irene said if I had too much to drink I'd end up with an upset stomach instead of an orgasm. She didn't think I'd come anyway because I'd be too scared and he'd be too inept. She had me convinced, and then I had a great idea. Diary, I'm going to give you the conversation I had with Irene about the idea I had. It went something like this: Me: "Irene do you still think Jon is a hunk?"

"If he's still like he was last year, I do."
"How would you feel about getting laid by him?"
"I could think of worst things."
"Even though he's a virgin?"
"I could teach him.—It might be fun for me and educational for him."

115

"Do you want to do it today?"

"You want me to take your place?"

"Yes. Will you?"

"How are you going to do that?'

"We'll both go to the motel in separate cars. I'll introduce you again and tell him you're taking my place because my period has begun and I'm not feeling very well. I'll tell him to carry on as though you were me and I'll leave and tell you both to enjoy the evening"

"Has your period begun?"

"Not yet but I feel it coming, and I know the feeling. How about it, are you game?"

Well, it didn't shock me that Irene was game. I called Jon and told him I was on my way and to be prepared for a big surprise.

We went right to his room. When he opened the door and saw the two of us his lower jaw dropped about a foot. In spite of what I told him he wasn't prepared for that kind of a surprise. He just stood there until I asked him if he intended to invite us in, so he did and closed the door behind us. I introduced him to Irene and they said they remembered each other. Diary, I'll repeat the conversation after that as far as I can remember it.

ME: "Jon, I want you to know that Irene knows all about us and what your plans were for a birthday party for me tonight."

JON: "You told her **everything**, Marge?"

ME: "Yes, **everything.**"

JON: "I hadn't planned this to be a spectator event."

ME: "It isn't going to be, Jon."

JON: "Oh, Irene is leaving now?"

ME: "No, I am."

JON: **"You** are?"

116

ME: "Yes, Jon. My period is beginning and I don't feel so well. Irene has agreed to take my place in every respect if that's all right with you."

Jon looked at her and she looked at him and smiled. She's a very pretty girl.

JON: "Irene, I had planned to make love to Marge, do you want me to make love to you?"

IRENE: "That's something we can decide after we drink your champagne."

JON: "All right. Marge, will you have some with us?"

ME: "No, Jon, I really don't feel very well. We'll make it another time, okay?"

JON: "Okay. I'm sorry you don't feel well, Marge, this is not what I had planned. There definitely will be another time."

We kissed and I left. Now I don't know how I feel about it. I can't wait till tomorrow to get a report from Irene.

Dear Diary,

Irene came over late in the morning and had breakfast with me. She told her folks she was spending the night with me but actually she spent it with Jon. From midafternoon yesterday to early morning today they made love *four* times! She said the first time wasn't so hot but by the fourth it was very good. She said Jon would like another session before she goes back to school so he kept the room for another day. She told her folks she wouldn't be home for lunch but she will join them for dinner. After breakfast with me she planned to go back and spend the afternoon with him. She said he was very accommodating, did well whatever she told him to; he was a quick study. She was also very impressed with his artistic talent. He had his sketchbook there and had been spending his time sketching while waiting for me. She saw the book, marveled over the sketches, and asked him if he would sketch her. He agreed and she modeled for him, first her face, then topless, then nude. After the nude one he couldn't wait any longer. That was the first time. After that they rested awhile, had some champagne, and went at it again. The second time was more leisurely and with instructions from Irene. It was a much better experience. They had some more champagne then went out for dinner. They were beginning to feel pretty affectionate towards each other. After dinner they went back to the room. Jon did some more sketching then they instructed each other in foreplay for almost an hour until they both were so excited they had to complete the process. After that they both went to sleep. Irene woke up first, early in the morning and woke Jon up for a repeat of the night before. That was the fourth one. I said to Irene I thought she did better than I ever could. She agreed and said it would be much better for me now that Jon had had some experience.

I feel better about it too—I think.

PATERNAL
GUIDANCE

"What is a father to do", I wondered, "or better, what is a father **able** to do when his twenty-two year old daughter is in trouble and comes to him for advice?"

The questions arose because that's just what happened. Jean, that's my daughter, called me on the phone and told me she had a tough decision to make and needed my help. It seemed perfectly natural for her to call me; we've had a good relationship ever since she was a little girl. And this kind of problem is something I've been trained for: eight years of college, four years of post-graduate work, and fifteen years to practice it. The difficulty for me was that I didn't know whether I could comfortably wear my clinical psychologist hat under or over my father hat.

Jean was finishing her senior year of college. It had begun with a very traumatic event. During her third year she had established a relationship with a senior student, Ray. This became cemented over the summer when they took a student tour of Europe together. In the fall two weeks after school had begun he was killed in an automobile accident. Jean was devastated but with support from Lily, that's my wife and her mother, and me she hung on at school. At Ray's funeral she met Bob, Ray's brother and ten years his senior. Bob was a bachelor. He was working in a brokerage firm and doing very well. A few weeks after the funeral he called Jean and suggested that since they had both suffered a great loss they had something in common. He thought they might be helped through their grief by talking to each other about Ray. They met and liked each other. Bob was an outgoing personable man, sensitive and caring. They began seeing more of each other and the relationship became closer. This spring Jean is graduating and they are talking marriage.

Jean had never spoken to me about how her feelings for Bob developed nor what part of them had to do with his being Ray's brother. Lily was concerned that the whole romance might be a rebound from the loss of Ray.

I thought perhaps Jean wanted to talk to me about deciding whether to marry Bob, but I couldn't figure out why it was so urgent that she would take a weekend off to come home and talk to me about it. She had told me she wanted to see me in my office because she didn't know whether she wanted to tell Lily. It wasn't difficult for me to arrange to be there on Saturday when she was arriving from college.

When she walked in I knew there was big trouble. The only other time I had seen her this agitated was when Ray had been killed. We greeted each other with a hug and a kiss and Jean sat down. The scene is vivid in my memory so I'll reconstruct it.

JEAN: Daddy, I'm in big trouble!
ART: (That's my name.) Tell me about it, Jean.
JEAN: You met Bob. What do you think of him?
ART: Both your mother and I like him. Do you have doubts?

120

JEAN: I didn't until a few days ago. Daddy, I thought I was really in love with him and maybe I still am, but now I'm terribly confused. *(She began to cry.)* I'm so upset! I feel like I did when Ray died.—(*I waited.*)—The night before I called you Bob said there was something about himself he had to tell me before we finalized any plans to get married. First he told me he loved me and always would and never would be unfaithful. Then he told me he had had several homosexual escapades. He said for awhile he was not sure what his sexual orientation was but had decided he was bisexual and with me could choose to be heterosexual for the rest of his life—now what do you think of him, Daddy?

ART: I still like him.

JEAN: Would you like him as a son-in-law?

ART: I like him and if you chose him as your husband I would still like him.

JEAN: Do you think I'm taking too much of a chance to marry him?

ART: How do you mean, Jean?

JEAN: He has had homosexual experiences in the past, what are the chances of having them in the future?

ART: He told you he would be faithful.

JEAN: Can I believe him?

ART: He has had heterosexual experiences in the past can you believe he will not have them in the future? Either you trust him or you don't. If you don't, then I think perhaps it would not be a good idea to marry him.

JEAN: It is easier for me to trust him in regard to other women than it is to other men. I accept there is something genetic in sexual orientation and that the drive may be so strong he will find it too difficult to stay in the heterosexual mode.

ART: Have you told him this?

JEAN: Yes. He said his reading has convinced him that homosexuality is a range of degrees from a slight tendency to one hundred per cent. He believes he has a slight tendency and his escapades were mainly exploratory.

ART: You weren't convinced.

JEAN: No, but I would like to be.

ART: How do you feel about his homosexual experiences?

JEAN: The thought is repugnant to me.

ART: Have you made love with him since he told you?

JEAN: No.

ART: Will this make a difference?

JEAN: I don't know.

ART: Do you want a family?

JEAN: Yes, and so does Bob.

ART: Are you concerned about homosexuality in the children?

JEAN: Yes.

ART: There seems to be a lot of negatives, what are the positives?

JEAN: Daddy, I've never met a man whom I felt was as close to being exactly what I would want in a husband. He has everything and I'm sure he loves me. Until he told me this I was halfway to heaven. Now I feel halfway to hell.

ART: Perhaps it would be helpful to think about why you feel abhorrence at the idea of homosexual activity.

JEAN: It's the physical aspects that repel me.

ART: Perhaps in the same way the physical aspects of heterosexual activity may repel a homosexual.

JEAN: I hadn't thought of it that way.—Do you think we ought to tell mom?

ART: I don't know how you can keep it from her, but if you don't want her to know I won't tell her.

JEAN: Does she know I came to see you?

ART: No. You asked me not to tell her.

JEAN: All right. I'm going back to school now, don't tell her. I'll think about this some more. Thanks, Daddy, you were a big help like I knew you would be.

After she left I thought about the interview. I was happy she thought I was a help but I don't know which hat I had been wearing.

A PEDIATRIC
CONSULTATION

The doctor, we'll call him Walt, was at his desk writing some notes on the chart of the patient who had just left his office. It would be a lot easier for him to dictate the notes into a machine so they could be typed in nice legible print by his staff which consisted of one secretary. Because he practiced psychiatry he was not willing to risk some breach of confidentiality so he wrote the charts in his own hand and kept them in a securely locked file cabinet.

Rita, his staff, was at the intercom. "Doctor, your next patient is a new one and will be the last for today. She has finished her questionnaire. Do you want me to bring it in first or shall I send her in with it? Are you ready for her?"

"I'm not ready yet. Bring the chart in and I'll let you know when you can send her in." He went back to his writing as Rita brought in the chart and put it in the in-basket on his desk. He finished writing, put the chart in the out-basket on his desk and stood up. He stretched then picked up the new chart and began reading the questionnaire as he walked around the room. He finished reading, returned to his desk, sat down, told the intercom, "Rita, you can send Mrs. Hall in now."

The door opened, Walt said. "Come in, Mrs. Hall, and sit down." He motioned to a chair. She said, "Thank you, Doctor." He noted her voice and facial expression and watched her as she walked in and sat down. He noted how she was dressed, her posture, how she walked, and how she sat. Once seated she was quiet.

Walt looked at her until he got eye contact then said, "Dr. Perkins asked me to see you. He's a very good pediatrician but doesn't often send me a parent. Before you tell me about it I would like your permission to tape our sessions. I will give the tape to you at the end of each session because I would like you to listen to it." She said that was okay so he set up the recorder

He resumed eye contact and leaned forward a bit. This was his usual procedure. He thought it conveyed to his patient that he was attentive and interested in what he was hearing. "All right", he said, "now you can go on."

Mrs. Hall as soon as she began to talk broke eye contact and looked down. "I'm very nervous, doctor, I expected your question and rehearsed what I was going to say so I could tell you my story coherently and concisely. I have three children: two girls six and four years old, and one son two years old. I have a wonderful husband and until my son was born we had a happy family. My husband had been looking forward with great expectation for a son so it was a specially bad blow for him when our son was born badly brain damaged. Early during my pregnancy I had had a severe viral infection, like the flu. Apparently it came at the time the brain was forming. We were told that was probably the cause of the brain damage. Unfortunately, I did not miscarry. We took the baby to a half dozen specialists There was no disagreement about the diagnosis or the prognosis. Finally we were told to stop going to doctors and accept that the baby would never function beyond the level he was born with. That was a nice way of saying that our son was classified as an idiot without hope of improvement."

She stopped talking and continued looking down while Walt waited. After a full minute with neither saying anything she resumed. "My husband finally accepted reality and wanted the child put into an institution but somehow I had bonded to the poor helpless little creature and was reluctant. We visited several places then I took my husband to the kennel where we kept out dog when we traveled. The contrast was evident; the kennel was so much better than the asylums. That's how things stand now. The family is in a shambles, my husband is very angry, my little girls are unhappy, and I'm depressed and frightened. I have an awful feeling that something terrible is going to happen."

She was quiet again and another minute of silence passed. Finally, she resumed. My husband has given me an ultimatum. If I don't have the boy out of the house by the end of the month he will file for a divorce and ask for custody of our daughters. He said he felt any court would agree that I'm not a suitable mother under our present circumstances."

There was another period of quiet then, "I think he's right."

More quiet and finally she looked up, "Doctor, that's my story, can you help me?"

"If there's something about how you're reacting that you would like to change I can help you make the changes but I can't make them for you. You have to do the work yourself."

Gloria Hall was thinking about what Walt had told her. She looked at him intently and said, "All right. I've got just two weeks to settle this. Let's get started."

"Good. Let me start with a question, does your son react differently to you then to anyone else?"

"He reacts the same to anyone: his father, his sisters, the cleaning woman, me. His reactions are the same: scream, yell, cry, spit, hit, or all five."

"In the beginning you told me you bonded with your son. My conception of bonding is that it's a two way street. Your son apparently gives no evidence of bonding to you."

"Well, maybe 'attached' is a better word"

"Does he ever smile or laugh?"

"No, I gave you his entire repertoire of reactions."

"How do you account for your attachment to him?"

"I carried him in my womb for nine months and gave birth to him. He's my child, he's living."

"But you said it was unfortunate that you didn't miscarry."

"Yes, I don't know why God made me carry this badly damaged baby and give birth to him. I can understand if I did something wrong and am being punished for it but why make my whole family suffer."

"Do you think there's a reason for you to be punished?"

"No. I thought I've led a good life."

"Are you a religious person?"

"Well, I believe in God." she hesitated. "I think. I admit I've got some doubts now. Maybe that makes me an agnostic."

"Do you belong to a church?"

"Yes, the First Reformed"

"Have you spoken with your pastor?"

"Yes, poor man is not equipped to help me. His answer to all such problems is to have faith, God will provide a way."

"What do you think of that? "

"Well, if there is a God I believe he will help those who help themselves. I know I have to provide the way. That's why I'm here, Doctor."

"Okay. Let's get back to your attachment. You said you're attached because you produced him."

"And he's living; his being alive is the important part."

"You said your whole family is suffering; how about your husband?"

"He's the most affected. He's been very patient with me but now he's very angry."

"Do you want a divorce?"

"No. It would be terrible for our children."

"Would it be terrible for your husband too?"

"I don't know. We haven't been sleeping together for over a year."

"No sex in over a year?"

"Oh, we've had sex but we're in separate rooms because I put our son's crib in my room so I could take care of him when he wakes up at night; that occurs when he gets hungry which is often." Gloria was quiet for a moment then continued. "I know my husband was deeply in love with me once. I don't know whether he is any more."

"Are you in love with him?"

"I don't know, I sensed his anger when we learned the diagnosis and prognosis of our son and I guess I've been reacting to it. At that time he wanted me to put the child away and I refused."

"What do you think about that now?"

"I made a bad mistake. He was right."

Walt looked at the clock on his desk. "I think that's all for today," he said. He stopped the recorder, took out the tape and handed it to her. "I'd like you to listen to this tonight. We're pushed for time so I'll see if I can get you in soon. Tell Rita I want see you again ASAP."

"Thank you, doctor." Gloria took the tape, stood up, and walked out quickly.

ASAP turned out to be a week. Gloria walked in this time with much more energy than she displayed at the first visit. She sat down while Walt turned on the recorder. She began talking immediately.

"A lot has happened this week, doctor. I listened to the tape that night and the next day began an intensive investigation of nursing homes throughout a much wider area than I had considered before. On my second day out I found one that confined itself to taking care of neurologically impaired patients. It was far from ideal but compared to the others I had visited was by far the best. There are some drawbacks. It is an hour away by car, and it is very expensive. It will cost as much per year as a good private college and he will be there for the rest of his life, no graduation for him. The commute is acceptable to me. I spoke to my husband about it and showed him the contract they had given me.

He said we could afford it for a year and then we might have to reconsider. In the meantime he said he would explore the possibility of getting some government financial help. I then called the place, told them that we would sign the contract, and arranged for the baby to be admitted ten days from now. Once the arrangements had been completed my husband became a different man. I too felt a sense of relief.

I feel terrible I delayed so long but I'm concerned about the expense. I see no way we can afford this year in and year out. However, I plan to follow my husband's lead and take advantage of a year's respite. The entire family needs a year to recover. It's been a terrible ordeal for all of us, and it seems so unfair."

"What about your attachment to your son?"

"That hasn't changed. Every time I look at him I feel guilty about what I'm planning to do."

Gloria paused for a moment. Walt thought she hadn't finished and waited silently. She did continue, "My husband reacted sympathetically when I told him about feeling guilty. A week ago he would have responded with anger or not at all. It was a welcome change for me. He told me I had no reason to feel guilt, I had done more for the child than even God would have expected. Besides the child would not even be aware that I was no longer around." Gloria paused but quickly continued, "I knew he was right but I can't help the feeling I have. I guess somewhere inside of me I still believe my son must be aware of who I am."

"Yet you told me that after carefully observing him on many occasions you were convinced he could not distinguish you from anyone else."

"Yes, I did and I still believe that's true. But I still have the feeling."

"Do you think that because your son doesn't recognize you that he's rejecting you?"

She thought about that awhile before answering, "I guess it does seem that way to me."

"Do you think you may be attributing more brain power to him than he has?"

Again some thought before an answer. "Yes, I suppose it's only natural that I like to think my son is better than he is."

"I think your son is operating on a very simple emotional level: pain or no pain. I doubt he is capable of feeling pleasure. He is certainly incapable of any such complicated emotional states as resentment or rejection." Walt paused then, "It may take you awhile to accept that."

He looked at the clock on his desk and turned off the recorder. He pulled out the disk and handed it to her. "I'm sorry, Mrs. Hall, I've been called to an urgent meeting at the hospital and have to finish this session early. The fee will be adjusted accordingly. I think Rita has found another appointment for you in a week."

"All right, doctor, I'll be here." She picked up the disk and left quickly.

In a week she was back, early as usual for her appointment.

This time when she walked into Walt's consultation room she looked as she did at her first visit, anxious and depressed. She sat down and made no attempt to speak after Walt started the recorder. After a long pause she began, "A lot has happened this past week that I want to tell you about. I decided I would do it in chronological order. When I got home a week ago I played the tape of the visit. I played it again that evening and did a lot of thinking about it. I played it again the next day and did more thinking about it. I spent more time with my son in his room. His room is really the dressing room leading to my bathroom. There is a gate blocking him from entering the closet and another blocking him from going into my bedroom so he has a little area where he can crawl around freely. My habit in the morning is to fill up his stomach and then go in and take my bath without being disturbed. When he's really full he may actually go to sleep for a little while. In any case he's not likely to yell or scream but may just crawl around. Of course anything he comes across on the floor he will put into his mouth and if there are things available he will stuff them all into his mouth until he chokes. That happened to me about six months ago. I had been giving him some crackers and left him to answer the phone. When I came back he was choking. I turned him upside down, stuck my finger in his mouth, pulled out a bunch of partially chewed crackers, and patted him on the back until he got over the attack Three days ago I filled him up from a box of crackers but neglected to put the box up out of his reach when I went in for my bath. My bath is the one time during the day when I indulge myself, and I spend a lot of time in it. I was not disturbed that day and when I came out of the bathroom I found he had discovered the box of crackers. He was quiet and I thought he was asleep until I saw some crackers coming out of his mouth." She stopped for a long pause, took a deep breath and continued. "I'll skip all the details because today will be a short session. It was very careless of me to leave that box of crackers where he could get to it."

She paused to think. Walt remained silent and after a full minute she spoke again, "Omar said a long time ago something like this, 'The Moving Finger writes, And having writ moves on. And all your piety and wit Can't bring it back to cancel half a line Nor all your tears wipe out a word of it.'" Gloria paused again, then "Rita has set me up for another appointment with you in a week. I'm going to need a lot of help, doctor. Now I have to go, my husband expects me to join him at a small private funeral."

Walt stopped the recorder and took out the disk. Gloria picked it up and quickly left.

THE VILLAGE
PRIEST

The meeting was planned to explore the meaning of aggression and more specifically to begin to delineate the behavioral effects of the newly discovered neurotransmitter which affected aggressive characteristics. The year was 2080. The participants were mainly neurophysiologists, psychologists, psychiatrists, and social workers but there was a large audience of interested observers. The press was also well represented. This was a hot topic with tremendous implications and the media was happy to fantasize on what effect this might have.

The first part of the meeting was devoted to the neurophysiologists who described how the neurotransmitter was discovered. It is an agonist which means it stimulates activity; in this instance that area of the brain involved in aggressive behavior. Work was in progress to locate the exact area involved. Animal work confirmed the potency of the chemical. In a colony of monkeys it was found that by injecting an animal on the lowest rung of the hierarchy it was possible to elevate him to the highest rung. This had been confirmed by many different investigators. By far the most important paper and the one that sent the science reporters to the phones was one given by Bion Yu, a Chinese investigator at Rockefeller Institute in New York City. From the time the agonist neurotransmitter had been reported a search had been going on to find or develop an antagonist which everyone expected had to be present naturally. This is exactly what Yu reported. An antagonist had been found. When the antagonist had been given to the top-rung monkey in a colony, he rapidly descended the ladder to the bottom rung. Work was underway to derive the formulae for these neurotransmitters.

The big unanswered question was how the neurotransmitters work in humans. After the hard data of the neurophysiologists, the papers given by the psychologists, psychiatrists, and social workers were speculative. It was evident that human experimentation would be needed to determine whether an injection would turn the office "gofer" into the company president or visa versa.

Exactly what role aggression played in human success was vigorously debated. In this respect many felt there was no analogy between the hierarchies of monkeys and men. Others felt aggressive behavior might lead to success in a chosen field but not necessarily happiness, good health, or long life. There was consensus that experimentation was needed but none on how to accomplish it or even whether it should be pursued. There were many who felt this could be dangerous. It was easy to see the possibility of a nerve gas that could transform a whole population to docile slavery.

The very nature of aggression was hotly debated. In a monkey hierarchy, position on the ladder of rank was important in matters of sex. The agonist drug made the subject monkey dominate sexually thus preserving the line of the most powerful. Does that mean that an aggressive spouse makes the best mate in human society, or that perpetuation of aggressive qualities necessarily strengthens the human race? Aggression in monkeys has to do with domination by physical means. It was agreed that in humans other traits were more significant in determining success in sex or any other endeavor. The conclusion was that whatever name was put on the behavior resulting from the effects of agonist neurotransmitter the nature of it could only be determined by observation of the results of experimentation. The meeting ended with all participants highly stimulated. They sensed history being made, a quantum leap for mankind.

As events turned out the questions of whether or how to experiment became moot over the course of about six months.

It was not long after the meeting that Bion Yu announced the synthesis of both the agonist and the antagonist neurotransmitters. For technical reasons the antagonist was much easier to produce and though sophisticated laboratory techniques were required, it would be possible to mass-produce it. There were no current plans to pursue that possibility although the military was definitely interested.

Bion Yu became the object of intense media interest, the main result of which was frustration on the part of the media and speculation on the part of the populace. His expertise was self-evident but his background was unknown except for what he said it was. He had appeared at the Institute and told a story that he had been a professor at the Chinese University in the city that had been completely destroyed in the recent earthquake. At the time of the quake he had been visiting his parents in a distant city. He never returned to the destroyed city but came directly to America because he felt only at Rockefeller could he carry on the work on neurotransmitters he had started in China. The Director of the Institute referred him to the Chairman of the Neurophysiology Department who after a two hour interview offered Yu a position in his department. He had discerned a genius, that was enough.

The Institute arranged for an apartment and Bion arranged for a young Chinese woman to keep house for him. He was a workaholic, spending days and nights in the laboratory, going home to sleep. The young woman would bring meals to his office. There were some periods when he worked at home and might not come to the laboratory at all. No one questioned his hours. He refused all social invitations and would not talk to the media.

With the neurotransmitters now readily available the question of human experimentation became more than academic. While the debate raged in academia, in the media, and in the legislative branch of government, nothing was decided and no experimentation was permitted until some decision had been reached. There was a general underlying fear that society had reached the point where it was no longer capable of coping with the knowledge developed.

All the debating turned out to be a futile exercise.

The Department of Viral Studies at the Institute was heavily involved in research modifying viral genomes. Whether this was related to what happened isn't known but circumstances suggested there could be a connection. A virus, ubiquitous in nature, had a change in its genome incorporating the antagonist to the neurotransmitter. Somehow the altered virus was released and spread rapidly worldwide in a great pandemic.

The experiment was now the actuality. How to arrange a sufficiently large, well controlled human study became moot.

The virus efficiently injected every human with a 100% effective dose of neurotransmitter antagonist and then took up permanent residence. This assured a continuing supply and ready transmission, including transplacental. The acute infection was not without discomfort. It caused a flu-like syndrome associated with generalized aching, a low grade fever, a loss of appetite, and especially fatigue. The whole episode lasted about a week during which the infected person, though able to function at a low level, slept most of the time. There was no specific system involvement; neither respiratory, cardiovascular, gastro-intestinal, musculo-skeletal, dermatological, nor neurological. As each patient recovered it became evident, first to observers and then to the patient, that a personality change had occurred. There were no more hostile outbursts, one-upmanship was no longer attractive, sadistic and masochistic behavior disappeared, violence was repugnant. There was no effect on intellectual function nor on any nonviolent emotion. Ambition was not lost but the march toward success was to gentler music.

Following the week of acute illness there were no further symptoms nor signs of infection although the virus remained a permanent boarder. The behavioral changes it produced would persist. Humanity was pushed into the promise of a Utopian era.

It was not long after the pandemic had covered the world that it became evident that the virus caused sterility as well as loss of aggressive behavior.

Panic was universal. The whole future of humankind was at stake.

Animals were completely unaffected by the virus so the earth would revert to the "lower animals". There were some who believed that this was God's way of indicating humans had made a mess of things and it was better to start over.

All efforts were directed towards discovering the nature of the problem and devising a method for resolving it. Bion Yu with others went to work full time on the project and it was he who discovered in the biochemical chain that maintained fertility the component neutralized by the virus. By supplying this element he restored fertility which persisted only so long as the ingredient was given. By the time this substance could be produced in quantity, profound changes had taken place in the world.

It was in the United Nations not long after the pandemic sterility that Russia had introduced the proposal for the implementation of the long sought goal of the World Federalists for One World Government. With what previously would have been considered surprising ease the proposal was accepted and plans were begun to make the dream a reality. With hostile feelings blocked, people came to believe that all humans were kin, to be cared for like brothers and sisters. It was not surprising that the Russian resolution was adopted; what seemed surprising was that this had not been done long before.

A World government was formed, modeled roughly on the English and American democracies with executive, legislative, and judicial branches. Several departments were organized to deal with the major world problems: Population Control, Education, Distribution of Wealth, Environmental Control, Health Maintenance, Food Production, Shelter Provision, Research and Development.

No Defense Department was needed but a small world police force was established.

It was the Department of Population Control that was given the responsibility for the distribution and use of the fertility drug as it was now called.

Bion Yu developed the method for mass production of the fertility drug and supervised the building of the plant. After that was finished he announced he was going to take a vacation. He took off with his young Chinese woman—and never returned.

The government established the criteria to determine which couples could qualify to become fertile. They would have to pass rigid mental and physical examinations and courses in human relationships and fathering and mothering. They would have to undergo counseling to assure to the extent possible that the union would be permanent. The criteria would include the density of the population where the couple lived and how many children were already in the family. Quotas were set up for different areas of the world and local authorities administered the distribution of the drug. Lotteries would be held to determine those eligible to submit applications for fertility. The numbers would be limited by the quota. Those who passed the examinations and the courses and were certified by the counselors would then receive the drug and would continue to be treated until a pregnancy occurred.

It was recognized quotas based on population density might prove a sticking point with the Pope. Central America with its dense population was mainly Catholic. However, India, Bangladesh, and China were equally affected. The Pope had strongly opposed the stopping of research directed toward the permanent reversal of the sterility but was not persuasive. That was not the only area of population control where there might be conflict with organized religion. There might well be objection to the use of, "couples" in the criteria rather than, "married couples". The government was not prepared to give ground in either case and the Pope was already coping with a far more serious problem, that of finances.

The Secretary of the Treasury was vigorously pursuing 100% taxation of all religious income above that needed to maintain existence. This applied to all religions but the Pope felt it particularly. He was protesting as vigorously as he could but he had done that in the past and had not been able to prevent the liquidation of all parochial schools. At that time he had warned the world was in danger of becoming Godless. The Humanists had responded and had indicated it was their belief that to become Godless was an opportunity not a danger. They took pleasure in pointing out the violent history of all the world's religions and the stubborn illogical resistence of religion to change and to acceptance of knowledge of the universe. The Pope carried on the dialogue and in another encyclical stated that without God there would be no faith and without faith there would be no hope, and without hope what would life be? The Humanists denied the validity of the syllogism. Faith, they said, must be in humanity not in some supernatural being. Is it any less idolatrous to worship an invisible idol than a visible one?

Parochial education was outlawed.

In the World Legislature the feeling was strong that World Government must be secular.

The little old priest in a small Central American village was troubled. Father Manuel sat on his straight wooden chair, his elbows rested on his ancient wooden table, his chin cradled in his hands. The big well-used official congregation Bible was open on the table in front of him and he was staring at it but not reading. He was thinking unhappy thoughts.

The whole village was nominally Catholic, all 1500 of them. To adhere to current world law his village was limited to six pregnancies this year. He knew this would come out to much less than the 10% negative world population growth which had been decreed; that was because the population density in Central America required it in the formula being used. This had all been spelled out in the schools for the children and the classes for adults who had not reached a satisfactory level of education. Regardless of the theory, the villagers considered the whole business unfair, but there were no pregnancies without the strictly controlled drug that reversed the viral induced sterility.

Because he was the most respected citizen in the village the priest was designated to run the lottery to determine which of the young women who wanted to have a child would be eligible to take the examinations and the courses which were held outside of the village. The first part of his job was to determine whether any of the applicants was ineligible to enter the lottery. This determination included an investigation of the husband. The second part of his job was to pick twelve for the actual lottery from those eligible: six to be sent for the examinations and courses, and six to be on a waiting list for replacements for those who might not pass. The winners had to be names picked by chance. The villagers had agreed that the number entering the lottery would be limited to the twelve picked by the priest plus one "wild card". That one was to be picked at random from those considered eligible but not chosen to be in the lottery. Every young woman was notified if she were considered ineligible. She had the right to appeal to a committee at the next higher level of government. At best that might mean the delay of a year.

It was decided by the villagers that no one would know the names in the lottery except the priest. In effect this left the decision as to who could try to become pregnant up to the priest. There were some nonbelievers who grumbled this was not the intent of the law but others who said the law permitted wide local latitude, and certainly the vast majority of the village population wanted the priest to do it and were confident his decision did not depend on whether the young woman was a good Catholic. The grumblers were not convinced but were outvoted. At least they got the one "wild card".

The old man was looking at the Bible in front of him but seeing the faces of young women who wanted babies. He was despondent. He felt he had been put into the position of an accessory to a crime against God. Every woman who wanted a baby should be allowed to try. Let God decide who would be successful. He didn't want this job in the first place. He had told the villagers' committee that he was opposed to the whole idea. He equated it to what he had read about the Jewish patriarch of the Polish ghetto who had been forced to select those designated for the concentration camps during the Holocaust of World War II. They told him that he was their patriarch and that he was choosing for life not death. He told them that was the reverse side of the same coin.

But when they asked Father Manuel whom he would suggest to do it, he could not come up with a name. He suggested the committee do it but they said that option had been considered and dropped because they knew there would be a conflict of interests that could not be overcome.

So he had agreed and now he was despondent. He had valid applications from thirty young women, 80% of whom would be disappointed. How could he call any of them ineligible? What woman did not have a right to have a child?

Because everything had to be in strict confidence one young unmarried woman had applied. He would like to call her ineligible but he didn't dare. If she appealed his decision she would win and he would be removed from his position and there would be great trouble in the village. The number but not the names of the applicants was public so there had to be the proper number of ballots in the lottery. Her name had to be put in for the "wild card". God would have to make sure it wasn't picked. What a commotion that would make in the village if it were. He would have to do some inspired preaching to assure his flock that this had been God's will.

God's will! He was finding it more and more difficult to understand God. Well, he thought, I'm just an old, not too bright village priest. I cannot expect that I will be able to understand God. I must be content to have faith. If I am to be their shepherd my flock must also be satisfied to have faith. Understanding is not required. This is what I preach and those who listen accept it. I only wish more would listen.

More and more don't even come to church. Yet they pick me to make their tough decisions. Well, that also must be God's will and I must accept that too.

That unmarried young woman, what an uncomfortable situation. She had not come alone but in the company of two equally young and also unmarried women. And the story they told. He felt queasy all over again just thinking about it. It appears there was a desirable young bachelor in the village with whom all three had an ongoing sexual relationship. He ran a comfortably successful farm with his father who was getting old. He was ready to get married but wanted to make sure he would be able to have children. He said he would marry the first one of the three who became pregnant. Initially each one of the young women wanted to enter the lottery. Patiently he had explained that each woman would have to have a partner because he too would have to receive the drug to become fertile. This did not seem a problem to them. They each did have a partner. They said they could see nothing in the rules that prohibited the same man from being a partner for more than one woman.

After that first visit he had told them he would have to think about it and to come back in a week. He had been uneasy about the whole business but had felt overwhelmed by three women better educated and probably smarter than he.

He had toiled and suffered over the problem for seven days trying all the possible scenarios for the consequences. When he saw them again he felt he had the answer which was simple and obvious. He thought they had been aware of the objection all along but thought they might be able to confuse him enough so that he would agree. He told them he could allow one only to enter the lottery because of the possibility that more than one might be a winner leaving only one man for two women. He also told them he would permit that one to enter only if both she and the young man agreed to get married immediately if she were one of the winners. There was immediate objection to this contingency from all three women. They would agree to just one entering but there could be no conditions. Reluctantly he had accepted the compromise but didn't feel good about it. He sensed that somehow they were planning to circumvent the rules. He thought two of them should have looked unhappy but none of them did.

Anticipating he might permit just one, they had already drawn lots as to who would enter and Maria was the one chosen. He had interviewed Juan, the young man, and could find nothing wrong with him. Although he did not agree with his behavior he could not fault him for it.

Maria was not one of the twelve he had selected for the lottery but it was God's will that, from the eighteen remaining, her lot was picked to be the "wild card". He sat up a little straighter put his palms on the table and slowly pushed himself upright. He would slowly drink a big goblet of wine, say his prayers, and go to bed. Tomorrow was the day he would pull twelve balls from a big bowl, one at a time, numbered one through thirteen. The names to match the numbers had been picked at random. The mayor would take the ball, open it, take out the paper inside, and read the number aloud in his big mayor's voice to the congregated villagers. Only the priest, the woman, and her man knew who held that number, and no one else would know for sure until some lucky woman became pregnant. The villagers would gather anyway and look at the young women and never see the mayor. They would watch the body language and try to figure out the ones chosen. Nobody would look at Maria.

He wondered what God's will would be tomorrow. He poured himself the wine and slowly drank it musing on the mystery of God.

The drawing was held in the church. The old priest felt comfortable there. This was his safe refuge. He knew everyone would be respectful even if they didn't feel that way. He also knew the day of the drawing would pull the biggest congregation of the year. He would get some prayers in even if the meeting were for another purpose. He felt good about that. Somebody might be listening and be touched.

The lottery went just as Father Manuel had anticipated. He got a nice long prayer in before and after the ceremony. He stirred the balls in the big bowl thoroughly before pulling one. He carefully handed it to the mayor who then slowly pulled the ball apart, took out the paper inside, straightened it, and then triumphantly read the number. After each one was read both priest and mayor stood silently for a moment for the significance to sink in and to allow the audience to look around at all the young women to see if they could identify the lucky one. So it went, twelve times, until only the unlucky thirteenth was left behind.

Father Manuel had felt his face flush when the mayor announced, "The number is eight", for the fourth ball picked. But no one was watching him.

Finally it was Maria's and Juan's turn at the Population Control Clinic. To maintain confidentiality appointments were scheduled so that people from the same district would not be there at the same time. Marie and Juan had waited among strangers. Fifteen minutes were alloted for each couple but Marie and Juan were with the doctor for forty-five. They came out with bottles and pamphlets like the other couples, but the others came out looking happy and they looked sober.

The way the drugs worked was that Juan would take his every day but Maria would take hers daily two weeks and stop for two weeks. If a period occurred then she would start for another two weeks.

It was four and a half months after the clinic visit that Juan came to see Father Manuel.

"Father", he said, "I came to ask you to perform a marriage ceremony."

"Ah", said the priest smiling, "she is pregnant." He added, "Maria must be very happy."

"No", said Juan, "Felicia."

The judge's chamber was a large room comfortably furnished. There were adequate places for the young people facing the judge sitting behind his massive desk. He had ushered them in and let them pick their own places to sit. Juan and his six months pregnant wife sat together on a settee, Maria, Raquel, and Roberto, the young clinic doctor, took separate chairs.

The judge began, "You are here because you have all been charged with improper distribution of the anti-sterility drug. Who will speak for the group?"

Roberto spoke, "Your Honor, with your permission, I will speak for the group. This began when Juan and Maria came to the clinic on their first visit. Maria told me of the arrangement made between Juan and Maria, Felicia, and Raquel. This had been discussed with Father Manuel who is in charge of the lottery in their district. Permission was granted for only one of the women to enter the lottery and Maria was chosen. However, the women had agreed among themselves that each should have a chance to become pregnant. The lots they drew gave Maria the first chance, Raquel the second, and Felicia the third. Juan had no objection and Father Manuel didn't know about it. I told Maria and Juan that they could not do this because Raquel and Felicia had not passed the examinations nor the courses.

After this visit Raquel and Felicia came to see me and Juan was with them. I admit they convinced me that allowing each woman a chance to become pregnant was the ethical course to take, based on the accepted ethical principle of justice. I arranged entrance to the examinations and courses for both Raquel and Felicia. Each had to take them with

Juan so I arranged them at different sites. Poor Juan went through this three times; just doing that indicated to me his sincerity. Both Felicia and Raquel passed.

I then saw the four of them together and told them I could not be a part of the illegal distribution of the drug. It was my duty to examine Maria each month and give her the next two weeks' supply of drug if she were not pregnant. It was not my duty to watch her take her pill each day.

What happened was that Maria took the pills the first month, gave them to Raquel the second month and to Felicia the third month. When Felicia did not get her period she came to see me and I found her pregnant. I then stopped the pills to both Maria and Juan.

Please note, your Honor, that no attempt was made by any of the accused to continue distribution of the drug once a pregnancy had occurred."

The judge looked at the others in the room. "Do any of you have anything to correct or add to what the doctor has said?" he asked.

Nobody spoke.

"Am I then to assume that you are all pleading guilty and are throwing yourselves on the mercy of this court?"

Roberto spoke up, "Your Honor, I will speak for myself and the others again. We consider ourselves moral people, innocent of any crime, who have acted in what we believe was an ethically proper manner. We admit we may have broken some rule but do not acknowledge that it was immoral to do so. Your honor, we are not lawyers. What do you recommend we plead?"

The judge hesitated a moment. "I cannot make a recommendation for you but I can provide you with a lawyer if you wish. However, this is an informal hearing for me to decide whether this matter should go further or be ended here. If it ends here there will be no need for a lawyer. Do any of you others have anything to say?"

No one said anything but there were nods of, "No".

The judge turned to the doctor. "Doctor", he said, "I am aware that you also broke some rules when you arranged for examinations and courses for Raquel and Felice. Because that is not the purpose of this hearing I can do nothing about it. But I suggest you do not do it again. The matter for which you are all here I will take under advisement. If further investigation is to be done you will hear from this court. You may all go now."

They got up silently and filed out, the doctor last.

THE QUIET ONE

It was a memorable party. That was a while ago, 1989 to be exact, and I still remember it vividly, better than any other party I ever attended even including the ones that we had given. We didn't even really belong at that party. The only reason we were there was that we were the next door neighbors for twenty-five years and very good friends. In fact Sue and I were intimately involved in the preparations for the party and were sort of auxiliary hostess and host for Marge and Charlie.

The party was Marge's idea and it was for all of Charlie's co-workers. Charlie was seventy years old, the age of mandatory retirement from the government position he had held. He had been feted on several occasions at work and Marge felt it was pay back time.

Charlie was a great neighbor but a very quiet man. Gardening was a passion with him. He had a beautiful flower garden, an extensive vegetable garden, and a remarkable herb garden.

He talked at length about his landscaping and gardens but never talked about himself. Any questions about his work were answered in very brief vague generalities. What I knew about our neighbors came from Sue's friendship with Marge who was not at all reticent about talking and answered any questions in great detail.

All that follows about the personal lives of Marge and Charlie I got from Sue who got it from Marge.

Marge was an English girl, born and brought up in a little town that turned out to be located close to what became an airfield for US fighter planes. Marge became one of a group of young women of the town in an organization something like the USO in the States. She met Charlie at an Officers Club Dance and a romance blossomed. During those somewhat rare occasions when Charlie would have a weekend off he would spend the time with Marge in her home. When after the requisite number of missions Charlie was to be rotated back to the States, Marge got very upset fearing she would never see him again. He promised that would never happen and to prove it asked her to marry him. They were married at the airfield with his whole squadron in attendance. She couldn't go with him but understood as soon as the war was over she would join him in America

In 1946 she did join him carrying with her a photo album given to her by Charlie's squadron at a farewell party for her. Shortly after Marge got here Charlie took advantage of the GI Bill and applied to law school. He had graduated college in 1941 a week before he enlisted in the USArmy Air Force.

During the few months they were together before law school began Charlie seemed the same as he was in England.but gradually as he attended law school he began to change becoming much more serious and quiet. In his senior year at school he got a request from the nearby VA hospital to fill out a questionnaire for a study that was being done. He filled it out and sent it in. About a month later he received a request to come in for an interview. He went in and ever since has returned periodically for interviews.

Of course, Marge was aware of this from the beginning. The study that was being done was to ascertain what happened after discharge to the physical and emotional status of soldiers who had especially stressful experiences during the war. From his answers to the questionnaire and his first interviews it was decided he was having a delayed onset of what used to be called Combat Fatigue but was later given the name of Post Traumatic Stress Disorder. He was referred to a psychiatrist who has continued to follow him. It was a big help to Marge to have an explanation for the occasional frightening nightmares Charles had, for his avoidance of any talk about his war experience, and his refusal to return to the album given to Marge by his squadron. He had, however, spent time studying it during those months before he went to law school.

After one particularly bad nightmare Marge asked him what it had been about. He said it was about him shooting a plane and watching it burst into flames. That actually happened sixty times, thirty in live time and thirty on tape when the camera attached to his guns was reviewed. He said it was the tapes that really burned it into his mind. During the war the tapes meant nothing to him except as a confirmation of his kills. A few years later, however, they came to haunt him as a reminder that there was a man in those flaming planes not very much different from himself.

When Charlie graduated from law school he had several interviews for positions in law firms. Before making a decision he made several visits to the VA and then applied for a government job which he obtained. He was thirty years old when he started work in 1949 and was seventy when he retired in 1989. All that time was with the government. He worked in various departments and was in his last office for ten years as the manager. He was a no-nonsense manager but kept a low profile and stayed aloof from any personal relationships with anyone in the department. He delegated to others all the stressful details of running the office but was aware of decisions made and had zero tolerance for falsehood, deceit, or bias. When he retired he was universally respected though not well enough known to be loved. The parties given him when he retired where subdued affairs as befitted the man they only knew as the quiet one.

Marge didn't expect that the party she was giving would be lively but hoped if the guests looked at the album they would discover a different perspective from which to view Charlie.

The party was for cocktails and hors d'oeuvres and scheduled for a Saturday beginning at 4:30. A bar was set up in the den; that's where the album was. I was the bartender. My job was to make the drinks, make sure nobody got drunk, and make sure everyone looked at the album. Marge and Sue were taking care of the food. I had everything ready by 2:30 so I had two hours to exam the album which before I never knew existed.

What I saw was perhaps twenty-five captioned photos of young US airmen of Charlie's fighter squadron. Charlie, Chuck in the photos, was in everyone of them, sometimes with one other airman, sometimes with several, sometimes alone or with "English Lass", his plane. He was identified in the captions as "Chuck, our Ace" or "Chuck, our Leader" or just Ace. Painted on "English Lass" were representations of planes which the "Lass" had shot down. Ace had thirty-five missions before he was rotated back to the US, and thirty silhouettes of German aircraft were painted on his plane. The squadron's mission was to ride shotgun for the heavy bombers and keep German fighters away. The album included a quote from Chuck, "Don't call me the Ace, that title belongs to 'English Lass'. Flying a Mustang against the

Nazis is like shooting fish in a barrel, they don't have a plane that can compete."

Marge told Sue she when she first met Charlie she asked him how he happened to get into the airforce. He told her he had always been crazy about planes. He began flying lessons when he was fourteen years old and got his pilot's license before he graduated high school. In college he started a flying club and remained the power in it until he graduated in '41. He expected war and enlisted right after graduation to be sure he would be assigned to the airforce. He was an outstanding air cadet and got what he asked for, classified as a fighter pilot and assigned to a squadron flying P51s, Mustangs, the hottest fighter plane in the airforce. When he got his plane he fell in love with it. When he flew it he felt a part of it, the two of them were just one entity. He named it "Thor" and had the plane decorated with an image of the god as a fierce warrior armed with his magic hammer. After Charlie had spent his first night with Marge he renamed his plane, "English Lass", and decorated it with an idealized image of Marge.

Looking through that album was a revelation to me so I was looking forward to the effect it would have on those who worked under him. The album was an immediate success. Word of it spread quickly, and I had no need to urge anyone to look at it. In fact it would have been better if I had had them draw numbers to take turns.

These are some ot the comments I heard: "I wouldn't believe it if I didn't see it. but the resemblance is unmistakable, that's our Mr. Morgan all right." . . . "Incredible, I can't picture Mr. Morgan as anything but a quiet, low profile man." . . . "I'm overwhelmed. I guess you never know a man until you've examined his past." . . . "That album is a look behind a curtain. I'm floored by what I saw." . . . "After looking at that I'm wondering if I really know anyone in our department, does anyone else have an album like this?" . . . "What an exciting time that must have been and what a handsome young man our Mr. Morgan was. Any young woman would have fallen for him, Marge was the lucky one." . . . "Mr. Morgan lost an opportunity. What a movie that album would make." . . . "Now that he's retired he should write a book, it would be a best seller." . . . "I can't believe it, our quiet Mr. Morgan a war hero. I wonder how many medals he got." . . . "I wish there had been a picture of him in dress uniform so we could see all the ribbbons he had."

After a few people who had looked at the album came up to Charlie and spoke to him he decided that was enough and retired upstairs asking Marge to make his excuses. She did this by announcing that Mr. Morgan wanted to thank everybody for coming to his party but that he, regretfully, had to leave it because an old war wound was giving him great discomfort and required some medication.

THE PATRON SAINT

We were driving in Mexico on a vacation trip. One Friday about noon we came into a little village well away from the main routes of travel. The road we were on was obviously the main street and was colorfully decorated for some sort of celebration. It was time for lunch so we looked for a place to eat and came upon what looked like a little grill. We stopped and learned we could get a meal there as well as beer. It was a small place with a short bar and a few tables that could seat four, and two tables for two. The man who greeted us led us to a table for two, acknowledged he was the owner, and excused himself to go into the kitchen and ask his wife what was available for lunch. We noted we were the only customers. He came back and told us what was available so we ordered it and some beer. We asked him what the decorations were for and he told us there had been a big celebration the day and night before. He said that was the reason we were the only customers this noon. He expected many would come in the evening. The decorations would stay up over the weekend.

He needed no encouragement to talk and pulled up a chair. The celebration was to honor the benefactor of the village who, although not a religious man, was called the village saint. He asked if we would like to hear about it and without waiting for an answer launched into this story . . .

Jesu was a big handsome boy of fourteen when he left the village and went to Mexico City to find work that would pay enough so he could send some money home to help support his parents and five siblings. He got a job as a caddy at an exclusive country club and began to play some golf. He had an exceptional talent for the game and the club pro took an interest in him acting both as teacher and coach. The pro got a few of the wealthy members interested and a corporation was formed to sponsor the boy. He was entered into a number of tournaments as an amateur and won them all. At the age of seventeen he became a professional. In his first year as a professional he won a major tournament. The corporation got him an agent. The agent took care of the commercial contracts. Jesu was becoming rich.

Early on he began sending money back to his family. When he was just a caddy the pesos were not many but when he became a professional and changed his first name to, "Juan" the pesos were many and after he won his first tournament they became a flood. He came back to his village for a visit when he was 20 and married his grammar school sweetheart. She did not want to go to Mexica City with him. She wanted to stay with her family in the village so he bought a bigger house for her and her family. He stayed for a month during which time his wife became pregnant. He left then and rejoined the golf tour.

He came back to the village quite regularly. He paid to have the main street paved. He set up a credit corporation to loan money at low interest so villagers could improve their homes. With money and influence he was able to get a new school built.

After the first baby his wife still refused to leave the village. She didn't wish to accompany him on the tour and saw no reason to move her home. He had a new home built for her and her parents and made her pregnant again.

On the occasion of their fifth wedding anniversary his golf game and his popularity were at their zenith. He arranged a celebration and invited the entire village. By that time he had four children. He set up a foundation to assure that the poor had adequate food, clothing, and shelter and had help in learning a skill sufficient to get a job and earn a living

The following year his golf game began to deteriorate. Reports began to circulate that he was living a fast life in Mexico City, including women and whiskey. His visits home became less frequent and lasted shorter periods. The credit union and foundation were running out of funds.

One day his father, Jose, got on a bus and went to Mexico City. He found his son in a luxury apartment with two servants and a beautiful young mistress. The old man was a strict father and Jesu would not cross him. Jose did not like what he saw. The first week he got an apartment in a poor section of the city and moved into it with his son. He got rid of the mistress and the two servants and put the luxury apartment up for sale, furniture and all. The second week he contacted Jesu's coach and with his help set up a training program. Women and whiskey were out, physical training and golf were in. The old man wrote home that he was staying with Jesu until he won another major tournament. He didn't like it but he went with his son on the tour. With the training program and the coach the golf game began to improve. Some minor tournaments were won and the money began to roll in again. The visits home resumed their old frequency. A home was built just for Jesu and his immediate family.

The credit union and the foundation were back in good shape. Finally, a major tournament was won and Jose came home.

Jesu continued with the tour.

Then tragedy struck. Jesu was killed in a car accident while traveling from one tournament to the next. The village went into a period of mourning. Jose sickened and died not long after. In his will Jesu left half his fortune to his wife and members of the family and the other half divided among his foundation, credit union, and the village.

When the will was finally settled and the village received the money, it was decided that once a year there would be a celebration in honor of the one responsible for the blessings bestowed upon the village. They considered their benefactor a saint and named the day in his honor

At this point there was a call from the kitchen and our host excused himself. He returned with our lunches which we immediately started on. He remained standing.

I said, "So yesterday was known as, 'St. Jesu's Day'".

"No, no", said our host, "It's St. Jose's Day. Jesu was no saint."

SEARCHING

My wife is a determined woman. Some might characterize her as an obsessive compulsive personality but she is not compulsive. She is deliberate, a deliberate determined woman. I suppose it could be said when she is determined enough about something she could be considered obsessed with it. Perhaps so.

Not too long ago we celebrated our fifteenth anniversary. I was financially comfortable when we got married, and since our marriage I have prospered. By most standards we are moderately wealthy.

Aimee, my wife, had told me she didn't want me to buy her anything for the anniversary. She said she had something else in mind and she would tell me on that day. When the time came she told me. It did not make me happy.

Before we were married Aimee had told me some things about her past. I had told her I didn't want to hear about her past but she insisted. She said when she was sixteen years old she had a baby out of wedlock. Arrangements had been made before the birth for the child to be adopted as soon as it was born. The sex was not known beforehand. Aimee learned the child was a girl and was healthy, but knew nothing about the couple who were to adopt her.

What Aimee wanted for our anniversary was my help in locating this girl.

Aimee was twenty when I married her, I am ten years older than she. We have two boys aged thirteen and eleven years. Assuming the girl were alive she would be nineteen years old.

I was skeptical about the wisdom of looking for Aimee's daughter. We knew nothing about her, not even her name. We had no idea of where she lived or even if she were in this country. If we pictured the best scenario: that she was brought up in a decent, loving, middle class family and was now going to college there would still be no assurance that she would welcome the existence and presence of her mother. She spent her whole life with the only mother and father she had ever known and, in this scenario, would be happy with them.

Aimee acknowledged all this might be true but pointed out there were many other possible scenarios, not the ideal one I had painted. She said she was now in a position to be very helpful financially and might even be a support emotionally. There might be a real need for that kind of help. More than that Aimee said she carried a terrible burden of guilt about the girl. After all she had deserted her, an indication the baby was not wanted. It was not difficult for her to imagine how she would feel if she were in this girl's position.

I asked Aimee how she would feel if she were the woman who had adopted the baby. Did she think she would welcome the biological mother intruding herself at this time? Aimee said she would not intrude, she would make herself helpful and in no way interfere with the relationships already established.

I had bad vibes about the whole business but knew I could not dissuade Aimee. I told her I could not help her but would not hinder her. This was all she had wanted for her anniversary present and was happy. She said she didn't need any help and really just wanted my approval for her to do it. I told her I did not approve, I just agreed not to hinder her. For Aimee not hindering meant approval. She lost no time getting to work on it.

First, on her own she tried to get some information from the hospital but her record was no longer available. She tried every adoption agency but turned up no record. She was told the doctor may have made the arrangements privately but found he had died and none of his records survived. She consulted several private detective agencies but received no encouragement. They would take the case on a fee for service basis but indicated it would be very expensive with little chance for success. They would have to depend almost entirely on advertising. Aimee had an idea of her own about that. She gave up the idea of outside help and began to implement her own idea.

Her first step was to hire a computer expert to give her advice on the kind of equipment to buy and then to tutor her in the operation of it. For her purposes the equipment was simple: a good personal computer and a modem. Starting from a point of complete computer illiteracy it took her a month of hard work to become proficient enough to use it comfortably. With her tutor's help she got online, joined World Wide Web, Prodigy, Delphi, and America Online, and began advertising on the bulletins of each service for information on the whereabouts of a young woman born on a certain day in a hospital in a certain city who never saw her mother but was immediately taken for adoption by a young couple. She began by offering a reward of a thousand dollars for information leading to her discovery. Communication was to be by e-mail. "Searching" was the name she used to identify herself.

Aimee began spending several hours a day with her e-mail. Most of the correspondence was frivolous or fraudulent.

The fraud was not difficult to uncover; two involved three people, one acting as the girl and two as the adoptive parents.

In early May, about a month after she had begun she thought she struck gold. She found a letter in her e-mail that read, "Searching: I think I have what you are looking for. If you are willing to up the ante, post a P.O. Box number and I will write you." It was signed, "Finder". She immediately obtained a box and listed the number on the bulletin board. Ten days later among the many wiseacre letters and ones advertising private detective agencies she found one from "Finder". He wrote his son discovered her ad and thought it fit his sister. The birthday was right and so was the adoption at birth. If "Searching" was willing to deposit twenty-five thousand dollars in escrow pending positive identification, she could write him at a box number he included and they would take it from there. He wrote that he arrived at that figure because it represented the cost of a year at college.

At this point Aimee came to me. She showed me the letter from "Finder" and asked my advice. I read it and told her I thought it looked genuine, but if she wanted my advice I would advise her to forget the whole business. She reminded me that I had promised not to hinder her and I reminded her that I had told her I wouldn't help, and added that she asked for my advice, I didn't volunteer it. She asked me to tell her why I thought she should drop the idea now that she was so close to success.

I told her that I thought it was going to be very expensive and risky. Risky not because of the money but because she was buying a pig in a poke. The girl may not turn out to be the kind of a daughter she would like to have. The girl might resent her and make her life miserable. Her sons could resent the time given to their new half sister. On top of that the adoptive parents could well consider her an interloper. They may not be pleased that she was interfering with the relationship they've established with their daughter. I thought it not unlikely she might be viewed as a money cow to be milked. It certainly seemed to be starting out that way.

Aimee thanked me for the advice, said she would think about it, and promised not to ask my advice again about this matter.

Aimee did think about it and began a correspondence with "Finder". She gave me copies of it:

Dear "Finder",

In your letter you indicated you are the adoptive father of the girl you think might be my biological daughter. I hope you're right and I'm willing to up the ante as you requested but I have misgivings and questions. First, I would like to know if she's aware of what you're doing, and if so what her reaction is. Second, since you contacted me I know you're interested in pursuing the matter but I don't know why nor what your expectations are. Third, I would like to know if the adoptive mother is aware of what you are doing and what her reaction is.

Please respond. I will be glad to answer any questions you have about me.

Sincerely,
"Searching"

Dear "Searching",

I will answer your questions and then I have a few of my own. First, my daughter is not yet aware of what I'm doing. Second, I am doing it because my daughter has a strong interest in investigating her biological parents although she has not made an intensive effort to locate them. She is now in her first year at college and I decided it would be better to wait until school was over before telling her about it. I'm afraid it would distract her. My expectation is that if the connection is established it will satisfy my daughter, but I also have misgivings. I am concerned about the effect it will have on her. I am also concerned about the effect it will have on her adoptive mother, and upon me. This whole business may be adding an unwanted complication to our lives. I answered your advertisement reluctantly but had no choice when my son brought it to my attention. We both knew how interested my daughter is in finding her biological parents. My wife knows what I am doing. She doesn't know what to expect and is ambivalent about how it comes out.

Now I have some questions: Why did you give up your baby? Are you married and is it to her father? If it is not to her father do you know where he is? Is it a sacrifice for you to come up with the $25,000 I asked for? Why are you interested in finding your daughter?

"Finder"

Dear Finder,

I will answer your questions then go on to other business.

I gave up my baby because I was sixteen years old and unmarried. I knew I could not take care of her properly. I assume the agency told you this.

I am married now but not to her father. I do not know where he is but he probably could be located.

Paying you $25,000 will not change my style of living.

I want to find my daughter because I want her to know that I longed to keep her but was compelled to give her up, she was not unwanted. I want to find her because if she needs help now I may be able to help her. I want to find her because I know if I were in her position I would want to know about my biological parents and my family back-ground.

166

Now, the other business. I have decided I will
go no further until your daughter knows about this
and wants to pursue it. I want to hear from her
directly.

Sincerely,
"Searching"

Dear "Searching",

Thank you for answering my questions.

I too have come to a decision. I will take this no
further until the $25,000 is deposited in escrow. My
lawyer has advised me that we shall have to identify
ourselves and since we live in different states he
suggests you have your attorney contact him and
together they will make all the arrangements.

If this is agreeable to you, let me know and we
can proceed.

"Finder"

At this point Aimee asked me about a lawyer. I told her
to use my lawyer and asked if she was prepared to come up
with the money. She said that was something she would take
care of with our broker when the time came.

Well, the lawyers made the arrangements. A contract
was signed and the money was deposited.

Correspondence continued without the need for P.O.
Boxes or pseudonyms. "Finder" turned out to be Robert Bayle
who lives in a suburb of Cleveland which is not exactly around
the corner from our home in a New Jersey suburb of New York
City. Only Aimee and her modem could have accomplished
the conjunction. A considerable bit of luck helped.

Aimee made copies of the correspondence for me:

Dear Mrs. Hurley,

Joan, my daughter, has been brought up to date
on what has been going on in regard to her. She has

read all our correspondence and was deeply moved by what you wrote about why you wanted to find her. From that letter alone she has developed a tender feeling for you. I'm afraid she will be bitterly disappointed if you don't turn out to be her biological mother. I think we should proceed quickly to complete the DNA studies you wanted. I am confident they will confirm what is already evident to me. I think it highly unlikely that two newborn girl babies would be adopted from the same hospital on the same day, even though it's a very big hospital.

Joan is composing herself so she can write you a letter.

Sincerely,
Robert Bayle

Dear Mrs. Hurley,

I can scarcely believe what is happening. It is the most exciting event of my life. Since I knew I was adopted and understood what that meant I have been dreaming and fantasizing about my "real" parents. I resolved that someday I would find them but I never even considered the possibility that my mother might come looking for me. I cried when I read why you wanted to find me. I'm crying now when I think about it.

I would like to meet you somewhere. We could have our blood tests together and learn for sure that we belong to each other. Please make it soon. I'm beginning to have nightmares that the tests will come out wrong.

I'm signing this the way I feel regardless of how the tests come out.

Love,
Joan.

Dear Joan,

Since I received your letter I am subject to the same nightmares as you. You don't have to guess the effect it had on me.

I'm enclosing a check to cover the cost of round trip first class plane tickets from Cleveland to Kennedy Airport, NYC. Let me know when you plan to come and I will meet you there. You will stay with me and I hope it will be for a week or so. It will give us a chance to get acquainted.

When you write again please don't address me as "Mrs." You already have a "mom" so please call me Aimee.

Love,
Aimee

Dear Mrs. Bayle,

I've been uncomfortable not knowing how you feel about what's happening with Joan. I know you two have a mother-daughter relationship and I have no wish to interfere with that. I would like to be like a dear aunt to Joan which would make me like a sister to you or your husband. My two boys are really half brothers to Joan but they don't know each other and really would be more like cousins.

Please write me and let me know your feelings. I would very much like to be a sister to you.

Sincerely,
Aimee

Dear Mrs. Hurley,

Thank you for your letter. I've been feeling guilty about not writing you and you have provided me the opportunity.

You wrote about a mother-daughter relationship between Joan and me. Of course we have one but it has not been good. Joan has been a very difficult girl for us to raise. The father-daughter relationship has been even worse than the mother-daughter. As an infant she was a pleasure but when she was a year old I unexpectedly was able to conceive and after my son was born her personality slowly changed. When she began to understand what being adopted meant she changed completely, becoming withdrawn and surly. She's a bright girl and concentrated on her books, more so since she had been told if she were to go to college it would have to be on her own. We could not afford to send her; both her father and I work, he teaches in public school and I am a librarian. She is making it on her own with the help of scholarships and loans. She equates herself to Cinderella and says we are saving our money to send our son through college. She says he won't be on his own when he reaches 18 years as she was. Of course she's right but if he were adopted we would feel the same way. She doesn't believe that.

I think Joan's fondest hope now is that you will take her to live with you permanently. My husband and I would both welcome that arrangement. Perhaps living with you would make a different girl of Joan. However, I must warn you if she doesn't change you will have a very difficult time with her.

One thing we all have in common is that we are all hoping the blood tests will confirm that you are the biological mother.

Sincerely,
Joyce Bayle

I am a naturally cautious man and have learned not to be trusting. When I read the letter of Joyce Bayle I smelled the possibility of a scam. Joyce Bayle wrote that the girl was paying her own way throught college yet Robert Bayle wrote he arrived at the figure of $25,000 because it was the cost of one year of college. The implication was $25,000 was what it cost him. Of course that was only implied, he never wrote that was what it cost him. Then I thought maybe he figured $25,000 was little enough to pay for raising the girl.

I knew testing the DNA could rule Aimee out as the mother but could not rule her in positvely without the father's blood. I did not tell Aimee my thoughts but I knew I would not recognize the girl as Aimee's daughter without her blood being tested against both parents, and I would not release the money from escrow without that being done.

Nor was I happy with the prospect of having this girl come to live with us. I anticipated she would be a disruptive influence in our lives. It was now early July.

> Dear Aimee,
>
> Thank you for the letter and the check. I have been working as a waitress this summer and had planned to keep the job until it was time to go back to school but I'm going to quit now so I can come to New York and get to know you a little before school begins.
>
> I would like to come next week on Tuesday. If that's okay with you I'll get the tickets and let you know the details. Of course I won't come first class, it's much too expensive just for a seat in the front of the bus.
>
> Love,
> *Joan*

Joan arrived as scheduled and I went with Aimee to Kennedy to meet her. I spotted her first and knew immediately she was Aimee's daughter. She looked just like Aimee when I first met her. The resemblence was so strong I could feel myself attracted to her.

Mother and daughter greeted each other with embraces and tears. After a few minutes Joan noticed me. "You must be Aimee's husband," she said without waiting for an introduction. She embraced me and kissed me, and then she said, "I like you already. Will you be my new father?" She caught me unawares and I blurted out, "I don't know, Joan, do you want me to be?" Then I caught myself. "Don't answer that," I said, "wait until you know me a little better." She laughed. "You mean you want to know me better before you commit yourself," she said, "Okay, I don't blame you. My reputation probably preceded me." She was bright all right.

Joan didn't want to waste any time in confirming the relationship. The first evening she asked about her father. Her idea was to have the three of them go to the lab together. She was aware Aimee didn't know where he was but had indicated in her letter that she could probably find him. "Well," said Joan, "let's find him. We need him and I want to meet him."

Aimee told Joan about the man she thought was the biological father: He is the brother of Elaine, a girl who was in her class in high school. His name is Tom Masters. He is five years older than Aimee and was a pilot in the U.S. Army Air Force when she met him. He seduced her with no difficulty at all. He was 21 and she 16. They were a consenting couple but legally she was not an adult. It was statutory rape. Soon after the seduction he was transferred to Germany and never was aware of her pregnancy. After he left the service he became a commercial airline pilot and still is. He's married to an airline hostesss and has no children. He is unaware of the existence of Joan. Aimee said she was still in contact with Elaine and through her could reach Tom. Elaine is also unaware of Joan's existence because before the pregnancy was well advanced she had moved out of town.

After Aimee finished this brief history Joan immediately said, "Aimee, call Elaine now." And Aimee did. She got Elaine on the phone and after an exchange of greetings told her she wanted to get in touch with Tom, that she had found something very valuable that she thought belonged to him. She said she could discuss it only with Tom. Elaine didn't know where he was at the moment but gave Aimee his home phone number in Atlanta. An answering machine picked up the phone in Atlanta and Aimee left a message indicating there was some urgency for him to respond and requesting him to call back at any hour.

Tom called back at 2:30 A.M. He apologized for the hour but said he had just arrived from a flight and was only following instructions left on the answering machine. After the initial greetings and a preliminary warning to prepare for some startling news Aimee told him about Joan. She said if Joan turned out to be her daughter there was only one man who could be her father and he was the one. When he got over the shock Tom said he would hitch a ride and meet them in New York later the same day if possible. He would call when he got in. Aimee invited him to stay with us. He said his wife might accompany him and Aimee said that would be fine.

Tom was able to hitch a ride and so was his wife, Ellen. They arrived in New York in the early evening after dinner. Tom rented a car and got to our place about ten o'clock. Aimee and Joan brought Tom and Ellen up to date and as they were getting acquainted I excused myself and went to bed. I was facing a very busy day of conferences starting early in the morning. I promised I would take them all out for a big celebration if the blood tests showed Tom and Aimee to be Joan's biological parents. It was evident to me that Joan was impressed by Tom and that before I went to bed I knew he had displaced me as the longed for father. I was happy to give up that designation. I was also aware that Ellen was less than enthused with Joan.

The following day while I was busy with conferences the

four of them went to a laboratory where blood was taken from the three principals. It would be several days before the results would be known.

Tom and Ellen decided they would go back to Atlanta but they couldn't get a plane until late evening so they had dinner with us. After dinner Ellen suggested we leave Joan to talk with Tom and Aimee so she and I went into the library to talk.

Ellen wanted to know my feelings about the situation. Joan made no secret that she didn't want to go back to her adoptive parents and Ellen told me she would not allow Joan to come with her. She said she didn't like her behavior and didn't trust her. I told Ellen I hadn't formed a judgment and that although I would not welcome her addition to my home I would not oppose it if Aimee wanted her to live with us. I asked Ellen what she would do if Joan expressed a preference to live with her father. Ellen wanted to know why Joan would ever express such a preference. I suggested she put herself in Joan's position. She would have a nice place to live. Both her father and stepmother would be away a good part of the time giving her more liberty than she would ever have here where her mother would be home most of the time and she would have two half brothers to contend with. Ellen said if Joan wanted to live with them it would be up to Tom. He could choose to live with his daughter or with his wife; he couldn't have them both. I told Ellen that if it turned out that Joan was my stepdaughter I would much prefer that we be good friends and not antagonists. I suggested it would be better that way for Ellen too. Ellen said she couldn't put her finger on it but there was something about Joan that she couldn't trust. She doubted she could ever be good friends with her. She thought it would be better for everyone if she stayed with her adoptive parents.

I was uneasy too, but I didn't tell Ellen that.

The blood tests came back. Joan was indeed the daughter of Aimee and Tom. When they got the news both Aimee and Joan were tremendously excited and jubilant. Joan immediately put in a call to Tom but had to leave a message. She said she would like to visit him before she returned to school and asked him to call her back. Aimee asked Joan where she would like to live and told her that her adoptive parents would not object to her living with us. Joan said she had seen the letter her mother had written to Aimee and had no desire to go back to her adoptive parents. She said she would like to make her permanent residence with her mother but would like to spend some time with her father.

Tom did not call back that night and we assumed he had an overnight someplace.

The following day was Saturday and we were all having breakfast together. Joan was unusually quiet and I asked her if she had something on her mind. She said she did, and now that she knew Aimee was her mother she thought she better come out with it. I didn't know what Aimee was thinking but I expected a shoe to drop. Joan said, "I don't know whether I'm going to go back to school this year." I waited for the other shoe. "I'm pregnant," she said.

That was it. Ellen and I had the sensitive antennae but could not avoid becoming involved. Joan's pregnancy entangled six people besides herself: two parents, two adoptive parents, and two stepparents.

Joan was early in her pregnancy. She probably conceived during a two day party following final examinations at the end of the school year. She did not know who the father was. Recollecting that party she said it was probably one of three but possibly one of seven. She became defensive about her promiscuity and asked why wouldn't she be looking for love since she never got any from her adoptive parents and didn't even know her real parents. Aimee asked her if she wanted a child when she didn't know who the father was. Joan asked Aimee if she had wanted her. Aimee said she wanted her but knew she couldn't keep her. Joan asked her why she didn't have an abortion and Aimee told her abortions were illegal at that time and very dangerous. She had been a very frightened sixteen year old and was paralyzed into inaction. Joan asked if conditions had been different would she have had an abortion. Aimee said she probably would have. She asked Joan if she planned to keep the baby. Joan said of course she did, how she could do otherwise knowing how she herself came to be alive, nor would she ever give it up for adoption.

I was angry. I knew where I stood and I made my stand plain. I said I was not up to having my home and my family disrupted and I would not welcome her to live in my home. I suggested she go back to school and said I would give her some financial support but that's as far as it would go. I told her I didn't think her father would take her either because Ellen had told me if Joan wanted to live with her father he would have to choose between his daughter and his wife. I got up from the table and left. I was glad our boys were away at camp.

At the door I looked back. Joan was crying, Aimee had that patient look of tolerance she wore when one of our boys had an angry outburst.

I came back to the table and apologized for my angry outburst. I sat down and said to Joan, "You look so much like your mother I can't help but be attracted to you. There must be a way for us to work this out. We know how we each feel. Let's not discuss it any more now. We can sleep on it and go over what the others said. Tomorrow we can talk about it calmly. I'm confident we'll be able to reach some agreement."

Joan stopped crying and brightened up. "I don't know how to address you, Mr. Hurley," she said.

176

"Call me, 'Stan'."

"Oh, that's good, 'Stan'. I'm so glad you came back. I'd like to kiss you again, may I?"

"I'd love it."

She got up and came over to me and kissed me on the cheek. "That's like her mother", I thought.

The next morning after breakfast, Joan couldn't restrain herself. "I was up half the night debating with myself. I took both pro and con of each option and I think I've decided what I would like to do. Stan, I would like to accept your offer to help me with college and I would like to use this house as my home base although I don't expect I will be here more than a few weeks a year during some of the time school will be on vacation. I won't need a lot of money and could get along without any help. I made my own way last year and could still manage it alone if I had to. Anyway, I would like this to be my home.

Last year I had a job at the school and they provided me with a dorm room which I still have. Most of my belongings are there and the job is available any time I want to go back. I think I would like to go to Cleveland now, pick up the stuff there that I want at school, say good-bye to my mom and dad, go back to school, and work there until the new term begins. Aimee and Stan, what do you say?"

Aimee said, "It's up to you, Stan."

I said, "Joan, I didn't hear a word about the pregnancy."

"There's somebody back at school I want to talk to about that."

"Fine, when you decide what you're going to do let us know and then I'll tell you about your making your home here."

"If I have the baby you don't want me here."

"That's right. If you go through with the pregnancy I think it will be a terrible mistake for you and for the baby.

I hope whomever you see at school will be able to convince you of that . . . . Now I've got to go to work. Joan, if you need some money I'll advance you a thousand dollars. I assume you'll be staying for a few days so I'll see you at dinner."

Driving to work I thought, "For hundreds of years we've heard, 'Let sleeping dogs lie' . . . . We still haven't got it."

SILVER ANNIVERSARY

Jane never particularly liked Flo. The woman seemed too self-satisfied, too critical of other women and their husbands. Gossip was the main topic of her conversation and she seemed especially to enjoy gossip about bad behavior in the circle of her friends. It was apparent to Jane that sometimes Flo stretched the truth.

So when Jane picked up the phone that day she wasn't prepared for what she heard. Flo indentified herself but didn't sound like Flo. Jane had always known her to be calm, cool, and usually somewhat patronizing. This time she was agitated and sounded teary. Confidence was gone from her voice.

"Jane," she blurted, "Oh, Jane, we're in terrible trouble!"

Jane heard her break down and cry. This was definitely not the Flo that Jane knew. "Flo, calm down and tell me what's happened."

No answer. Jane waited, she could hear the crying. She wondered why Flo chose to call her, she certainly wasn't her best friend; and what was this business about, "*We're* in terrible trouble."

Finally, Flo came back on the phone, "Jane, please come over right away. I can't talk about this over the phone.

"I can't come over now," Jane answered, "I'm expecting a guest for lunch and I'm in the middle of preparing it. If this can't wait you'll have to tell me over the phone. Nobody's listening, our phones aren't tapped."

Flo's voice rose, "No, Jane I can't do it. Now you cancel your lunch and get over here. This is a lot more important than a lunch."

Jane felt her anger mounting and sensed Flo's vulnerability, no longer was she her usual intimidating self. "Flo, compose yourself. When you settle down call me back. I can't talk with you any longer now. Good-bye." She hung up and immediately afterword took the phone off the receiver. She felt good about the whole conversation. She ordinarily would have had little to do with Flo except that Larry, Jane's husband, and George, Flo's husband, were old friends back to their college days. On occasion Larry and George would take a long weekend for golf and once a year took a whole week off for fishing.

Jane's guest was a woman who was helping her arrange her silver anniversary party. It was to be a party that Jane insisted she was going to give by herself. She told Larry she had had a wonderful twenty-five years with him and this was to be a celebration of her amazing good fortune in having married him. She really felt that way too, although Larry insisted he had been the lucky one. They compromised. Jane would give the party and Larry would pay for it.

It was midafternoon before the woman left. After she was gone Jane remembered she had not put the phone back on the receiver; it had been off more than four hours. Jane thought about calling Flo but decided not to.

Larry came home early from work He didn't say anything but Jane knew with one look that he was very upset. Her heart began to pound. "Larry, what's happened?" she asked, afraid of what he would say.

"George called me this afternoon, did Flo call you?"

Jane felt relieved. It was only about George and Flo. "She called but I was busy and couldn't talk to her. She sounded very upset."

"She's upset all right. She and George are splitting."

"Splitting? All of a sudden, just like that? I had no idea they were having any difficulty."

"They weren't until this morning. Now Flo is on her way to her sister's, half way across the country."

"My God, did George try to kill her?"

"You know George wouldn't even step on an ant."

"Did he tell you what happened?"

"Yes, but I think he wants it kept confidential."

"Apparently Flo doesn't expect to keep it confidential. She called me to tell me and she isn't even a good friend of mine. I wondered why she called me of all people."

Larry was puzzled, "She didn't say anything at all to you?"

"She said, 'We're in terrible trouble'. I wondered why she said, 'We're' but apparently she was referring to George and herself."

Larry was quiet. Jane waited. Finally, Larry said, "Flo will call you again so I better talk to you before she does. Let's sit down, this is going to be difficult." They sat down at the breakfast room table. Larry took a deep breath and began, "First, Jane, let me tell you I love you. I loved you since we became engaged, I love you now, and I expect I'll love you until one of us dies.

Jane was frightened; her mouth was dry, her insides were shaking, she felt her pulse pounding in her temples. She sat rigidly and said nothing.

Larry continued, "When Flo mentioned, 'We', she was not referring to George and herself she was referring to you and herself. By snooping where she should not have, she discovered that George had been having a homosexual affair. From the evidence she found she figured it had been going on for thirty years, and she deduced that I was his lover." He stopped speaking.

Jane managed to get a few words out, "And she was right?"

"Yes."

Jane got up from the table and went shakily into their bedroom and shut the door.

About two hours later Larry was still sitting at the table staring into space when Jane came out of the bedroom.

"Are you all right?" he asked.

"I think I'm still in a state of shock. I'm so confused I don't know what I'm doing.—I know it's time for me to be making dinner and that's what I came out to do. I thought if I began doing the routine things it would help me get oriented."

Larry stood up, "Would you object if I came over and held you?" he asked.

Jane looked at him uncertainly, "I don't know."

He went over and took her in his arms. She responded to his embrace and began to cry. "Oh, Larry," she sobbed, "I just don't understand. Will you explain it to me?"

"I'll do the best I can," he said, "do you want to go into that right now?"

"Yes, please. I have to get some things off my mind. I can't eat now anyway."

They went back to the breakfast table and sat down again.

"In two hours you must have thought of a lot of questions," he said, "why don't you start by asking them and I'll do my best to answer."

Jane composed herself. "I developed some very angry feelings," she said, "Let's dispose of them first. Before we got married I was honest with you and told you I would never be able to have a family, why weren't you honest with me? You were George's lover before you ever met me."

"I gave that a lot of thought, Jane. I agonized over it. You were the first, and only, woman I ever fell in love with. I had never before experienced the feelings I had developed for you. I became convinced that the affair I had been having with George was just an exploratory investigation, obviously in a different category from what I felt for you.

I was convinced it was only an isolated episode in my youth, just a footnote in my personal history. I debated with myself the consequences of telling you or not telling you. I saw great risk in telling you and very little in not telling you about a footnote. George had been the only homosexual contact I had had and I've never had another. For two years after our marriage I did not see George although we kept up a correspondence; I knew he also had gotten married. When he and Flo moved back here he urged me to resume our affair; his marriage was not a good one. My old strong feelings for George were not gone, just hidden, and after about six months I persuaded myself that I needed and could have both your love and his. As it turned out I was right, at least for the first twenty-two years. If it hadn't been that he married the wrong woman it may have lasted the rest of our lives. If he had married a woman like you we could have remained four happy people as long as we lived."

Jane was quiet.

Larry asked, "Do you have another question?"

"Yes, now that I know, what do you plan to do?"

"I don't plan to do anything. The question is what do you plan to do? Flo lost no time in making her move."

"Flo did not have a happy marriage. Up until this afternoon I did."

"And now?"

"Now? I don't know."

"Jane, I don't understand. You say you had a happy

marriage. Nothing has changed over the last twenty-two years yet suddenly you have discovered you don't know whether your marriage is happy now."

"I don't know whether I can share your love."

"For the past twenty-two years you've been happy sharing it. What's different now?"

"Oh, Larry, you know what's different. Now I know. I know and the knowledge is destroying the marriage."

"If the marriage is destroyed it will not be the knowledge that destroys it; it will be your reaction to the knowledge."

Jane was beginning to feel angry. "How would you like me to react to the sudden revelation that my husband is gay and for most of our marriage has been having an affair with a man?"

"Not gay, Jane, bisexual. If I were gay I couldn't be in love with you like I am."

"Okay, bisexual, but unfaithful none the less for twenty-two out of twenty-five years." Now she was really angry, "How do want me to react?" she yelled. And broke into tears again.

Larry waited. This time Jane did not get up and leave. After several minutes she stopped crying and composed herself.

Larry spoke very quietly, "Jane, I would like you to react with understanding."

"How do I understand infidelity?"

"I don't consider it infidelity. It would have been if I had had a mistress all those years. I never had another woman than you. My affair with George occupies a different compartment in my mind and life. It has nothing to do with you. For me, being bisexual is like being two people of different sex, each with a need to be loved."

"I don't want to be married to two people. I want just one who will give me all his love."

"You want me to give up George?"

"That's right."

Larry looked the picture of dejection. Jane softened. "Larry, you've been a wonderful husband and I don't want to lose you but I couldn't go on this way. Can't we move away and have the next twenty-five years somewhere else? I expect Flo will lose no time in publicizing why her marriage broke up. It will be uncomfortable to stay here."

Larry said, "I don't know, Jane. I guess we both have a lot to think about." He got up. "Jane, will you come out and have dinner with me?"

Jane brightened and managed a smile. "Of course, Larry, I feel better now and I didn't want to make dinner anyway."

That night as they were getting ready to go to bed Jane said, "Larry, I would prefer you sleep in the guest room until you decide whether you stay with me or George."

"I'm sorry you feel that way, Jane."

"I'm sorry you haven't made up your mind. Good night."

"Good night."

The next day George came to Larry's office. When they were alone the first thing George said was, "Did Flo tell Jane about us?"

"Not yet, but I'm expecting her to any time now."

"Wonderful! She told me the truth." He burst out with a great big smile. "Well, we're in the clear now. Don't worry about Flo, she won't call."

"What happened, did you shoot her?"

"I didn't have to. I promised to send her a considerable sum of money every month unless I learned Jane found out about us. I'm confident that for once in her life she will keep her mouth shut. She will tell nobody. Larry, don't look so upset! You're free now to go on with your happy married life . . . . I'm looking forward to your silver wedding anniversary party. Just tell Jane not to expect Flo; I'm sure that won't break her heart . . . . Larry, Larry, what's the trouble?"

SISTERS

I have a sister who is four years older than I. We don't
see each other very often; she lives in a different world as
befits her position as a winner in life. My world is more in
keeping with my position as a loser in life. This business of
winners and losers must be so because she's told me often
enough. It began when we were kids. She drilled it into me
incessantly and proved it when we were grown by seducing
a very wealthy man. The man I seduced had very little money.
He's a cabinet maker now and makes a decent living. We're
not suffering for lack of resources. My sister's husband now
has even more money than when she married him. She seems
to have everything: three beautiul homes well equipped with
servants and cars; one home for the winter, one for the
summer, and one for the spring and fall. I just have one
modest home, one car, and no servants.

As I said we don't see each other very often but I get
cards from my sister as she travels the globe. Picture postcards
from Paris, Prague, Madrid, Berlin, Hong Kong, Singapore,
Shanghai, Gibraltar, London. Think of a world city, I'll have
a card from here, all signed, "the winner".

Well, a few days ago, like an unexpected clap of thunder, I got a phone call from her. It must be at least fifteen years since she phoned me, maybe longer. In fact I don't remember. She may have called me before she got married. Anyway you must have gotten the idea we are not loving sisters I don't count her among my best friends, in fact I don't consider her a friend at all. I don't even like her.

She told me she was calling from her suite at the Plaza Hotel in New York City but she didn't sound comfortable. She said she wanted to see me on an urgent matter and wanted me to come to New York. She said she would send first class plane tickets for my husband and myself and would reserve a suite for us at the hotel. She said to plan to stay a week or ten days.

"Flo, (that's her name), Flo", I said, "what's going on?"

"Bert", (that's my name) she said, "I can't tell you over the phone."

"In that case I'm not about to come to New York. If it's that important you better come here to see me. My house isn't big enough to put you up but I'm sure you can find a suite in a hotel here."

"It will be very inconvenient for me to come to you."

"If this is just a matter of convenience why don't you forget the whole thing"

"Bert, (in a parental voice) don't be difficult!"

"Okay, I won't be difficult. I see no reason to continue this conversation. If you change your mind, call me. Good-bye."

I hung up before she had a chance to reply.

About ten o'clock this morning I got another call from her. She was in a suite at the best hotel in town. "Bert, I just got in. I have a ticket to return to New York late this afternoon. Will you please come down here to see me. We can have lunch together. I'll send a cab for you. Don't change your clothes, we'll eat right here in my suite. Please, Bert, this is very important."

I couldn't refuse.

When I walked into her suite, I barely recognized her, but then I couldn't remember when I saw her last. I thought she had aged poorly, but she may have thought the same of me. More than the ageing she looked very tired. She was sitting when I walked in because when I knocked she called out for me to come in. She didn't stand up, just asked me to sit down.

"Bert", she said, "I've been rehearsing what I'm about to say to you. Please hear me out before you say anything." She hesitated, took a deep breath and continued, "Today there will be no pretense on my part, and I hope when you speak there will be none on your part. Bert, there has never been any sisterly love between us. I've resented you from the day you were born. In my mind you were an interloper. Until you came along I was the queen of the realm. After you appeared I lost my crown and scepter. I perceived you as the favorite and deeply resented you. I did everything I could to beat you down until you were justified to resent me as I did you. When we grew up I didn't change from my childhood mindset and acted towards you no differently than I did as a four year old. You have every right not to feel kindly towards me. Now, after all these years I've come to you under difficult circumstances to have an urgent talk. I'm sure it's obvious that I've come to ask something of you. You have a right to gloat that the 'born winner' has to ask the 'born loser' for help. In your place I would gloat but I don't think gloating is in your nature.

"Now I'll get to the point. I have money, lots of it, but you have two things I'll never have: two lovely children and two good kidneys. I'm not going to ask you for one of your children but I am asking for one of your kidneys."

"One of my kidneys!?" I blurted out, then "I'm sorry, Flo, that just came out, I didn't mean to interrupt you. Please go on."

"Well, I've had kidney trouble for a few years. Last week

the doctor told me I will have to go on dialysis. He said I need a new kidney but my chances of getting one are very slim. There are too many better qualified people waiting for an organ, and the supply is very limited. The only chance I would have of getting one would be if one of my close relatives donated it to me.

"That's my speech, Bert. Now the floor is yours."

"I haven't had a chance to think about this, Flo, so I'll talk off the top of my head, no pretense. I thought you had the idea that with enough money you could get anything you wanted. Apparently this isn't so for a kidney. Can you fill me in on this?"

"My husband is willing to pay a million dollars for a kidney but apparently it's against the law to buy and sell organs from live people. It's okay to donate a kidney and apparently okay to give a gift in return. However, it's politically incorrect and probably illegal to advertise for a donor. We're left with the hope that some relative can be induced to offer his or her kidney."

"What inducement is being offered?"

"A hundred thousand and all expenses to be tested. A million and all expenses if the kidney is acceptable and the surgery done."

I didn't say anything for maybe three minutes, I was thinking about the offer. It didn't seem right. Finally, I said, "That would be for an ordinary kidney. My kidney is extraordinary. Of all the kidneys in the world mine is the most likely to be a satisfactary and successful transplant for you."

"Okay, so how much do you want?"

"Off the top of my head a million for each of my daughters and for my husband, two million for me, five million in all. Of course this has to be with my husband's permission."

"All right. We both will have to talk to our husbands and they to their lawyers to arrange the gifts. . . . Will you have lunch with me?"

"No, thanks. It's still early and I have a morning's work ahead of me. I'm going to run along. Have a good trip home. I expect I'll hear from you. Good-bye Flo."

That evening I told the whole story to George, he's my husband, and asked him what he thought. He was quiet for a few minutes. Finally, he said, "Bert, this is a decision you have to make."

"I know that but I won't give up a kidney without your permission."

"I can't give you my permission without knowing a lot more about it. What are the risks to you of such an operation and the risks to you of living with only one kidney? More than that what is your relationship to Flo that you would risk your life for her? Finally, what bearing does the money have on your decision? . . . . How much thought have you given to these questions?"

"Very little. Let me think about them now and tell you my thoughts as they come. First, I don't know the risks to me of the surgery or to living with only one kidney. I presume the surgical risk is very small. Living with one kidney may be a much greater risk, like driving a car with no spare tire. The risk probably increases the more miles you drive or the more years you live. So far as Flo is concerned, we have never had a loving sister relationship; on the contrary we don't even like each other. Finally, the money is probably the crucial factor."

George looked grim. "Because the money seems to be the crucial factor, let's talk about it first. What's so crucial about it? Why do you want so much money?"

"I guess I want the money so we can all feel secure."

"We will all feel secure when you're undergoing surgery and thereafter will live with only one kidney? Speaking for myself I would never feel secure about you if you had but one kidney. I would never choose to drive a car with no spare

191

tire, how do you think I would feel it you had no spare kidney? If you told the kids you had only one kidney they would have nightmares about losing their mommy. Why do we need all that money for anyway? We're not financially insecure. If something were to happen to me you're well protected with insurance . . . . I'm upset just thinking about it. If you're not going to do this without my permission, Bert, you're not going to do it."

"All right, George. I'll call Flo and tell her I can't do it, it's too big a risk for my children. I admit I hate to call her and tell her I won't give her a kidney."

"Tell her the truth, your husband won't agree. I'll be happy to take the responsibility for your decision. I'll have no hesitation telling her."

"No, George, what you told me convinced me. It's my decision."

The next morning I called Flo. Her private secretary picked up the phone. When I told her who I was she asked me to hold the line, that she had been instructed to put a call from me through at once.

In a moment Flo was on, "Tom is talking to his lawyer this morning." Tom is her hus band. "He's also talking to his financial advisor. He doesn't know whether what you want can be arranged."

"Tell him not to bother. I've decided not to do it."

"You decided not to do it! You can't do that. You already set a price. What is it, George wants more?"

"Flo, I decided it's not fair to my children. Money is not involved. I'm sorry to turn you down, Flo, but my children are more important to me than you are."

"How much more money does George want?"

"You're not listening. I said 'money is not involved.'"

"I'll talk to Tom and find out how much more he can come up with."

"Don't bother, Flo, good luck on finding a donor. Goodbye."

I hung up before she could answer. I expected to hear from her again.

I didn't hear from her but the next day George got a call from Tom who wanted to set up a meeting. George said he was not interested and would appreciate no further calls. He made clear the matter was settled.

I never did hear from Flo again, not even any more picture postcards from "the Winner". I don't know whether she's on dialysis, whether she got a donor, or even whether she's alive.

I look at my daughters and my husband and I'm glad I have both my kidneys.

OLD SOLDIERS

I walked into the health club room thinking I would ride a stationary bike for awhile but when I saw someone on one of the treadmills I decided I would try that. I got on the one alongside this rotund man who despite his blubber was swinging along at a good pace. He gave me some help and I got started. I worked up speed slowly and finally reached a military pace. And when I arrived there I found I had walked myself back fifty years. I swung into the rhythm and heard running through my head, "Someone's in the kitchen with Dinah". I silently sang through what I could remember of that, keeping in step to it of course, then went into, "I've got sixpence, jolly, jolly sixpence". I did what I could with that one, and it wasn't much. Those were the only two songs I could remember that we sang as we marched along in the Army Air Force Officers Training School in Miami Beach in 1942. "My god," I thought, "fifty years, I don't believe it."

I marched along on the treadmill and wondered how many men in that class were alive four years later to be mustered out, and how many were still alive now on this fiftieth anniversary. Musing on those days I suddenly became aware my fellow marcher and I were in step. I turned to him and said, "We appear to be marching together like soldiers. Is this something you have done in uniform?"

"Yes, a long, long time ago."

"Then we must have been in the same war. I was just thinking this is the fiftieth anniversary of when I first marched."

"I'm a few months past my fiftieth. Your draft number must have been a little higher than mine."

"I enlisted."

"Patriotism or escape?"

"Conscience."

"Are you sorry now?"

"I was lucky so I'm not sorry. Perhaps if I hadn't been so lucky I would be sorry—or dead. Are you sorry your draft number was so low?"

"Yes, I'm sorry because I was not lucky."

"Wounded?"

"Wounded? I guess you could say so."

"Did it get you an early discharge?"

"No, just a ten day hospitalization when the battle was over—then back to full duty—that was considered the best treatment.—Ten days in the hospital and the rest of my life living with the painful scars."

"Which battle was it that was over?"

"Guadalcanal."

"I don't understand what kind of wound you had."

"Nothing physical—an emotional breakdown related to battle stress. I think we marines who were there from the beginning all went to the hospital to be checked over. I can't imagine any of us not being affected."

"What are the scars?"

"Today the name is 'Post-traumatic Stress Syndrome'. They called me back a couple of years ago for a medical check-up and asked me a bunch of questions. They decided

I had it and gave me a disability pension. Unfortunately that didn't stop the nightmares."

We marched along together in silence for awhile then he continued, "I don't get them so often anymore but my wife still won't sleep in the same bed with me—not that I want her to, I think I'm more scared than she is. When I have one of those dreams I can get pretty violent; I could kill her in my sleep—and I never know when they're going to come."

"You're entitled to a pension. Did they make it retroactive?"

"Yes, they did. It came to quite a hunk of money. I guess the funds were available because there are not too many of us left."

We marched another quarter of a mile quietly thinking. He wasn't finished, "My wife doesn't think it was a nightmare about Guadalcanal that night when I beat her up in my sleep. That was the first nightmare I had after we were married— and the last time she slept with me. Of course we didn't stop making love but afterwords we're each in our own bed."

"What does your wife believe?"

"She believes it's because she's my wife."

"I don't understand."

"When I went into the army I was engaged to be married to someone else, someone I was madly in love with. While I was overseas she married, a guy deferred because of an essential defense job. I got her 'Dear John' letter while I was in the hospital after Guadalcanal. That letter kept me in the hospital another four days. I've never heard from her again, don't know what happened to her, don't know whether she's still alive. Anyway, my wife thinks I'm still so angry at her that in my dream I think it's she who is in bed with me. Originally, I think my wife really meant it because she felt I didn't love her like I did the other one, and she was right. Now after all these years she knows I love her, and she's right again. When she mentions it now she's just teasing or perhaps recognizes I'm no longer angry. Anyway, I recognize I have a wonderful wife and I suspect the other would not have made me happy.—Right now after talking to you—after marching along together with you—I think maybe I wasn't so unlucky after all. Maybe tomorrow if we march again you can tell me how you were lucky too.

STEEL

That was a significant day for me. I completed the sale of my business.

I've been in the steel business practically my whole life. My father started it as a junk yard and expanded it into scrap steel. He talked about it incessantly at home so before I was old enough to go to school I knew about the steel business. My father used to take me to work for brief visits and introduce me as the men's next boss. As I became old enough I began to work part time in any capacity I was fit for, beginning with office gopher. I slowly became familiar with every aspect of the operation at the same time I was becoming educated academically. I got my MBA and began making some changes even before I took over. When my father retired many more changes were made and the business prospered greatly. I have a son and a daughter but I didn't train them to take it over like my father trained me. Perhaps because of this or perhaps for other reasons, neither of them are interested in it. They both encouraged me to sell. My wife was noncommittal. "Make up your own mind," she said. In business, steel was my whole life, I never realized I would also be dealing with it at home.

Steel is so much a part of my life that sometimes I wonder whether subconsciously I was attracted to a woman with a core of steel. Perhaps it was intuitive for when I first met Kate and fell in love with her I didn't appreciate the nature of her inner character. She was born and brought up in New York City and educated in private schools. She was bright and went on to Wellesley. I met her when she came upstate to visit a college friend. At that time she was at loose ends. She had been out of college two years, had decided on no career because she wanted to get married, have a home of her own, and have children; but she had found no man she cared about enough to marry. I don't think she was attracted to me as I was to her but she must have considered me suitable husband material: someone who would make a good father, who could provide her with the kind of home she wanted, and who would cater to her wishes.

She was right on all counts. I built a home for her to her specifications and furnished it the way she wanted it. We had the family she wanted, raised the children her way, and educated them largely by her direction although she did it so cleverly the kids thought the choices were their own. We took vacations as she planned them. I was content to let her run everything outside of the business. I considered it a happy marriage. Shortly after the kids were grown and left home her father died. Her mother was alone in New York City and Kate is the only child. Her mother refused to move upstate and was content to stay alone where she was. Kate went down to stay with her for a little while after the funeral. I went down weekends to stay with her and ran the home here. After a few weeks there it became clear to me that Kate did not plan to come back home. She said she could not leave her mother but would come back to be with me alternate weekends. I didn't like the arrangement but made an adjustment by hiring more help at home. The weekends with her were good, both in New York and here at home, and I had a degree of freedom I didn't have when she was at home with me.

We went along this way for about four months until one weekend she told me she was starting law school in New York. She had to do something to make use of her time productively. Her father had been a highly successful lawyer and had always wanted her to become a lawyer. She had disappointed him, but maybe now this would honor his memory. Her weekends were consequently taken up with study so commuting became less frequent. We were together now maybe every four to six weeks. This seemed to satisfy her completely but I didn't like it. That's when I began to think about selling my share of the business. She was going to be in law school for three years and I was ready to move to New York to be with her rather than to be separated as we were. However, I knew I couldn't go there without something to do so on one of my weekends in New York I spent some time making inquiries among those doing business in steel internationally. I learned enough from those inquiries to form a corporation as a trade consultant for the steel industry. I located the office in my home upstate.

I hired away a secretary, Elaine, from one of the companies doing business overseas. I gave her shares in my new corporation and made her an officer in it. She's a bright young woman, speaks four langauges, and has a talking acquaintance with key personnel in steel companies in France, Germany, and Italy. Now that my business was sold I could pay full attention to marketing my expertise as a consultant. I envisaged enlarging my firm to include consultants in every facet of the steel industry and was already on the lookout for prospective colleagues. I decided a trip overseas was essential. Elaine, now the official secretary of the corporation, was a thirtyish divorcee without children. A paid trip to Europe to accompany me was welcome to her. I believe neither of us had any romantic ideas about the other. Our relationship up to that point had been purely professional. I treated her like I would any junior partner.

Katie knew I planned to sell the business and when I told her the deal was consummated and that I had formed a new corporation she barely reacted beyond saying, "Good for you." When I told her I was going to take a trip overseas to investigate business possibilities she asked if I was going alone. I told her I was going with another officer of the corporation. She asked about some details of the trip and told me to be careful. She never inquired further about the other officer. She was deep in the work of a first year law student and didn't even express any regret that she couldn't go with me.

Elaine and I spent six weeks in Europe doing business and sightseeing. Elaine had been in Europe many times and acted as my guide. I was her escort and paid all the bills. We always got two bedroom suites in the hotels where we stayed. The chemistry between us was good and by the middle of the third week it was apparent to me that Elaine was developing some tender feelings towards me. I began to be concerned that I may have got myself into a dangerous situation. I didn't know Elaine well enough to be sure she wouldn't start a suit against me for sexual harassment. I decided to talk to her about it. The occasion occurred one evening after a leisurely dinner following a highly successful business day. We were both exhilarated. The conversation went something like this:

ME: Elaine, something about us has been bothering me and I want to talk to you about it.
ELAINE: All right, Ted, I'm listening.
ME: I like you and I think you like me, right?
ELAINE: Right.
ME: I'm concerned that our relationship might become sexual.
ELAINE: Why does this concern you?

ME: I don't want to be accused of harassing you.

ELAINE: It's too late for you to be concerned about that. I could accuse you now. You're my boss and we've been sharing a suite. Ted, if you don't trust me why did you risk taking me with you?

ME: Obviously, even if I don't know you well, I trust you. I guess really it's myself I don't trust. I'm feeling some sexual desire, and I find you're appearing more and more attractive to me.

ELAINE: Ted, I have some sexual desire myself, and you've always been attractive to me.

ME: I'm old enough to be your father. Am I attractive to you as a sex partner?

ELAINE: Attractive enough to be a candidate. That's as much as I can tell at this point.

ME: I don't make passes. If sometime you think you'd like to try me my door will be open. You will always be welcome.

ELAINE: I'll give that some thought. Thanks for the invitation.

That was all that happened at that time.

A few days later Elaine came into my bed. It turned out to be a highly successful venture. We were both eager for the encounter. After that I made no advances but she joined me two or three times a week.

Meanwhile from a business standpoint everything was going extremely well. I had so many tentative contracts that I knew I would have to expand my firm quickly. I couldn't possibly handle everything by myself. I contacted a law firm in New York specializing in business contracts overseas and engaged their representatives in each country we went to. They were kept busy in contract negotiations.

Elaine had an apartment in New York and up to the time we went to Europe we had kept in contact by phone and fax. Now we had to decide whether I would move the office to New York or Elaine upstate. I decided the best solution would be to have an office both places so I got one in New York as soon as we returned and kept the one in my home upstate. I recruited three top associates by giving them each a piece of the firm. I put Elaine in charge of the New York office. The firm became very prosperous. More associates were added without giving away any more pieces of the firm.

I was spending more time in New York but the living arrangements were not good. Katie's mother's apartment was not satisfactory for more than a weekend and she, Katie's mother, would not consider moving to a bigger place. During the summer after Katie's first year in law school I suggested she find a place for us in New York. She was unwilling to do this and leave her mother. I told her I wanted to sell our home upstate and she didn't resist. I suggested she find an apartment in New York that would be suitable for us after her mother died and which I could live in meanwhile. She agreed to do this and worked with an efficiency that frightened me. In the course of six weeks she got an apartment and furnished it by moving the furniture she wanted from our home. I sold our home upstate and disposed of the remaining furniture by giving the kids what they wanted and giving the rest to charitable organizations.

Now I was in New York. Katie was in an apartment with her mother, I had my own apartment, and Elaine had her own apartment. Katie was back in law school and was not interested in seeing me during the week nor on some weekends. We contacted each other a couple of times a week on the phone. She wouldn't stay with me overnight in our apartment because she wouldn't leave her mother alone at night but she did spend some Saturday afternoons with me in our apartment. We would make love and afterwords go out to dinner. I never invited Elaine to my apartment; I was afraid Katie would know another woman had been there. I think women have a special intuitive sense about that, or maybe it's a hyperacute sense of smell that alerts them to a different perfume. If I had Elaine in bed with me I suspect her perfume would permeate the mattress and Katie would smell it out.

Elaine and I frequently spent evenings together. Sometimes it was just for dinner, occasionally we would take in a movie, or a play, or a concert, or even an opera. We spoke a lot about business and I valued her judgment. When she invited me I would spend the night with her at her apartment. I kept a change of clothes there.

The months passed. Katie arranged to have a summer internship at a law firm in the city after finishing her second year.

All my associates who held shares I now designated as partners and we held regular meetings. At one of these meetings a partner suggested it was time to investigate the possibilities in Russia, China, and Japan. I didn't mind investigating but I was skeptical about the reliability of any people I would be able to do business with. I liked to travel and the idea of another six weeks with Elaine appealed to me. Elaine was pessimistic about the possibility of doing business in those countries but said if the partners were willing to spend the money she would go and at least enjoy the sightseeing.

Elaine and I were in Tokyo in late April when I heard from Katie that her mother had died following a massive stroke. She told me not to interrupt my trip, which I had no intention of doing in any event. The trip was not successful so far from a business standpoint but Elaine and I were having a wonderful time. In mid June Elaine and I were in Moscow. We had returned from dinner to find a note at the front desk that Katie was in our suite. She had shown her passport convinced the manager that she was my wife, and was allowed into the suite. Elaine and I walked into the bar, had a drink, and talked over how to handle this. We decided to treat her as a welcome addition but indicate this was a purely business trip and she would pretty much be on her own for amusement. This done we went up to the suite to find Katie in a very deep sleep which we attributed to fatigue and jet lag.

The following morning I had breakfast sent up to the suite. Katie was still very tired but got up to have something to eat with us. I introduced the women who looked at each other warily. I could see Katie was miffed but Elaine was relaxed and solicitous of Katie's jet lag. Katie said she came to Moscow on the spur of the moment. She had had an altercation with the firm where she was interning and quit. The same day she arranged the trip. She had tried to reach me but was unable to. After breakfast she went right back to bed. Elaine and I had a business appointment but I told Katie we would be back and all have dinner together. As it turned out our business appointment wanted to have dinner with us and discuss more business. I called Katie and invited her to join us but she declined. We got back late, Katie was asleep but there was a note for me. She had signed up for a tour leaving early the next morning. She would see me in New York. The following morning she was up and out while I was still asleep. I thought it had been stupid for her to come and was glad she had left. Two weeks later Elaine and I were back in New York. I had not heard again from Katie but learned her tour was for two weeks so she may not have had a chance to reach me. Anyway she said she would see me in New York. I tried not to let Katie's visit interfere with the pleasure I was feeling in the company of Elaine. Elaine did not appear in the least upset by the episode. Her behavior showed no change. We both greatly enjoyed the remaining days we had in Russia. Elaine did once mention she thought Katie was well aware that we had developed a sexual relationship. I agreed. Neither of us speculated on whether a divorce was in the offing.

It was more than two weeks after I returned before I

heard from Katie. She said she had been in her mother's apartmene for a few days but wanted to recover from the trip before calling me. She reached me at my office and said she would be home by the time I got there from work. She suggested we go out for dinner. At dinner the matter on both our minds was brought up by Katie. The conversation as I remember it went something like this:

KATIE: Ted, what are we going to do?

ME: Do about what?

KATIE: Don't answer with a question. You know about what. Do you want a divorce?

ME: The answer is, "No." Now can I ask a question? Do you?

KATIE: No, not if you give up Elaine; yes, if you won't give her up.

ME: Katie, I need her in my firm, but I'll give up the social relationship.

KATIE: How can I be sure of that?

ME: You can't, you'll have to take my word for it.

KATIE: That's not acceptable. I want you to fire her.

ME: I can't do that. She's a very important officer in the firm.

KATIE: More important than keeping your marriage?

ME: I don't think I have to make that choice.

KATIE: I know you do.

ME: You're presenting me with an ultimatum: fire Elaine or I will file for a divorce. Don't you leave any room for compromise? I don't want to marry Elaine even if she were willing and I have no reason to believe she is. I certainly don't want her as a mistress and she would have none of that in any event. I told you I would give up the social relationship, what more do you want? You have no reason not to trust my word. In all the years we've been married have you ever had reason not to trust me?

You've finished two years of law school; look back at the years since you left me to come to New York and live with your mother and tell me if I have grounds to divorce you. Think about it Katie. I don't want a divorce but if you do I won't contest it.

KATIE: All right, Ted, I'll give it some more thought. Maybe you're the one who should be going to law school.

Well, apparently she gave it a lot more thought because she never brought the subject up again and we went on living as though nothing had happened. She went on to her final year of law school and I discontinued the sexual relationship I had had with Elaine. Elaine said she missed me and saw no reason why we couldn't continue as we had. She was confident Katie would never bring the subject up again. I told her I was sorry but I couldn't do it.

Graduation came and Katie was busier than ever preparing for the law boards but finally they were over too. Katie got a job with a good law firm in the city. My firm continued to do well. I should have been content but I had an uneasy feeling that I couldn't exactly identify. There was something in the behavior of Katie and Elaine that somehow didn't seem right. I began to see that Elaine had a core of steel just like Katie. I visualized they were forging swords from their steel.

I was right. Within a week they both struck and when the blows came I was actually relieved. Katie filed for divorce, her first official act, and Elaine announced she was leaving the firm to start one of her own and was taking my best men with her.

My belief is reinforced: the hardest steel is found in the cores of women.

UNTIL DEATH

I met him my first day in school. It was his first day too, like it was for all the kids in our kindergarten class. All the mothers were there that day and some of the kids really needed them: the frightened kids and the crying kids. Ralph and I didn't need our mothers. We were eager beavers who wanted the action to begin. Our mothers left early knowing they weren't needed. Ralph and I had discovered each other almost immediately and have remained close friends ever since—and that was more than a half century ago.

We were born here in this small town, went to school here, and have settled here. Ralph went into his father's hardware store after high school. I went off to college and law school but came back to practice here, and Ralph was one of the reasons to come back, and Ida was the other. Ida was my girl friend in high school and when I went away to college she went to nursing school. When I went to law school she came to the city where I was and got a job in the hospital. We got married there, but only after I had agreed to come back here to practice—which I would have done anyway. Ralph had married his school sweetheart, Ethyl, two years after graduating. We live in a nice neighborhood just a few blocks from each other. Ralph and Ethyl are our closest friends.

About two years ago, before even Ethyl was aware, Ida told me she didn't like the way Ethyl looked. It was Ida who persuaded her—dragged her would be a better way to describe it—to see her doctor. Ethyl was found to have a cancer. She had all the radiation and all the chemotherapy she could have, and still had the cancer. Ida was devastated, Ralph was in a state of despair, and I was pretty depressed myself. I never realized depression was so contagious.

Ida spent a lot of time with Ethyl. She was there a good part of every day and went back after dinner to help Ralph with her. I didn't spend much time at their house. I couldn't find how I could make myself useful. Anyway, I used to have lunch with Ralph every day. When Ida left after dinner I would go out for a walk. It was summer and walking was pleasant.

Flo lived next door to us. She was a widow, nice looking and very pleasant. She was a good friend of Ida's and would have liked to help with Ethyl but felt unwelcome there. Ralph and her husband, Sam, had had a falling out.

Sam and Flo ran a Mom and Pop general store across Main St. from Ralph and Ethyl's hardware store. One fall about five years ago they abruptly became competitors. Sam opened a hardware department and Ralph opened a soft goods department. They each blamed the other for starting it. That ended the friendship. There was no contact between the couples ever since. When Sam died two years ago Ralph and Ethyl never went to the funeral, they belonged to a different church anyway. In those two years nothing changed. Flo continued running the business and got some help for the heavy work.

I would see Flo sitting on her porch the evenings when I walked and we would exchange greetings. One evening she invited me up on her porch and we talked for an hour. I could see she was a pretty lonely woman. As the days went by it became a routine. On my way home from my walk I would stop at Flo's and we would talk. Before I left we would go into the house and have a cup of tea and some cake or cookies.

Towards the end of the summer Ethyl was getting worse making it more difficult for Ralph. He hired a nurse's aide during the day and after work with Ida's help took care of her himself. Ida was spending more and more time there as Ethyl became more confused and finally became unaware of anything except the strange little world inside her head. Ethyl had been dying for a couple of weeks with Ida coming home later and later so that I no longer waited up for her.

One night while I was having tea with Flo I could see she was troubled.

"What's the matter, Flo?" I asked.

"Oh, I guess I'm upset by some gossip I heard today."

"I don't let gossip upset me."

"You might this. I've been debating whether to tell you."

"Don't. I don't want to hear it."

"Then you already know?"

"Know what?"

"That Ida and Ralph are having an affair."

I could feel the blood rushing to my face. I just looked at Flo. She saw how I looked and got frightened.

"You didn't know," she said, "I shouldn't have told you."

"That's ridiculous," I said, "that's vicious gossip. Does Ida know about it?"

"Not that I'm aware. I just heard it today."

I thought awhile and decided that Ralph and Ida should know about it. I told Flo I was going to Ralph's house right then.

She said, "Please don't say I told you. Ralph will think I started the gossip because I don't like him."

"I'll tell them you just repeated what you were told—who told you?"

"Emma."

"Emma. I might have known. Poor woman leads a troubled life, and works hard to get other people to be equally unfortunate."

"Please come back, George. I'll wait up for you."

It was about ten o'clock when I got there. I thought Ethyl might be asleep so I didn't ring the bell. The door was open so I walked in. I heard a radio upstairs and again fearful I might wake Ethyl didn't call out. I walked upstairs. There was a light in Ethyl's room so I walked in. She looked like a cadaver but I knew she was asleep because I could see her breathing. It was her radio that was on but she was alone. I walked into the hallway. Ralph's bedroom door was closed. I quietly walked down the stairs and left the house slowly closing the door behind me. I went back to Flo's and told her what had happened.

"How do you know they were in the bedroom?" she asked, "Did you see them?"

"Where else would they be?"

"Did you look in the kitchen?"

"No."

"They could have been having a cup of tea, just like you and me."

"I suppose it's possible."

I went home and waited for Ida. She came in a little after eleven.

"How about a cup of tea with me?" I asked.

"Oh, I can't. I'm full of tea. I've been drinking it with Ralph the past hour and a half—poor man, I'm so sorry for him."

"What do you do, have it right in Ethyl's room?"

"Oh no, we have it in the kitchen."

"Aren't you afraid to leave Ethyl alone?"

"No, we have the intercom on in her room. We can hear her if she begins to stir.—You look tired, how come you stayed up tonight?"

I told her what Flo had told me. She was shocked.

"That's vicious," she said, "George, do you think I could do that?"

"No, Ida, I don't."

"And poor Ralph. Making love to me or anyone else must be the farthest thing from his mind right now. He was so in love with Ethyl. He treats what's left of her so tenderly. What a pity she isn't aware. It's breaking my heart, George, I hope it doesn't go on much longer. It's wearing me out, I don't know how much more I can stand. I don't know how Ralph endures it."

"Do you think Ethyl is suffering?"

"No, the doctor has told Ralph to make sure she gets her pain medicine right around the clock even though she doesn't show any signs of pain. He said it's easier to prevent the pain than try to relieve it once it occurs."

Ethyl's aide would leave at three o'clock and Ida would stay with Ethyl until Ralph came home from work at six o'clock. During that time she would give Ethyl her pain medication at four o'clock, and make dinner for Ralph.

A few days after I had made that night trip to Ralph's I got a call in my office from Ida at about 5:30. She said Ethyl had died just a few minutes before. She said she had called Ralph who was closing up and would come right home. She thought it would be helpful if I came too.

I got there the same time as Ralph and we hurried in together. Ida met us at the door quite distressed. She broke into tears when she saw us. I took her in my arms to comfort her, and Ralph rushed upstairs. After about ten minutes he came slowly back down.

"The Lord has finally taken her," he said.

Ida and I were sitting on the couch in the living room. I had my arm around her and she had stopped crying. Ralph sat down in a chair close to us. No one said anything. Finally Ralph spoke.

"Ida, I looked for the pain medicine but couldn't find it. You know the doctor wanted me to flush it down the toilet right after Ethyl died."

Ida said, "I know that's what he wanted so I did it. I guess I must have thrown out the empty bottle."

Flo had asked me to ask Ralph if he would be upset if she came to the funeral. He said of course he wouldn't so she came. She even talked to Ralph and told him how sorry she was. Ralph just nodded.

After the funeral Ida and I helped Ralph as much as we could to get him over the roughest times and to adjust to his life without Ethyl. Both he and Ida were acutely aware of the gossip so were careful not to spend much time together without someone else being present. I thought that was ridiculous and told them I resented that they felt it necessary to adjust their activities to suit some busybody gossip. I told them if I didn't object they didn't have to pay attention to anyone else. Gradually they relaxed and were no longer concerned about being together alone.

Both Ida and I felt Ralph would eventually feel the need for someone to replace Ethyl, and to our way of thinking Flo would be the perfect wife for him. We thought maybe we could bring them together but couldn't figure out a good way to do it. We decided we would wait six months and then start doing something although we weren't sure what. As it turned out an opportunity arose at about the time we had set.

Steve ran the only hotel in town: the two floors above his restaurant, and usually the top floor was unoccupied because there was no elevator. The days I worked I had lunch at Steve's place. This day Steve came over and sat down with me.

"I heard something I think maybe you oughta know," he said.

Steve's restaurant had a bar along one wall and guests at the hotel would frequently spend an hour or two there. Steve often tended the bar himself.

"I've had two salesmen staying here the past couple of days," he said. "Last night they came down to the bar and had a few drinks. They hadn't seen each other for awhile and began talking over old times. 'Hey,' one of them said, 'do you remember the time we introduced competition to this town?' The two of them then put together this story. They had come into town on the same train and became acquainted. One sold hardware to Ralph and the other software to Sam. Ralph would never buy software nor Sam hardware because they had agreed they would not compete. On that train these two guys devised a plan. The software salesman told Ralph that Sam had placed an order for hardware and wondered whether Ralph would now like to place an order for software, and the hardware salesman told Sam that Ralph had placed an order for software and thought maybe Sam would now like to place an order for hardware. That's how Ralph and Sam became competitors, and each blamed the other for breaking the agreement."

I told Ida Steve's story and we decided I would talk to Ralph and she would talk to Flo. Their reactions were predictable: anger and resolution to do no further business with those salesmen. Ralph asked me to draft a letter to the salesmen's employers, and wondered if he could sue them. Flo's anger was tempered by sorrow at what Ralph and Sam had done to one another, each too stubborn to ask the other how this had come about. She cried.

I suggested to Ralph it would be appropriate for him to approach Flo and talk about returning to the terms of the old agreement so they could stop competing.

"I don't know," Ralph said, "my software department is doing well. I've been thinking about expanding it."

"Are you thinking of putting Flo out of business?" I asked.

"If Flo goes out of business it will be because she doesn't

know how to run it, not because I put her out. My software department never amounted to much when Sam was running the business."

"Okay, Flo can't run the business like Sam did, but she's a mighty fine woman. You and she could become good friends. You're both lonely, Ralph, you'd be good for each other. Be a gentleman, make the first move."

"Maybe, I'll think about it. I'm pretty shook up by this. I gotta think."

Nothing happened for a week. Ida and I thought we had to do something. We invited them both to dinner without telling them who else was coming. It was pretty awkward at first but things had warmed up a bit by the end of the evening, and before they left we had played a couple of gin rummy games: the men against the women. When their spouses were alive we used to have regular games with each couple. They agreed we could start again with them. Flo said she would have the next one and would make the dinner. Ralph said he would have the one after that and do the same. He said he had become a pretty good cook when Ethyl was ill.

The next day Ralph called me and said he wanted to see me. I dropped in to see him on my lunch hour, he had his lunch right in his store. He told me he was up all night thinking about Flo and decided he was going to back out of the dinners and gin games. He said the chemistry wasn't right between Flo and him. They were business competitors and always would be. I told him they didn't always have to be competitors, that he could get together with Flo the same as he had with Sam. He said there was no reason for him to do that now. Flo's business was going to go right down the tube.

He said, "I'll tell you the basic problem. I can't see Flo as a woman; I see her only as a business competitor—and you can tell her that."

"What do you want her to do," I asked, "go out of

business? She needs the income to live on. Who's going to support her, will you?"

"No, I don't want Flo. Look, I know she's a widow and I'm a widower, and we both need a mate. But I don't want her."

"Is there anyone you do want?"

"Yes, I want Ida."

"Ida?!!—my Ida?

"Yes, your Ida."

"Does she know that?"

"No. I don't think she even suspects it. I think I fell in love with her when she was helping me with Ethyl."

"Do you plan to tell her?"

"No."

"Do you want me to tell her?"

"How do you think she would react?"

"I don't know whether she would feel anger or sympathy."

"Are you angry?"

"No, I don't blame you. Ida is attractive to me too. _ Flo is also an attractive woman, Ralph."

"She is. Perhaps under other circumstances—but that isn't the way it is."

"What other circumstances are you considering?"

"I'm not, George, I don't want to start with her.—Suit yourself about telling Ida what I said to you."

When I got home that night I told Ida that Ralph had backed out of the dinners and rummy.

"That's interesting," Ida said, "I stopped in to see Flo today and she backed out too. What was Ralph's excuse?"

"He can only see Flo as a disagreeable competitor."

"That's about the same as Flo. Flo is convinced he means to put her out of business.—We don't seem to be doing very well as match makers."

"That depends on whose getting matched up."

"What do you mean?"

"Ralph admits he's lonely and wants a woman but he doesn't want Flo. He wants you."

I thought I knew Ida well enough to be able to tell how she felt about something just by watching how she reacted, but this time I didn't have a clue. She said nothing and didn't change her expression.

"You're not surprised," I said.

"No, I'm not."

"Has he told you this?"

"No, but he showed me in other ways. I don't know what's happening. Flo told me she wants you—has she told you that?"

"No, but she showed me in other ways."

"I didn't know you knew her that well."

"We got acquainted when you were spending so much time with Ethyl—and Ralph."

"Flo and I had a long talk."

"Ida, Ralph said he wanted you, do you want him?"

"I want you, George."

"I didn't ask whether you wanted me."

"I know."

"Well, do you want Ralph?"

"I guess I want you both. Do you want Flo?"

"I suppose I could say the same. I would enjoy having you both."

"Would you allow it if it could be managed? That's what Flo and I talked about."

"My god, you two are way ahead of me. It sounds like you're both strongly for it.—Okay, let me have it."

"We thought two nights a week, say Wednesday and Saturday I would cook dinner for Ralph in his house, and Flo would cook dinner for you here. If it suited us we would stay over Saturday nights. We thought we could try it for a few months and then decide if it was working okay or if some changes would have to be made.—what do you think?"

"I think you must have some feelings about the marriage vows you took."

"I do and I'm concerned about that. We vowed to be faithful to each other 'until death doth you part.' How do you reconcile your vows with what we've planned?"

"Well, I could consider that we are no longer bound, death has supervened. The death was Ethyl's but it was death none the less."

"You are playing the role of the defense attorney. That's good enough for me, I'll go for it."

"If you and Flo are for it I'll go along. We are all consenting adults. I can't see where it will do any harm, and I can see where it will make Emma very happy. But I have one condition: Ralph and Flo must settle their business differences."

"What has that to do with us?"

"If they don't it will poison the relationship you and I have with each other because you will feel you must support Ralph and I will feel I must support Flo."

·

Ida agreed and the next day I told Ralph and Ida told Flo. Nothing happened. A few weeks later Ida suggested if they were working it out we should get started on the plan. I agreed so one afternoon I went back to Ralph and Ida to Flo. Neither endorsed the idea. Each said they were in the middle of negotiations and wanted to settle the business matters first.

At dinner after we had told each other what had happened, Ida said, "George, you make a good defense attorney but I don't think a crime will be committed. I think the case is going to be thrown out of court. I'm convinced Flo and Ralph have discovered each other. You and I are going to be stuck together until death doth us part."

I didn't answer, just smiled.

"You don't act surprised," Ida said.

"I'm not. I anticipated this. It's the way I planned it."

The hell it was.

TRUE BELIEVER

"Hell," I thought, "it's time to quit."

I had been at the books all night and had definitely reached the point of diminishing returns.

I figured it would be a good idea to walk down to the corner neighborhood bar and have a beer nightcap. It was eleven o'clock and I was hopeful there would still be an interesting character or two hanging out there. I wasn't disappointed.

When I walked in there were two guys at the bar with about five empty barstools between them. They both looked like they were in their early fifties and they way they dressed advertised what they were: one a white collar worker, one a blue. I picked a spot between them, one away from white collar. Both were drinking beer.

"Hi," said white collar

"Hi," I replied

"Warm night."

"That it is."

"Coming from work?"

"I suppose I could say that though I'm only a block away. I've been working at home. How about you?"

"Oh, I get out of work at five o'clock. I live in the neighborhood too and usually about this time walk down here for a nightcap and maybe find somebody I can talk to. Mind if I talk to you?"

"Not at all."

"Will you listen?'

"Sure, for a while."

"Sometimes when people start listening, they don't listen very long. How long is, 'a while'?"

"No more than an hour."

"Oh, that's wonderful."

He went back to his beer without saying anything more, and I went to mine.

After a couple of slow thoughtful swallows he began, "I've just been collecting my thoughts to plan how to start." This was said in a whisper as an aside to me. He continued now in a voice easily heard by the bartender and by blue collar. "Have you ever thought that there is a voice inside of each of us.?"

"A voice that is not ours?"

"That's right."

"Do you have one?"

"Of course, each of us has one."

"Have you heard yours?"

"Yes, many times."

"What does it say?"

"That depends on what I ask it."

"You ask it questions?"

"Just the tough ones. I don't bother it with the minor ones, those I can figure out myself. It's a tremendous help to me, it guides me in all the tough decisions."

"Sounds like you have a genie inside of you. Is it a man's voice or a woman's?"

"I don't know, it's hard to tell. I get the message but I

don't actually hear a voice. Messages can be transmitted by other means than voice, you know."

"Do you think that's just a receiver inside of you, or is there an actual presence you're harboring?"

"There's a presence, all right, but I'm not harboring it, it's harboring me—more than 'harboring', it owns me."

"There's something inside of you that owns you?"

"That's right. I'm renting my life, and when I die this 'something' will take it back."

"This is a little difficult for me to grasp.—Do you talk to it?"

"Of course, frequently."

"Does it answer?"

"Not always."

"Do you talk out loud to it?"

"Sometimes."

"But it never answers in a voice?"

"Once in a while I thought I heard a voice, but I might just have imagined it."

Blue collar had been quietly listening to all this; now he spoke up, "No goddam 'presence' inside of me owns me. I think you bin talking a crock of shit.—Hearin' voices, you must be crazy."

White didn't answer blue, just looked at him in a patronizing way. I began to wonder if blue wasn't right. White seemed to have a well established delusional system and probably was hallucinating.

"You said that we all had a voice within us," I said.

"That's right, only some of us don't listen for it."

"Is the voice in me the same as the voice in you?"

"That's right, the same 'presence'."

"It's in me, and at the same time it's in you?"

"That's right."

Blue broke in, "Same guy in two places at once. Man, you're weird."

I went on, "And it's the same in everyone, in every human being?"

White smiled, "You're getting it," he said.

Blue moved over two stools, he was warming up. "So this guy inside of you owns the whole human race.—Does he own any real estate?"

"The whole universe," white replied calmly.

"That's a lot of real estate," said blue, eyeing white suspiciously. "Does this guy ever tell you what to do?"

"Yes, and I try to do his bidding."

"Does he ever get violent?" I asked.

"He has been known to."

Blue moved back to his original place.

"Has he ever told you to do anything violent?" I asked

"No, but if I heard a clear, loud message to take action, I would."

I went back to my beer and he to his. Blue was staring at white. Nobody spoke.

I finished my beer, got up, and turned to white. "It was nice talking to you," I said, "Good-night."

"Good-night," he said, "maybe we'll talk again some time."

I walked out quickly.

TRUST

This was the day Stan was picking up his wife, Amy. He had told her he would be waiting for her outside the gate at 12 noon. She had said that's when she would be getting out.

He was sitting in his car outside the gate at 11:30. He had gone into work early, done what had to be done, and at 10:45 told his secretary he would be gone for the rest of the day and left. He could do that, his position was high enough in the state bureaucracy that he could set his own hours, and he had been there long enough to be known as someone who was completely reliable. As he waited his thoughts and feelings were as jumbled as they had been three years before when he got a phone call from Amy telling him she had been arrested.

Amy was an attractive woman: pretty face, well proportioned petite body, out-going, and upbeat. She came from a background of poverty. Her father died in an industrial accident when she was two years old and her mother was in a constant struggle to support herself and her two small daughters. Amy inherited her mother's optimistic outlook on life and except for the absence of a father did not consider her childhood an unhappy one. She took a business course in high schcol and when she graduated got a jpb with the state. She had a position as a secretary and it was at work that she met Stan when he had his foot on the lowest rung of the bureaucracy's executive ladder. Two months after they met they got married. "That was thirty-five years ago," Stan thought, "It doesn't seem possible." Two years after they were married Amy quit her job and had a son; Andy; and two years after that she had a daughter, Angie. When Angie began school Amy began taking courses in bookkeeping and medical secretaryship. She thought her obstetrician was so wonderful she decided she wanted to work in a doctor's office.

Amy finished her courses and with help from the school got a job with a group of five family practitioners. She was well liked; an efficient, dependable worker with a pleasing personality. In ten years she had worked herself up to bookkeeper and office manager. She was with them another twelve years before she was arrested.

The arrest was the result of unforeseen circumstances. The IRS was conducting a routine audit of the office as was done five years before. This time, however, there was a new young diligent auditor. Whereas the previous audit was done in five days, this young man took two weeks and came up with evidence that considerable skimming was taking place. The way the office was run Amy was obviously the one doing the skimming. When faced with the evidence she readily confessed.

She had been skimming for twelve years but was completely unable to estimate how much money was involved. Her home finances were thoroughly investigated and it was evident that all expenditures were accounted for by the legitimate income of Stan and Amy. When questioned about where the money went she said she gave it away to the Medicaid patients of the group.

She said from examining the charts she was well aware

of the sometimes deplorable home conditions of the patients. She decided who needed the most help and gave the money to them. This was a weekly event done on Sunday mornings when she told Stan she was going to church. He was not a churchgoer. She did it anonymously by working through the children in the neighborhood. She would pay some child to deliver the envelope with the cash, and watch to see that it was delivered. When asked to identify some of those to whom she gave money she refused. She said it would spoil everything for them to know who gave the money and that it was stolen.

Stan was also closely questioned and claimed complete ignorance of what had been going on. When asked if he was surprised he said that "surprised" was too mild a word, "astounded" would be a better choice. However, he said he could understand it because from how his wife had spoken over the years he knew she had some sort of Robinhood complex. In any event Stan was not charged with anything.

The doctors were unaware that anything had been skimmed and were not interested in prosecuting Amy, but this was a criminal matter. Her lawyer told her she could avoid prison if she told to whom the money went but she refused. Now, she had served her time and was being released.

Stan thought the whole business was bizarre. He wanted to believe Amy but there were doubts. He was upset that she hadn't confided in him and had been deceiving him all those years. She said she couldn't tell him because she knew he would make her stop and put all the money back into the office, and she didn't want to do that. She said the doctors wouldn't miss it (which turned out to be true} and the poor people badly needed it. She said it made her feel good, that she was doing something worthwhile. She was glad she did it even though she went to jail, and she would do it again if she had the opportunity.

That attitude frightened Stan. He wondered what sort

of moral standards Amy had. If that's the way she thought she might not have any compunctions about lying. Maybe the whole story about giving the money away was a lie.

He had asked Andy and Angie what they thought. Andy said he didn't know whether Amy was telling the truth but didn't see any sense in doubting her story. He said it was a good story even if it wasn't true. Angie said of course she believed her mother. She said it was just like her to do something like that. She thought it was sort of wonderful.

Stan tried to figure out what happened to the money if Amy made up the whole story about giving it away. She obviously hadn't spent it on herself, she was not a gambler, and he couldn't come up with a way she could have hidden it. Amy's sister obviously didn't get any of it because she was as shocked as Stan when she heard about it.

So for lack of a good reason to doubt her story, Stan accepted it. From the beginning he acted towards Amy as though he believed her implicitly.

At exactly twelve noon the gate opened and Amy walked out. She was wearing the same clothes she had worn three years before when she went through the gate in the other direction. She walked quickly to the car, opened the door, threw her small bag into the back, and got in beside Stan. He didn't know how to greet her so he didn't say anything. She said, "Let's get away from here—fast!"

He took her to lunch at a high class restaurant where she could have a good meal and they could talk quietly. They each got a drink before ordering. Stan thought those three years had changed Amy. Before she would have been exuberant coming for lunch to a restaurant like this and would be talking incessantly. Now she was subdued and wasn't saying a word.

"What are you thinking?" Stan asked.

"I've been wondering how I'll ever pick up my life again."

"You must have been wondering that for a long time. Have you come to any decisions?"

"I want to hear from you first. You must have been thinking about it too, and I trust your judgment better than I do my own."

"I *have* been thinking about it, and a few weeks ago something happened at work that has made reaching a decision much easier. I was offered a gold parachute to take an early retirement."

"Did you take it?"

"I didn't want to do anything without talking to you about it first."

Amy was quiet for a minute. Finally she said slowly, "Stan, I don't want anything to do with that decision. You're going to have to make it by yourself."

Stan took another sip of his drink. "I thought if I took an early retirement it would make a difference to you. Are you telling me it doesn't matter?"

"That's right. I can't stay in this town but you're 62 years old, you'll be retiring in three years anyway. I would get a place and wait the three years for you to join me."

"All right, Amy, you don't want me to take an early retirement . . . . Have you also thought where you want to go?"

"Yes, I have it all picked out. It's going to be outside of Tecuala, Mexico. It's a little fishing village on the Pacific. I met a girl in jail who comes from there and whose family is still there. She got out of jail a couple of months ago and I've kept in contact with her. She's there now and plans to stay. She writes it's beautiful, peaceful, quiet, and inexpensive to live there. She writes that if I have a little money I could have a beautiful home built in a location of my own choice, and she knows the people who could build it. She is urging me to come down. I think I will go down and look it over . . . . I can't bear the thought of going back to our house here." She finished her drink.

Stan was quiet. He finished his drink in one gulp and said, "Amy, that place sounds wonderful to you, but it doesn't sound good to me. It sounds too far from civilization, I wouldn't be able to find enough to interest me, I would be bored and unhappy."

"You may be right. I want to go down and look."

"Do you want me to go with you?"

"No. that doesn't make sense. It would take too much time from your job.

"How soon do you plan to go?"

"As soon as I can get plane tickets."

"Aren't you going to need a car?"

"If I need one, I'll pick it up there."

"You're going to need money."

"I have enough in my bank account, I'll use it."

"And if you decide to buy land and build a house?"

"Don't worry about it, I'll handle it."

Stan was full of conflicting thoughts, he felt his heart beginning to pound. He said, "I think I want another drink. Do you want one or do you want to order?"

"I guess I can use another one."

After a long silence while he collected his thoughts, Stan said, "Amy, you've changed so much I don't know you."

"Three years in jail can do that. I've become acquainted with a different world."

"You've become acquainted with a different world and I see you as a different person. You haven't smiled once since I picked you up. That's not the Amy I used to know. I have some wild thoughts about what's troubling you."

They ordered second drinks and started on them in silence. Amy looked at Stan intently. "Do you trust me, Stan?" she asked.

"I have up until now."

"You've been a fool."

"I'm beginning to realize that. Where is the money, Amy?"

"In a Swiss bank account."

"Where did you learn about Swiss banks?"

"One of the doctors I worked for taught me."

"Did he also coach you on the story to tell?"

"No, that was my own idea. I have it copywrited . . . . Stan, does this mean it's all over between us?"

Stan didn't answer but slowly finished his drink while making up his mind. Finally he asked, "Amy, do you trust me?"

"You're transparent to me, Stan, I trust you implicitly."

Stan hesitated only a few seconds, "Amy, I'm not the only one who's been a fool."

"My girl friend was right! She said no man is going to stay alone for three years. Do I know her, Stan?"

"No . . . . Let's have lunch. After lunch I'll take you to a travel agency."

TWO GRANDMOTHERS

Sometimes a member of a family of generations of old wealth may marry and have but one child. This might also happen to a member of a family of generations of poverty. This is a story of a member of each category who marry each other.

Richard Preston is the one who comes from old wealth. He was brought up with such a strong feeling of security that without difficulty he ignored the family tradition of entering the Real Estate Development business of his father, Charlie, or the banking business of his mother's family. Instead he became a philosopher with a PhD, a professorship, and a published book. His widowed mother is Victoria of the Clarke banking family. She has a good figure and carries it well, but she has a homely face and her disposition does nothing to make her attracive. She blames her husband's father for instilling into Richard that spirit of independence which led the young man to throw over the family tradition. When Richard was three years old his paternal grandfather moved in with Victoria for two years. During those years Richard and his grandfather became buddies. Victoria says that's how Richard was directed away from banking. After his grandfather left the house Richard never agreed with his mother on anything.

How Charlie Preston came to marry Victoria is another story. Gossip has it that a huge Preston Development went sour and a Clarke bank had financed it. To avoid bankruptcy the two old line families agreed to settle everything amicably if Charlie married Victoria. Charlie figured the business would go on and the marriage didn't have to. The marriage was consummated, Victoria became pregnant and had Richard. There were no other children.

Peg Mullins Preston is an outstanding beauty. She is the one who comes from generations of poverty, which substantiates the obvious that you don't have to have money to be beautiful. She is a nurse who met Richard Preston when he was in the hospital following an auto accident To avoid family problems Richard decided they would elope. They did and Richard firmly resisted his mother's request that they have a big wedding even after the elopement. She said she would take care of everything including the cost. She thought Peg would make such a beautiful bride it would make up for her family deficiency.

Peg and Richard have two children. Carl was born the year after they were married and Mary a year and a half later. Peg's mother, Millie, suddenly widowed. moved in with them when Peg was pregnant with Mary. Millie has no education beyond grammar school but she's a excellent housekeeper and a good cook. She has a cheerful disposition, a great sense of humor, and is wonderful with her grandchildren.

Victoria was not happy when Millie moved into Richard's home but figured Millie was really a live-in housekeeper, cook, and nanny. When Victoria was at Richard's for a meal or to visit with the grandchildren her attitude towards Millie was distant at best. She acted as a guest and made no effort to help with the slightest chore. From long practice she played her role as a highborn lady with perfection. Millie accepted her as a guest and treated her as she would any guest. She did not consider her part of the family. The grandchildren adopted Millie's attitude and when they were by themselves made fun of Victoria.

Victoria was a socialite, active in the very exclusive counry club circle made up of only old money families. Charles died ten years after Richard had married. A year after he died Victoria began thinking perhaps she would marry again. The single life was not good socially, but after being available for two years she had found no good husband material who had any interest in her.

It was about at that time that she had a talk with Richard. She said she had been feeling lethargic and consulted her doctor who worked her up completely then sent her for a consultation with a psychiatrist because he suspected a depression. That diagnosis was confirmed. It was recommended she move out of her big house where she was alone and move in with her family. After a few weeks on an antidepressant she felt well enought to consider the suggestion carefully. She told Richard she would like to build an apartment for herself attached to his house. If he agreed she would sell her home and take care of all expenses associated with building the apartment.

Richard spoke to Peg and Millie about it. Although neither expressed any enthusiasm for the idea each felt she couldn't veto it. It took seven months from start to finish and Victoria moved in. The apartment was beautiful with its own private entrance. It was like an upscale small home except for a double door access to Richard's house from kitchen to kitchen.

The end of the week that Victoria moved in she had Richard's whole family, including Millie over for dinner. The whole affair was a surprise in that it was catered and done formally, complete with crystal glasses, fine chinaware, and gold settings. Everyone except Victoria felt uncomfortable.

The second week Victoria set up the following arrangement. She would come for dinner twice a week. She would have the grandchildren, Carl now fourteen and Mary twelve, once a week for dinner and once a week for lunch. She would have the whole family once a month for dinner. All the meals at her place were catered. The occasions when she had the grandchildren she used to teach them the niceties of proper manners in high society and that included proper language. They addressed her as Grandmother. They addressed Millie as Grams.

Victoria was patient and a good teacher. What was originally a chore for the children to go to her place for dinner became dress-up fun. Victoria never told them to dress up they just decided on their own it would be more enjoyable, they would feel more comfortable, more in keeping with the way the caterer served, and the table was set. The meal itself was always delicious. Victoria arranged the menus so that the children would learn how to handle every kind of food that was presented to them.

With table manner instructions going well Victoria extended the lessons to social behavior toward adults. How to greet adults, how to answer questions, how and when to speak, when to remain quiet, what to do in the presence of adults when adults were talking to each other. As Victoria set up different menus to handle different foods, she presented different scenarios for different situations to challenge social behavior. She enlisted the grandchildren to supply conditions they thought they might encounter.

The kids no longer made fun of grandmother behind her back, but they began to correct Grams. That didn't get very far. The first time Carl said something Millie looked at him and said,

"Carl, it appears you'd like to teach me some of the things you learned from your grand mother. Is that right?"

"Yes, Grams, I guess it is."

Millie went on,

"Mary, you think that's a good idea?"

"Yes, Grams, I do."

Millie thought about that for a moment and decided to go on,

"Kids, first I want to tell you I think what you would like to do is wonderful, it shows me how much you love me . . . . I think now I better tell you something about your Grams. I probably should have done this a long time ago. I was born and brought up on a little farm in Ireland. The Lord provided me with a good brain but in those days society did not provide me with a good education. I was taught to read and write and do a little simple arithmetic. That was it. My Ma taught me all the essentials: how to keep a clean house, how to sew, how to cook, and how to take care of the barnyard animals and the little vegetable and flower garden. We were a hard working family but we had our own little house and farm and enough to eat. Then a time came when the crops failed and my Pa decided it was better to take a chance and move to America than stay in Ireland and starve. We ended up in New York City. I met and married your Gramps who neither of you knew, and had your Mom. Your Gramps worked as a bricklayer and I cleaned house for the rich people. It was not an easy life but we got along fine. Your Mom was the only child I had. I can't say I was sorry I missed an education. I was happy with your Gramps and your Mom, we had a decent place to live, and always plenty to eat. We lived in an Irish neighborhood and had lots of friends. If your Gramps hadn't been killed in an accident I would have been happy to stay there the rest of my life. As it was he died a short time before you were born, Mary, so I came here to live and help your Mom. I've been as happy here as I was back in New York. I don't think learning what your Grandmother taught you would help me be any happier. However, I think what you're learning from her is very important for you. Times have changed and you're going to be leading a much different life than I did. For your happiness you need to learn what she's teaching you. You're going to be living the kind of life she did.

"So, thank you very much for your kind intentions, but 'no, thanks'"

And that's the way it remained. Carl and Mary made no more attempts to educate Millie.

As summer approached Victoria arranged for her grandchildren to attend an elite golf and tennis camp for two months. Victoria said that golf and tennis were the two sports that well bred men and women must learn to play well.

Carl and Mary went to those camps until they entered college. They became excellent golfers and tennis players.

Richard Preston paid close attention to his children's school work from the time they entered school. He was interested in evey course they took and discussed each course with them. He was a scholar and from him they learned the value of scholarship. Carl learned it better than Mary; he was the student, she was the athlete. In college Mary was the star of both the women's tennis and golf teams, Carl was Phi Beta Kappa. On graduation Carl was headed for a PhD in philosophy, Mary was headed for a position as coach.

Carl married a girl he met in graduate school and became a professor like his father.

Mary married a man who coached at the same college she did.

Neither Carl nor Mary ever made full use of the lessons taught by Victoria nor did either of them lead the life foretold by Millie.

UNFINISHED BUSINESS

It had been a long and busy afternoon and the man behind the desk was tired. He thought, "I guess I'm getting old, I never used to get this tired this time of day." He pressed the intercom, "Jane, how many more?"

"There's just Mrs. Livesy left", came back the answer.

"All right, send her in."

Mrs. Livesy was a woman in her early forties, a small woman and attractive. If you walked behind her on the street you might guess her to be in her twenties. She had the carriage, gait, and figure to go with that guess. If you were walking toward her you might think, "There's an attractive young woman", and place her age in the midthirties. She had small features, smooth skin, dark black hair, and large brown eyes. She dressed neatly, conservatively, and well.

She walked into the room quickly, smiled warmly at the man behind the desk, closed the door which separated the rooms, and sat down in the chair alongside the desk facing him.

As Mrs. Livesy sat down she was thinking, "He's such a nice man and not bad looking, but he's getting old. I wonder how he would be in bed." Then she immediately thought, "My God! I never thought of him that way before. Just since Tom stopped sex I'm beginning to think that way about every man. Goddamit, I've really got hot pants."

The man smiled at her. "Well, Marge, have you got a problem?

In the beginning he used to address her, "Mrs. Livesy" but after he had seen her many times and she had confided so many highly personal things to him it seemed more comfortable to address her, "Marge." Before he did that first time, he had said to her, "Mrs. Livesy, it seems more natural for me to call you by your first name but I want you to call me by my first name if that's what you would like to do."

She replied that she would like him to call her by her first name but she wouldn't feel comfortable calling him by his first name. And that's the way it had been ever since.

Marge answered, "I guess I do have a problem. I came to talk this time, Dr. Charles. You've always been so easy to talk to, and you've been so helpful to me."

Dr. Charles leaned back in his chair which tilted with him. He was glad she had come to talk. He didn't feel like getting up and examining another patient. It wasn't that he was physically that tired, "just lazy" he thought.

He didn't answer Mrs. Livesy, just leaned back and waited. He had trained himself to be patient. He just kept looking at her and waited. His expression was calm and sympathetic. He understood sometimes it took awhile to get the thoughts organized and then awhile longer to put them into the right words.

She began to speak softly and slowly. "I'm moving away. My husband is being transferred to Chicago. I don't want to go but I really have no choice. I'm concerned about my mother. Of course she's getting worse almost daily and I know it just won't work out to take her with us. Besides, my husband has practically given me an ultimatum. For the last six months he has been wanting to put her away and he says, 'now is the time'. Before she got so bad and while she could still understand I promised her that I would never put her into a nursing home. She told me, 'I would rather die than go into one of those places.' Right now I don't think she would know whether she was in a nursing home or the Plaza Hotel, but I don't feel right about it. I promised her."

The doctor sat up straight, the back of his chair following him with a little squeak.

"Have you thought about what options you have?", he asked.

"Yes. I could put her into a home here. I could take her to Chicago and put her into a home there." She hesitated then went on, "I could keep her with me here and let my husband go to Chicago by himself—I could tell my husband that if he wants me he has to take my mother too.—that might end up that she will go to Chicago with us or that my mother and I will stay here and I will have a divorce." The doctor waited. It appeared to him she had not finished. He thought, "There's something more going on here."

Mrs. Livesy was beginning to appear agitated. Color came to her cheeks, she began to breathe faster, and her lower lip began to quiver, but her voice came on strong and loud, "I've got other options. I could kill my mother, I could kill my husband, I could kill them both." With the last sentence she broke into tears, not a quiet gentle rainfall but a torrential thunderstorm with sobbing and shoulder heaving.

The doctor leaned forward, opened the lowest drawer of his desk and took out a liberal supply of kleenex tissues laying them on the desk next to her chair. Then he leaned back again and waited.

Marge Livesy was born Marge Nolan in a poor section of New York. She was the youngest of three girls. There would have been more but her father left when she was just a year old. Her oldest sister, three years older, remembered only one incident about her father. Father was a big man. He worked in a factory and liked to drink. One evening just when his oldest daughter was getting ready for bed there were sounds of an angry argument in the kitchen. The little girl sneaked to the kitchen door and looked in. Father was red in the face and shouting. Mother was standing with her back to the stove, one arm behind her. She was a small woman but did not appear frightened, just angry. She didn't say anything. Father came towards her and raised his arm to strike her. Her arm came from behind with a heavy iron frying pan which came down solidly on father's head. As he melted to the floor the little girl with wide open eyes and mouth came into view. She was hustled off to bed without a word. She doesn't remember ever seeing father again; doesn't know whether he just took off or got kicked out. Mother just said, "Father's gone away." Just matter of fact as though that were the most natural thing in the world. Marge heard the story many times and pictured the scene with strange mixed-up feelings.

Mother was tough. She raised her three daughters and made a living by being a cleaning woman for those who could afford a cleaning woman. There were many fringe benefits working for some families: outgrown clothes, discarded toys, leftover food. Annie and her girls got along.

And the girls were tough too; they had to be in their neighborhood. Marge was the youngest and the smallest but also the toughest. Maybe there was a relationship.

There were fights of course when some kids got beat up. Marge was going to get beat up once by a big Amazon but she grabbed a bottle and broke it. Amazon called her bluff and got slashed. It took fourteen stitches to pull her together. Marge didn't have much trouble after that. It wasn't so much that she was able to defend herself as the way she did it. No shouting, no swearing, no threats, just action. And no hysterics afterwards, and no regrets.

Marge grew up there in the same neighborhood, there never was enough money to move out. When she was old enough she got a job after school in a little Mom and Pop restaurant, first working in the kitchen then filling in for some waitresses, then being a regular waitress. After she got out of high school she decided she could do better. She was attractive and she was a good waitress. She got a job in a better restaurant, and after a year there got a job in a still better one. She learned quickly and mastered all the amenities of a good waitress.

When she was still in school, boys and men took an interest in her. She didn't bother with the boys but with some of the men she returned the interest. She had a strong sex drive and didn't hesitate to indulge it. This increased her popularity tremendously. In her own mind she was discriminating: she wouldn't go to bed until the third date at the earliest, and then only if she really liked the guy. Once in bed she didn't have any hang-ups, she tried anything she thought she might like. There was just one thing she was meticulous about: no sex without a rubber. She insisted on it because she didn't want to take any chances on getting pregnant. There was a fringe benefit she didn't realize. She never got a venereal disease.

All the sleeping around stopped after she met Tom. He used to come into the restaurant every night alone to have dinner. He would go wherever he was seated until by chance she had served him a few times then he asked that he be seated at one of her tables. She decided she liked him and there was much about his appearance for a young woman to like. He looked to be in his late twenties. He had a boyish face with a well proportioned straight nose, blue eyes, and a great mop of blonde hair. Marge figured from the clothes he wore and the way he spoke and the size of the tip he left that he must be well off. She thought, "This is the guy to marry." And she set about to do it.

Tom Livesy was "well off". He came from a small town where his father was one of the first citizens, an officer in the older and larger of the two banks. Tom went through high school there and was a star on the football team. He was broad and rugged and could run well. He went on to college but didn't even try out for the football team there. He knew he couldn't compete against the scholarship athletes and besides he couldn't take the time from his studies. Encouraged by his father he was determined to become a lawyer and he wanted to do well enough in college to get into a good law school. He did well enough and he got into a good law school. Between his junior and senior years he got a clerkship in a large law office in New York. He was invited to join the firm when he graduated and he did. He had just been working there six months when he met Marge.

He was attracted to her when he first saw her in the restaurant. He admired her figure and the way she walked and he thought her face was beautiful. He liked the way she smiled and laughed. He thought she was probably not the kind of girl to bring home to mother but he sure would like to know her better. After he got himself seated always at her table they began to talk about things other than the menu. They found out they were both unattached. She found out he was a lawyer. He found out she was just a waitress, had gotten through high school, and came from a poor family. One Saturday night he asked her if she was busy after work and would she like to go out with him afterwards and have a drink somewhere. And that was how it began.

After the third date she went to his apartment and spent the night with him. She was the teacher and he was an apt student. She was clever at leading him slowly and gently with frequent expressions of pleasure at his skill as a lover, so that he did not suspect her experience. It was no more than a month before she seduced him into inviting her to move in with him. They got along fine. She flattered him and catered to him and never made demands of him. She was determined to marry him but never mentioned marriage. She never brought him home to her mother. She said her mother did not approve the living arrangement. She said she wasn't talking to her mother.

Tom became very fond of her and not just as a sex partner. He began to dislike her being a waitress and wanted her to get more education. He found he was beginning to think of her as a wife. He told her he would support her and pay for her education. She was jubilant inside but outwardly hesitant. What would happen she asked if after awhile he got tired of her and sent her packing? He said she would have to trust him, and anyway she would be no worse off. And so she left her job and became a student. It worked out well. Tom loved to talk to her about her studies and was proud of her when she did well which she did most of the time.

The holidays came and Tom took Marge to the office party. She was a great success. Even a couple of the senior partners were impressed and told Tom so. He began to think maybe she was the kind of a girl he could take home. Before the holidays were over he did take her home. She was on her best behavior. She told his parents everything truthfully but did not mention that she was not talking to her mother like she told Tom. In fact she spoke to her mother almost every day and she was finding Annie was getting a little forgetful. And she really wasn't that old. In any event Tom's parents thought Marge was nice even though they were not happy about her background. Tom's father asked Tom if he were serious about her. Tom said he didn't know and asked if there were any objections. He asked in a challenging way and his father backed off and assured him there were none.

"After all I came from a poor family myself."

Back in New York Marge and Tom slipped into their old routine. Marge never mentioned marriage and neither did he. Their life together was a good one. They both were working hard doing their own thing. There was not too much togetherness and when they were together it was fun.

Marge was already a junior in college when Tom began getting some pressure from his folks about getting married. They knew he had been living with her and thought it was about time he made it legal and settled down or else broke it off and found someone he could marry. They would like some grandchildren. Tom was doing well, had a good position and was advancing in the firm. It was time he got married. Tom didn't know about children. One night he asked Marge how she felt about a family. She said she could go either way and would do whatever he wanted. She thought, "I don't want a family in the city, but if we had a house in the country that would be different." She thought he was about ready to ask her to marry him. It wasn't long afterwards that he did ask her and of course she was ready. They had been living together five years.

They got married elopement style at Marge's request. After she finished college they moved to a suburb. But no children came. They didn't investigate why but just accepted it. Instead of children Marge's mother came.

Annie had been getting progressively more forgetful and was no longer able to take proper care of herself. Marge's sisters had both moved away and neither could take her. Tom didn't like the idea but grudgingly accepted her on a tentative basis. She was not an unpleasant woman to have

248

around and Tom admired her pluck. Once she settled in, her condition seemed to deteriorate more rapidly. She began to have trouble talking. It was then Marge took her to Dr. Charles. He told Marge it looked like dementia but sent her to a neurologist to rule out a tumor or some other remedial condition. The work-up confirmed the diagnosis: Alzheimer's Disease.

Tom was as upset as Marge. He wanted her out. Marge pleaded with him that she could take care of her and would keep her out of the way. At least it could be tried that way and if Tom ever thought it wasn't working out then a nursing home would be found.

A year went by and it was getting very difficult for Marge. Her mother was a constant care now. Tom didn't say anything about a nursing home, but never seemed to be in a good mood anymore. He was increasingly absent from home and though Marge knew he was working hard she began to get suspicious that there was another woman. Then one day she inadvertently found some evidence. She did not confront him with it, just went about her usual activities without any change in her behavior. But she was angry: angry at her mother for having Alzheimer's, angry at her husband for having another woman. She understood now why he hadn't said anything more about a nursing home; he wanted her home and busy taking care of her mother.

Marge picked up a couple of the tissues, stopped sobbing, blew her nose, wiped her eyes, took a deep breath, and apologized, "I'm sorry. I don't know what got into me. I've never done that before." She regained her composure quickly.

Dr. Charles waited a little longer but she seemed to have no more to say. "What you would like to do?" he asked, accenting the "like".

"I guess what I would LIKE would be to take her with me

to Chicago and put her in a nursing home there. I think what I SHOULD do is take her with me and take care of her myself." She thought, "I don't know whether I can do it much longer. Should I tell him that?" She did.

"The real trouble is I don't know whether I can manage her alone much longer, the constant incontinence is the worst part and I can't leave her for a minute. She's very unsteady on her feet and she's very restless. Anytime she decides to get out of bed or out of a chair I've got to be right there or she'll fall. She'll move enough by herself but if I want her to move she won't. I just can't make her understand and she doesn't talk at all anymore. I'm sure she knows me though, and I just can't bring myself to put her into a nursing home."

The situation was all too familiar to Dr. Charles. Marge was not the only child with responsibility for an Alzheimer parent. He thought there was something Marge had said that that might be of more interest than her problem with her mother. He was thinking how to work into it. "Could you arrange to have help at home?" he asked.

"No. The agreement was that if things got too difficult at home she would be put into a nursing home."

Dr. Charles thought, "Now I can confront her." Without changing his manner or tone he asked, "Is this why one of your options was to kill your mother AND your husband?"

"No, not really." she replied softly.

Dr. Charles leaned back. He thought, "Maybe this is what she really came to talk about."

"What's happened to your marriage, Marge?" he asked gently.

He had known Marge a long time and she had come in to talk with him many times. Tom had sent her in the first time. He had seen Tom for a checkup right after he came to town because a senior partner of his firm wanted him to have a doctor and recommended Dr. Charles. Tom sent Marge in for a checkup before he let her move in with him. He thought it would be the sensible thing to do, and she had no objections so long as he was paying for it.

Marge and the doctor were sympatico. She came to look upon him as a wise and gentle father who was nonjudgmental. She would often make appointments just to talk and Tom never objected to paying the bills. After they were married his insurance picked up the tab.

Over the course of many visits Marge told her whole life story, including her early sexual experiences and how she reacted to them. The sex part came out when she began to talk about her difficulties in managing the early sexual relationship with the inexperienced Tom. That she managed so well in teaching Tom was largely because of Dr Charles' advice. She soon fell into the habit of consulting him on all her minicrises: going to school, meeting Tom's parents including how to act and what to say, getting married and then what kind of a wedding to have. She consulted him about moving into the suburbs, about getting pregnant. And she spoke to him many times about her mother. She became well versed in Alzheimer's Disease and knew what to expect. But when the expected appeared it was still difficult to cope with. However, until this moment she had not spoken about Tom. Not that she hadn't wanted to, it was just that she had been so involved with her mother and the real evidence she had was so recent that she just hadn't had the opportunity.

Marge looked back at the doctor. She thought "I don't think he can help me this time but I've got to talk to him about it."

"The trouble with the marriage is that Tom has another woman." This came out angry; no weeping with this statement.

Dr. Charles thought, "So that's it. It's too bad, but not too surprising." "Did Tom tell you this?" he asked.

"No, I found out myself." She sounded both angry and triumphant to the doctor. He needed more information.

"Did you confront him about it?"

"No, not yet." Marge was thinking, "I've got something on that bastard and I'm not going to waste it. I'll wait for the right time and that's not yet."

The doctor thought, "She's saving it and that's probably smart. If she wants to save the marriage she might want to save that information forever."

"Marge, do you want to stay married to him?" he asked.

"I don't know." And she didn't know. She was talking now as the thoughts came to her, no rehearsing in her mind first. In the past she had found this was the best way to talk. Ideas came out then that she never realized she had been thinking.

She continued after a short pause, the doctor waiting, "He's really been sort of ignoring me recently. And as for any sex, HA!", the last word came out with disdain.

Dr. Charles looked at his desk clock. He thought he had better bring a closure to this visit and arrange for another appointment. "Marge, you've told me about two problems: one, what to do with your mother; and two, what to do about your marriage. I think your mother is the more immediate problem and it may also have some bearing on your marriage. I suggest we concentrate on the mother problem and declare a moratorium on the marriage question for now. Is that agreeable?"

Marge spoke her thoughts, "I don't know. If the marriage goes down the tube I may want to stay in New York with my mother."

Dr. Charles thought, "This may take a little longer. Looks like I may be late for dinner again."

Jane was on the intercom. "Do you need me for anything else, doctor?" "No, Jane," he answered. "you go on home,

I'll lock up." "All right," came through the intercom, "good night." "Good night, Jane." He responded. Then he turned back to Marge.

"Shouldn't rush it," he thought, "not enough data to make a good decision."

"How soon does Tom have to be in Chicago?" he asked.

"The office would like him to be there in a month."

Dr. Charles hesitated for a moment, thinking back over the earlier conversation. "You mentioned earlier that Tom had given you an ultimatum about your mother, that now was the time to put her into a nursing home. That seems to imply that he expects you to come with him, that he is not thinking about breaking up the marriage".

"I guess that's right." She thought,"I really didn't think about it that way. Maybe if we go to Chicago and he leaves that woman here and I put my mother into a nursing home things will work out."

Dr. Charles went on, "Marge, you might think about getting some information on nursing homes in Chicago and New York. If you decide to make the move you're going to have to put her in one place or the other at least temporarily, and if you decide not to make the move you will have lost nothing."

"Yeah, I guess so." This was said with a sigh and an air of resignation. Marge thought, "He doesn't think I ought to break up the marriage. Maybe he's right. He thinks I ought to put Mom into a nursing home. Maybe he's right there too." She sat quietly.

Dr. Charles thought,"I may get home on time after all."

"All right," he went on, "You look into nursing homes and give some thought to what we've talked about. I think I would like to see you again pretty soon. You have a lot of unfinished business to take care of."

An appointment was made for a return visit in ten days. Marge left and Dr. Charles spent ten minutes writing a note on her chart so that on her next visit he would have good recall on what took place. He finished, closed up, and took off for home. He was only fifteen minutes late, not bad.

Tom never got over being upset about Annie, Marge's mother, after Dr. Charles diagnosed her as having Alzheimer's. Early on he really felt so sorry for her and for Marge that he didn't want to send her away. But as time went on and she required more and more of Marge's time and concern he became resentful. Before Annie came he got all Marge's attention and after Annie he developed the feeling of a second class citizen.

On several occasions he had asked Marge to send her to a nursing home, but she kept putting him off. He appreciated Marge's feelings toward her mother but he felt he should have number one priority and he didn't. His understanding of the agreement he had made with Marge was that when her mother became too difficult she would go to a nursing home. He thought she was too difficult now, but apparently Marge didn't. Every time he came home and saw Annie he felt angry. His anger and Marge's frustration and fatigue didn't conduce to good feelings between them.

And things at the office were pretty hectic. He was becoming a good lawyer and was very busy. Marge used to be interested in what was going on at the office and he would tell her about some of the cases. Now if she asked it was in a perfunctory way and he felt her mind wasn't really on what he was saying. After a while he would just say, "Oh you wouldn't be interested." And Marge wouldn't contradict him. He still initiated sex periodically but more for a physical relief than as an act of love. Then Louise came.

Louise was a new young lawyer in the firm. She was bright, aggressive as a lawyer but not as a woman. In a social situation she would not be picked out as a professional woman but just as a tall, poised, well dressed, sophisticated woman who spoke well and knowledgeably. She was assigned to the same department Tom was in so they began to see each other often. Eventually there was a case that they were both working on. Louise was assigned to help Tom and she proved to be a big help. They frequently went out to lunch together and so began to learn something about each other. Louise was single and though she had had a few men in her life nothing had developed into a meaningful relationship. When she joined the firm there was no one special. She was living in a small apartment by herself. Her home was in upstate New York.

It seemed inevitable that one night they would have to work late and have dinner together too. When that happened Tom told her about conditions at home. Louise listened sympathetically but only commented, "That's a tough situation."

Before Louise ever came to the office Tom would occasionally stay in the city overnight. This would happen if the work piled up and it got too late or if it were just somewhat late and the weather was very bad. Before Annie, and if Tom knew ahead of time he would be late, Marge would sometimes come into the city and they would have dinner together and spend the night in a hotel. In a hotel sex was always good and they both enjoyed these occasions.

So Marge didn't think much about it when one winter afternoon Tom called and said he would have to stay in the city that night. He gave her the name of the hotel where he would be staying. He did not tell her he would have company.

Tom was excited to have Louise in bed with him. She was not the sex kitten Marge was, but she was a new experience and he felt good about being the teacher. He taught her to ask him to do the things that gave her pleasure and instructed her in the ways that pleasured him. Once during the love making he thought, "God, I learned this from Marge."

It was a very enjoyable evening, and not only for the sex. The dinner was good and the conversation was stimulating. Tom wondered a little why he didn't feel guilty.

That was the beginning, the continuation followed easily. Whenever the opportunity arose they would have dinner together and spend the night in a hotel, or he might come into town on a Saturday to work. He might or might not work but he would always end in her apartment. He wasn't ready to tell Marge about Louise because he wasn't sure he wanted to break up the marriage.

Louise never indicated she wanted him to make any changes and seemed perfectly content to let things go on as they were. She never suggested any of the meetings but usually made herself available when he wanted to be with her. However, there were a couple of times when she said she wouldn't be able to make it, and he wondered if there were another man. He never asked her but her independence bothered him a bit. He was used to Marge deferring to him and catering to him, although since Annie the catering wasn't like it had been. Still he felt once Annie was gone things would get back to what they were with Marge, and Annie would have to be gone pretty soon. No way was she going to Chicago with them.

Marge was back in ten days right on time. Dr. Charles had this time deliberately arranged for her to be the last patient of the day so the visit could be open-ended if he needed more time. They greeted each other as Marge came in. She closed the door and sat down. She appeared grim.

She looked at the doctor and said, "I've had an awful time. I really couldn't do anything in Chicago over the phone, so I decided it would be better to put Mom into a nursing home here in New York at least for now. Besides I don't know what the Medicaid situation is in Illinois. I thought it would be better to wait until I got out there and then make arrangements for transferring her. So I went around and looked at places here." She paused and grimaced. "They're awful! Besides being awful they're full and they all have long waiting lists for Medicaid patients. We could get her in quickly if we paid the full freight but Tom says, 'Nothing doing.' He says it would cost thirty-five thousand dollars a year and we would probably have to sign a contract to pay for at least two years before she would be able to go on Medicaid. So that's out."

Marge paused. Dr. Charles said nothing.

She continued, "Those places are really terrible." She sounded angry. "I think if Mom knew what was going on she would rather be dead. It just isn't fair. Mom was such a great woman. She was tough and resourceful but full of affection for us kids. And she had a terrific sense of humor. Boy, she was sharp. And now what is she? It would kill her if she knew. She would never want this."

The anger was gone now. Marge just sat there. Her eyes filled up and she seemed to shrink into a little girl.

Dr. Charles reached into his desk drawer and took out some tissues, laying them on the desk. Marge quietly helped herself to some. The doctor waited. He felt genuinely sorry for her, little girls who cried always evoked sympathy.

Finally, Marge took a deep breath and went on, "What shall I do?" she asked.

Dr. Charles answered in a straightforward way as though he were giving clinical information, "You've told me a number of important things you've already done." Then sounding more like a proud parent he went on, "and I think what you've done is great!" He paused for a moment but never took his eyes from hers. He thought, "she knows what she wants to do. She's stronger than she's letting on."

Then he continued, "YOU tell ME what you're going to do."

Marge looked a little surprised but there was a faint smile. "He's not going to let me depend on him too much," she thought, "or maybe he thinks I'll do what I decide to do no matter what he says."

She answered after some hesitation, "For now I'll keep Mom with me. Tom will go on to Chicago and see if he can find a place for us." She stopped and thought, "He better not take that woman with him." She went on, sounding more assured now, "I've spoken with the social service people and they're helping me find a place for her. I guess that's all that can be done for now." She paused a moment, smiled and said, "I think I feel better about it now." There was another short pause. Before Dr. Charles could comment she said, "I would like to ask you something about Mom's physical condition. I notice she's been getting a little short of breath lately."

"When do you notice that?", Dr. Charles asked, and added, "I know she hasn't been able to do anything physical for quite a while."

"It happens when she lies down. Lately I've had to use three pillows."

"Are her ankles swollen?"

"They have been for some time. Maybe they're a little more so now."

Dr. Charles thought, "It sounds like she has some heart failure. I guess I'll have to treat her. If I could give her back her brain for five minutes I wonder if she would want me to. Well, I can't give her back her brain and she still gets some joy out of living: Marge says she loves her ice cream. It may not be the quality of life I would want or even the quality she would have wanted before but it's the quality she has now. Who am I to take it away from her?"

Finally, he said to Marge, "I think she better be seen by someone. It's going to be too difficult for you to get her in to see me. Maybe I can get a visiting nurse to see her. I probably can get enough information from the nurse to make a decision about what should be done."

He had another thought and went on as he was thinking,

"If the social service people found a place for your mother, would you put her in a home right away?"

"I guess if it seemed like a good one I would. Places are hard to come by. But I wouldn't put her into a dump." Marge was emphatic about that last statement.

The doctor thought, "Well, I guess I can't wait until Annie gets into a home to take care of the heart failure." He said, "Marge, I'll call the Visiting Nurses and have someone stop and take a look at your mother. Now, what's been happening between you and Tom?"

Marge looked at the doctor and began talking her thoughts: no thinking first what she was going to say or how she would say it, "I found out who the other woman is, she's a lawyer in his firm and works in his department under him." She paused, realized what she had said, then with a faint gallows smile put in parenthetically, "working 'under him' is a good way of putting it." She stopped and getting angry thinking about it came out with, "I get so damned mad when I think of Tom . . . . making love to her."

She hesitated before saying, "making love". She was ready to say, "fucking" but couldn't say that word to Dr. Charles. She had never heard him swear and it didn't seem an appropriate word to use to him. Yet she thought "fucking" was a better word in this instance. It better described what a whore, or this woman, was doing with her husband. She stopped again, giving herself time to calm down. The doctor waited quietly.

She went on, "Tom doesn't know I know and I don't plan to say anything to him, yet. I'm hoping that when we move to Chicago and it's just the two of us again things will go back the way they were before. What do you think, doctor?"

"I think that's fine," Dr. Charles answered, "it doesn't appear to me that either one of you want to break up the marriage at this time."

Marge was quiet for a moment then spoke up again, "I

don't know what I'll do if that woman moves to Chicago with him. Do you think I should tell him I know and ask him to leave her in New York?"

Dr. Charles thought how he might help her make the decision herself. "You told me you hadn't confronted him because you thought things might work out after you got to Chicago. You think if this woman moves to Chicago then things might not work out?"

"Well," Marge answered, "the only difference will be that we'll all be in Chicago instead of New York."

The doctor responded quickly, "I think there will be more differences than that." He stopped talking and looked at Marge. She knew this meant that he thought the ball was in her court now.

She picked it up after a little thought, "Well my mother won't be with us," she said quietly, then nothing else. She looked down. It appeared that volley was over.

Dr. Charles decided to make an observation. "It seems to me," he said, "that you may have discounted the effect your mother had on your relationship with Tom. It might be quite different in Chicago without a demented woman in the house to whom perhaps you paid more attention than you did to your husband."

The doctor thought, "That's a rough statement, but she has to realize her mother is demented. Well, I'm into it. I might as well plow through." Marge didn't answer so he continued, "Marge, I think it would be helpful to you to realize that the woman you knew as your mother has died. You're taking care of her body but she has left it. It might be better if you let someone else take care of the body. There is nothing to be gained by your taking on the burden, and there is much to be lost." He thought, "That's a long lecture," and stopped talking.

Marge was looking at the doctor while he was talking. She was thinking, "He's right, you know, it's not Mom, it's a zombie." She could feel her chin quivering. Her eyes filled up and she reached for a tissue in her pocketbook. "Well," she thought, "I'm going to put her into a home so that will be that. It would be better to put the body into a grave, bodies belong in graves, not in homes." She blew her nose and looked up at the doctor. "I know you're right," she said, "but it's hard. The body still bears a resemblance to Mom. It's hard to tell myself it really isn't Mom."

"I know it isn't easy," Dr. Charles said gently, "but that's the way it is and it has to be faced. I think it's important for you to get on with your life, her's is over." He thought, "That was a minilecture, I can't tell whether that's good or bad, but that's what seems to come naturally to me."

Marge was quiet for another minute, she seemed to herself to be thinking about six thoughts all at once and at the same time having all mixed-up feelings. Mom was a zombie, Tom was cheating on her, Louise was a whore: depression, frustration, anger. "I know you're right," she said, "but it just doesn't seem fair."

"No one ever promised you the world would be fair." Dr. Charles replied.

"I know," Marge said, "I know, and it sure isn't. It's just not right." She said the last with such determination that it seemed to imply to Dr. Charles that she planned to do something about it. But she did not appear to have anything more to say.

"Let's get back to your question, Marge." Dr. Charles addressed her again, "Do you think you should talk to Tom about 'that woman'? Incidentally, do you know her name?"

"Her name is Louise." Marge said with evident disgust.

"Okay, do you think you should talk to him about Louise?" the doctor asked.

"I don't know what to do. I want you to tell me." Marge pleaded. "I'm so mixed up."

"Marge, you're going to have to make that decision, but I'll see if I can help you," the doctor went on, "first we'll consider what might happen if you tell him, then we'll think about what may happen if you don't tell him, and then you might be able to make a decision. First tell me what you think might be the likely consequences if you tell him."

Marge thought and said, "Now you're going to make me work again." Then she began to talk as she was thinking it out,"Okay, if I tell him I know, and tell him what I want him to do, the best thing that could happen would be that he would admit everything, say it would be all over, and agree to leave her in New York. The worst thing that could happen would be that he would say that he's taking her with him and I could stay in New York and we could get divorced.— And I'm afraid of the worst thing so I guess I better not tell him." This all came out slowly as the thoughts were organized. She continued, still thinking about it, "But I'm also afraid if I wait to tell him and she's already there, he'll say, 'Why didn't you tell me that in New York?'" She stopped.

Dr. Charles prompted her, "You've already told me the worst thing that could happen if you don't tell him, now what's the best thing?"

"Oh," Marge picked up, "the best thing would be that he would not have taken her with him and the whole affair would be over and I never would have to mention it."

"Hmm," the doctor signified he heard then asked, "So now what do you think is the best thing to do?"

"I guess for now I better ignore it," Marge replied, "anyway I'm too chicken to bring it up just yet."

Dr. Charles felt that question was settled for the present. He saw it was about time to close the session. "Marge, what's next?" he asked.

"Well," she answered, "next week Tom goes to Chicago. He has a lot of work to do there and he's going to try to get an apartment for us. I'll probably be alone with Mom for ten days or so. I won't mind. It may give me time to find a place for her and do some quiet thinking." She stopped, looking grim again.

"When do you think you may move?", the doctor asked.

"Probably the end of next month, another six weeks," Marge replied.

Dr. Charles leaned back, "Would you like to see me again before you leave?" he questioned.

"Oh, yes!" Marge answered quickly, "I'll have to. There's still a lot of unfinished business."

An appointment was made for the last hour of the day in three weeks' time. By then the doctor figured Tom would be back from Chicago and the move would be settled. Marge might even know if Louise were also moving.

Marge left and Dr. Charles spent five minutes writing in her chart the cues he needed for what had been said.

Early the following morning Dr. Charles called the Visiting Nurses and had one of them stop in to see Annie. The nurse called that afternoon from Annie's house. It was evident that Annie was in heart failure. Her breathing and heart rate were more rapid than normal; her ankles were badly swollen; and there were rales at her lung bases, the sign of lung congestion. The doctor ordered a diuretic and a digitalis preparation. He gave careful instructions to the nurse and then spoke to Marge. He had her write down exactly what he told her and then had her read it back to him. He impressed on her how important it was for Annie to get the medication. He told her he thought Annie would respond well but that he would put her into the hospital if she didn't show rapid improvement. He told Marge to call him the following day.

Marge did call the next day and told him Annie was improving just as he thought she would. She said the visiting nurse would not have to stop back. She kept in touch with the doctor over the next several days, and as Annie got better the medication was adjusted to maintenance doses.

Four days before Marge was due in for her appointment she called Dr. Charles early in the morning. She sounded frightened, "Dr. Charles, Mom is gone, she's dead, she's gone. I went in just now to wake her up and she's gone. She's not breathing, her body's cold already. What shall I do?"

Dr. Charles knew well what to do. The necessary arrangements were made, he signed the death certificate, "arteriosclerotic heart disease", and Annie's body was duly buried. Everyone was greatly relieved that Annie had died—except maybe Annie.

Marge's appointment was postponed a week because of all the turmoil associated with Annie's death. She came into his office appearing subdued, tired, and pale. She managed a faint smile greeting the doctor and sat down looking depressed.

"How are you feeling, Marge?" Dr. Charles asked quietly.

"Oh, I'm doing all right," she replied, "but you know even though you've always realized it could happen any time, when it comes it's a shock."

"Marge," the doctor said, "it's much better this way. There was a very poor quality of life for her. It's not even possible to know how much she was aware of. I've often thought it's a very small transition between life and death for these people. I think Annie would not have been aware that she was dying. And after death none of us will care.—Now it will be a lot easier for you as well as for Annie."

Marge was quiet for a few minutes thinking while the doctor waited. Finally she looked up at him and said, "I know, it has solved a lot of problems. In a way I'm very grateful it happened before I had to put her into a home. And I know what you're thinking. You're thinking that now I can get on with MY life." She continued looking at the doctor but seemed to have no more to say.

Dr. Charles took up the cue. "Tell me what's happening in YOUR life" he suggested.

"Tom couldn't find the kind of place he wanted," she began then kept on, "He arranged to store our furniture in Chicago until we find a suitable house. Meanwhile we'll stay in a hotel. His firm is paying for all this. He's getting to be a big shot in that firm, you know. This transfer to the Chicago office is a big promotion for him. I'm not happy about living in a hotel but in a way it will be better, at least temporarily. It will give me a chance to catch my breath and then to look around carefully for the kind of home I want." She paused briefly then went on with another thought, "I'm worried about Tom. He doesn't look good. He's working too hard and comes home exhausted. I never heard him complain before but now he tells me he's getting pains in his chest coming up the stairs. He attributes it to being in poor shape but I think he's concerned about it. One of the partners dropped of a heart attack just a couple of months ago. I asked him to call you but he said he would see somebody in Chicago that one of the partners recommended. He didn't think it made much sense to see you when he was in the process of moving. But I'm still worried about it, what do you think?"

"I don't know," Dr. Charles answered, "it sounds as though he may have angina. Certainly he should see someone soon. In general I think it's a good idea that he see someone in Chicago but if he is having a lot of pain I don't think he should wait. Why don't you have him call me. We can talk about it on the phone and then make some decision."

"Well, I'll tell him what you said," Marge offered, "but I don't know whether he'll call you." She said the last with a tone of resignation.

Dr. Charles was thinking, "She hasn't mentioned Louise, I wonder if it's too painful? I guess I better confront her on it".

"Marge, you haven't said anything about Louise," he ventured.

"I know," she answered with a sigh, "I was going to—

she's already in Chicago. Tom didn't tell me, I found out myself." The last came out again with that tone of resignation. "What shall I do?" she asked.

"It sounds to me as though you've already made up your mind what you're going to do for now," the doctor said. "You told me that you're going to go to Chicago, stay in a hotel, and look around for a house."

"Oh, that's just for now," Marge replied, "I mean what am I really going to do about Tom and our marriage." She paused for a minute, then without taking her eyes from the doctor's went on, "You know I have to have a place to live and whether or not I stay married I want a home. And believe me I'm going to have a good one." The last sentence came out with an angry determination.

"What do you have in mind?" Dr. Charles asked.

Marge thought, "Hell, I might as well tell him part of it and get his reaction."

She went on, "I plan to get settled in the very nicest house I can get, Tom's credit is good. I plan to be on my best behavior with him, Mom isn't here anymore so I can devote full time to him. Then I'll see how he reacts. And I'll take it from there."

"You've thought this all out very well," the doctor noted, "you don't need anyone to tell you what to do."

Marge thought, "He's right. I don't need him or anyone else to tell me what to do. I know what I'm going to do. I'm going to take care of Marge." To the doctor she said, "I guess I do know what to do, at least for now. And if I get stuck, you'll be the first one I'll call. There may still be some unfinished business.

"When are you leaving, Marge?" asked Dr. Charles, recognizing that this was the end of the relationship.

"Hopefully within two weeks," Marge answered, standing up.

The doctor stood up too. "Good-bye, Marge, and good luck. If you ever need help that you think I can give you just call me. I expect, though, that you'll make out okay." He said this smiling.

Marge held out her hand which he took. She smiled back at him. "I WILL call you, doctor," she replied, "just to let you know how things are going even if I don't need any help. Good-bye." She walked out quickly, closing the door behind her.

Dr. Charles sat down at his desk again and wrote a final note on her chart. He thought about Tom, "A real Type A personality. There may be something to the belief that this is a risk factor for coronary heart disease." He wondered if he still smoked so much, that was the real risk factor. Of course having an extramarital affair was the kind of stress that has long been known to conduce to sudden death. More prominent men than Tom have been struck down in the act. "It could happen to Tom." the doctor thought. "What Marge told me certainly sounds like angina."

He didn't expect Tom to call him. He hadn't seen him for a few years. The firm had arranged for all the partners to be examined regularly at a clinic. Tom had apparently been well and had seen no need to see any doctor between clinic visits. And the Type A patients Dr. Charles had known seemed to him to have a lot of denial about the possible significance of any symptoms. However, he thought Tom might be pretty scared if one of his partners had recently had a heart attack. Well, maybe he would call.

It was the end of the day. Dr. Charles decided he wouldn't think about Tom or Marge any more now. Or any other patient for that matter. It was time to go home and relax.

It was in September that Marge was last in Dr. Charles' office. Tom never did call and the doctor wasn't surprised. One day in March when Jane brought in the mail she left unopened a letter marked "personal", handwritten. The doctor opened it and read:

"Dear Dr. Charles,

"It's three o'clock in the afternoon. Tom is asleep and this gives me a chance to write to you, which is something I've wanted to do for a long time now.

"You've probably already guessed why Tom is asleep in the afternoon. Yes, he's had a heart attack. It happened three weeks ago and he's been home a week now and really far from well. He had a rough time in the hospital; the doctor said it was a very severe attack. I'm concerned they may have sent him home too soon but he was very anxious to get out and they thought sending him home would be better than keeping him in the hospital and letting him get more upset. I suppose they were right but I worry about him home. He has a bunch of medicine to take, some of it the same as you had given to Annie, and I'm the medication nurse. I take care of giving him all his pills. He doesn't like medicine and doesn't want to know anything about them. He just takes what I give him.

"I'm very upset about the whole thing and I don't think I'll ever get over how it happened, or how I think it happened. It was on a Saturday afternoon. Tom had gone into the office after lunch to do some work. At 4:30, which must have been about three hours after he got there, I got a call from Louise. This was the first time I had ever spoken to her. When she told me who she was my heart began to pound. She told me Tom was on his way to the hospital in an ambulance. She said he and she were alone in the office working together when he developed a severe chest pain and collapsed. She said she had called the rescue squad and an ambulance. The rescue squad got there first. They didn't have to use resuscitation on him but they gave him oxygen. When the ambulance arrived with the paramedics they started an i-v on him and called the hospital emergency room and spoke with them on the shortwave then put something else into the i-v. Then they put him on a stretcher with his i-v and oxygen and took him. She sounded pretty upset. She told me what hospital he was being taken to. She said she was going there too and would meet me there. I told her please not to come, that there was nothing she could do there, that I would have someone with me, and that she must be very upset and had better go home. So I never did see her. But I think I was almost as angry as I was scared. I could just imagine what their "working together" consisted of.

"Well, I had some very rough days in the hospital, hanging around the waiting room to the intensive care unit with all sorts of mixed feelings. The only thing I think I felt thankful for was that there were no children. I asked the doctor not to allow any visitors except the immediate family, that was me, so Louise never came to see him. Before he left the hospital he got some get-well cards from her. I never tried to intercept them. After he got home I know he spoke with her on the phone because the nurse we have told me he made a number of calls when I was out. I think that's one reason he wanted to get home so soon.

"Tom's still asleep so I have time to bring you up to date on what happened before the attack. We've got a home, just like I wanted. And if I say so myself it's furnished beautifully. The only thing I take credit for is hiring the interior decorator. It cost a small fortune but Tom's credit is good. He didn't complain about the cost at all. He just let me take over and do whatever I wanted to. He was really very nice but never worked up much enthusiasm about it. He always seemed so preoccupied. When the house was all settled we gave a big party for the partners. He invited Louise too but she couldn't make it. The party was a great success. I get along fine with all the partners, especially the senior ones.

"I hear Tom stirring so I'm going to close. I haven't confronted him about Louise and he hasn't said anything to me, but we're not the same couple we used to be. There's still some unfinished business.

Sincerely,

Marge"

The doctor took a deep breath, picked up the letter and put it into Marge's file himself. He didn't feel happy about what he had read. He wasn't surprised about Tom's attack. He thought, "I'll bet they were making love when it happened, that would have been awful tough on Louise, whoever she is. Marge thinks they were making love too. I can understand her mixed feelings. It's very, very tough on her too. And poor Tom, what a blow for him. Boy, that's a bad situation all around."

In October another letter came from Marge. Dr. Charles put it aside until the end of the day when he would be able to read it leisurely and without interruption. After his last patient had gone he opened it up and read:

"Dear Dr. Charles,

"I thought so much about you in August but I couldn't pull myself together to write to you until now. I still feel trembly inside whenever I start to write it but I know I must get over that.

"Tom is dead.—There, I wrote it.

"It's been twenty minutes since I wrote that sentence. It took me that long to compose myself again. It's so hard to realize Tom is dead. But he is dead and I have to go on living. And I will.

"I'm going to write you how it happened. I think

270

it's good for me to go over it and over it again and again. Certainly, I don't react so strongly to thinking about it now as I did.

"Tom's recovery from his first attack was slow but by the time summer came he was feeling pretty good. In fact he was feeling good enough that he bought a little cabin on a lake in the woods. He loved to fish and he thought that was a place he could go just to rest and fish. It was small and sort of primitive and very isolated but it was a comfortable little place. The real problem with it as far as I was concerned was that it had no phone. I went up there with him right after he bought it and was immediately unhappy about no phone. The nearest neighbor was five miles away across the lake and along a miserable dirt road; going by boat to that neighbor was not much better. I made him promise me he would never go up there alone. I have no interest in fishing but I told him if he couldn't get a fishing buddy to go with him I would go. He bought the place in June. I went up with him one weekend in June and then over the 4th of July. I didn't go up there again until that last weekend in August. The other times he went he told me he had one or the other of the fellows as a fishing buddy. That last weekend I didn't have anything planned and didn't feel like hanging around the house alone so I told him I wanted to go up with him. I told him he didn't have to cancel with his buddy that I would go up and cook for them. He wouldn't hear of that. He said it would be a good chance for us to spend the weekend together without any distractions, that he had been wanting to talk me about something important anyway and this would be a good opportunity. He called his buddy and cancelled the arrangements he had made. I was thinking he wanted to talk me about Louise. I thought, 'Well, so be it.'

"The day we went up was a beautiful one and it was a lovely drive but we didn't have much to say to each other. I guess he was thinking what he would say to me and I was thinking the same thing and how I would respond.

"When we got there we brought in the supplies and then he went out to check the boat and I checked the cabin. In one of the clothes hampers I found some lingerie that didn't belong to me. 'Louise's', I thought. I wondered if she had done it on purpose so he would have to tell me or if it was an accident. I left it there and didn't say anything, but I was seething. I thought I had been so good to him ever since Annie died. I catered to him just like in the old days, and nursed him through those terrible days after the heart attack. Now he was spending those quiet weekends making love to Louise, his fishing buddy. Well, we had dinner that night and went to bed early. We were both very tired and there was little talking. The next morning we were up early. Tom was going to get some fishing in before breakfast and went down to get the boat into the water. Then I heard him calling. He sounded like he was in trouble and I ran. He was lying by the boat holding his chest. He told me he left his medicine in the car. I ran up and got it but it didn't help. I knew I had to get him to a hospital but that would be a good two hour trip to a little hospital that probably didn't have decent facilities anyway. And I thought just moving him might be too much for him. But I couldn't leave him where he was. I thought I would just have to take the chance of moving him. Once I got him out of the woods I knew there was a police station where I might get some help and there was a volunteer fire department somewhere along the line. I drove the car down as close as I could to where he was lying. He was unable to help himself at all but I was able to drag him to the car and little by little drag him into it. I didn't have the strength to get him onto the back seat but I did manage to push and pull him all the way in on the floor, all crunched up. He looked awful. He was blue and breathing hard. There was a little froth at his mouth. He looked like he wasn't even conscious. Somehow I got out of the woods and on to the paved road. I was driving pretty fast but there were no cops out to stop me. I came to a volunteer fire station first and pulled in there. Fortunately it was the volunteer ambulance service too and there were two men there. They took a look at Tom and pulled him out of the car. They examined him for a couple of minutes then said he was gone and it was too late to try to resuscitate him. I had told them I hadn't heard him breathe for the last ten minutes. I knew he was dead.

"Well, that's how it happened.

"That was two months ago and I'm just now beginning to pick up the pieces. I never did meet Louise. She sent a condolence card but didn't call. She may have been at the funeral, I may even have seen her, but there were many people there I didn't know. In any event that's one piece of business that's finished.

"I still have one piece of unfinished business. Maybe someday I'll tell you about it. I know you've always told me how important it is not to leave unfinished business, but I'm not quite ready yet to finish this one.

"Thanks for reading this, I feel like I've been talking to you.

Sincerely,
Marge"

Dr. Charles sat for a minute after reading the letter then picked it up and put it into Marge's file. He thought, "She must have been left pretty well off. She'll get along. It won't be too long, she'll be married again. She's an attractive woman and probably a very desirable sex partner. She'll get a man." He wondered about Louise but shrugged it off recognizing that was one of the many questions he would not be able to answer. That got him thinking about unanswered questions. He figured it must be part of a doctor's training somewhere along the line to learn to deal complacently with unanswered questions; they're faced with so many of them. "Well," he thought, "it's time to go home and I'm ready."

One morning in April of the following year Jane had a message for Dr. Charles. When he had time to talk he was to call Mrs. Marge Stewart at her suite in the Plaza Hotel. He didn't know any Mrs. Stewart who would be in a suite at the Plaza Hotel, but the name Marge struck a bell. "It must be Marge Livesy," he thought, "it didn't take her long to get a man, and he must be a good one. A suite at the Plaza Hotel is not bad living."

It was a busy day and the doctor didn't have time to talk leisurely until he was finished in the office late afternoon. When his charts were all cleaned up he leaned back and put in the call to Mrs. Stewart.

A woman picked up the phone and said, "Hello."

Dr. Charles recognized her voice. "Hello, Marge", he said.

"Dr. Charles! I'm so glad to hear your voice. Thanks for calling back. This is a good time to talk too. Randy is in taking a nap before we go out. I can hear him quietly snoring." She had been talking rapidly and paused now to take a breath. She went on without waiting for any comments from the doctor. "This seems just like when I used to come into the office the last patient of the day so I could talk. Well, I'm

274

going to talk now if its okay with you. I rehearsed what I want to say and I want to get it all out before Randy wakes up. Okay?"

Dr. Charles smiled, settled back and said, "Okay."

Marge began, "First, I'll tell you what you already know, I'm married again. Dr. Charles, he's a wonderful guy. He's fifteen years older than I am and retired. He was a banker and he doesn't have to work. His wife died about two years ago. They had no family. And Dr. Charles, he's crazy about me. Anything I want I can have. It's so different. HE caters to ME. Boy!" She paused a minute to enjoy that thought then continued, "We're on our honeymoon. We're taking a trip around the world, starting from New York and ending in New York. We have no timetable. If we find a place in France or Spain or Italy or anywhere we'll stay there for as long as we like it. We could even buy a place anywhere and settle in."

Marge stopped. She changed gears then went on with a lower pitch to her voice. "I've avoided what I really called you for. I have a piece of unfinished business I'm going to finish before we leave tomorrow. Then it will be a permanent 'good-bye' Dr. Charles. I couldn't write you this because after I tell you I'll deny I ever said it. But for me the business will be finished."

Dr. Charles raised his eyebrows and wondered but said nothing.

Marge didn't stop. "You remember when Annie got sick at the end. You told me what to do and what you expected would happen. You wanted me to call you every day so you could make sure she was getting better as you expected she would. Well, I called you every day and told you what you expected to hear. But that isn't what happened. I never gave her the medicine and she didn't die suddenly. She died over the several days she was supposed to be getting better and she never knew the difference.

"Don't say anything, I'm not finished.

"Now I'm going to tell you about Tom. It wasn't like I wrote you, though part of it was. What happened was this: when we got there that afternoon, like I wrote you, he went down to look at the boat and I went into the cabin to get things in order. I found the lingerie and stood there holding that bikini and burning up when I heard him call. I ran down to him still holding the bikini. He said, 'Run up and get me the pills I put under my tongue, hurry!' He was on the ground holding his chest and I just stood there looking down at him. 'What are you waiting for?' he gasped. 'Here,' I said, 'put this under your tongue,' and I threw the bikini in his face. I walked slowly back up to the cabin thinking what I should do. I stopped and took the keys out of the car before I went inside and closed the door. I'm not one to interfere with nature. I figured if he were having a bad attack I couldn't save him anyway and if it were not a bad one he'd get over it. Well, he must have gotten a little better because in about a half hour I heard the car door slam. I was glad I had taken the keys out. I didn't hear anymore. After about another half hour I either got chicken or curious and went out to see what was going on. He had gotten into the back seat apparently to get his medicine out of his coat pocket and had collapsed on the floor. I wrote you what he looked like there. I figured then he would never make it. I didn't want to leave him there all night. I thought he might die and rigor mortis would set in and then there might be questions. I cleaned up the cabin, repacked everything, locked up and took off. By then he was in a coma and gasping for breath. I drove carefully and after a while I didn't hear him breathing any more. The rest was like I wrote you.

"Don't say anything, Dr. Charles. The unfinished business is finished. Good-bye."

Marge hung up.

VOODOO CURSE

I was in my midfifties when it happened. I had a lucrative profession, was my own boss, worked at my own sweet pace with time off for as long as I wanted whenever I wanted, and had practically no stress from my work. I thoroughly enjoyed every minute of it. I was a master craftsman and my craft was in much demand. I reconditioned violins of great value and made violins of lesser value. I am a violinist of sorts. I reached my peak as the concermaster of a small city symphony orchestra. I decided in my early forties that I was a better craftsman than a violinist and enjoyed it more—much more. After a while I also had the additional perk of playing on instruments I previously would never have been able to touch. Some of my customers were well known museums so you can appreciate the reputation I had developed. I had a loving wife, a young son, a somewhat younger daughter, a well behaved spaniel, and a nice home.

Well, that's the way it was but it all changed when it happened. I'm going to tell you what happened, and how it was brought about.

I met Carl while I was playing in the symphony. He's a good violinist, good enough that he's able to make a living at it, playing in the orchestra, in chamber music ensembles, even in a gypsy restaurant. Carl owns a good violin, no masterpiece but a very decent instrument. He brought it to me periodically to keep it in good shape. As my fee got higher with my reputation, I continunued to take care of Carl's violin at the price he could afford. He knew he wasn't paying the full freight. One day when he picked up his violin I had worked on, he paid what I asked and told me he had something extra for me and put down ten lottery tickets along with his check. "These are for you", he said, "as long as you're not superstitious."

"I'm not superstitious", I said, "but how come?"

"I've got two big faults", said Carl, "one is being superstitious, and the other is being addicted to gambling. Well, maybe you know for the past ten years or so I've been living with a young Haitian woman. We're not married but the past few years she's been acting like we are. She doesn't mind that I'm superstitious but she's become very angry at my gambling. When she found these lottery tickets she exploded. 'I'm going to curse these tickets', she said, 'so you better throw them away'. She was brought up in Haiti, the daughter of a witch doctor, and well versed in voodoo. She bought a live chicken and somehow used it in some sort of bloody ceremony with the tickets and put a curse on them to cause misfortune if they were used.

"As I said I'm superstitious so I won't use them. If you're not superstitious I suppose the curse won't work so you can have them."

I figured the worst that could happen is that I wouldn't win anything so I took them and thanked Carl. There was an extra big lottery coming up so I guess that's why he bought ten tickets.

Doubtless, you've already guessed what happened. One of those tickets hit the big one. The first thing I did was call my lawyer. I arranged for him to bring the ticket in and I insisted I not be identified. We didn't know how many others had the same number so we didn't yet know the value. The next thing I did was call Carl.

"Carl, one of your tickets hit for some money; I want to split it with you."

"Don, I've been thinking about those tickets; I'm sorry I gave them to you. Do me a favor, don't turn in that winning ticket. The money you get will be cursed."

"Ask your woman what it would cost to remove the curse."

"I've already asked her about removing it. She said it can't be done for any amount of money."

"Okay, how much money would it take for you to overcome your superstition?"

"Money won't do it, Don. Look, if you cash in that ticket, you do it at your own risk. I don't want any part of it. I wish you wouldn't ever mention those tickets again. I feel guilty about the whole business."

Well, I tell myself, I tried to split it with him. I didn't dare tell him I won the jackpot because then word would get out all over. I had to tell my wife, Kate. That night after the kids were in bed I decided that was the time.

"Kate, I have to talk to you and what I say you must keep strictly confidential, that means you tell no one, not your closest relative, not your very best friend. If you think you can't keep this absolutely secret tell me now and that will be the end of it."

"Why do you have to tell me?"

"I don't have to. However, I foresee some problems associated with it may arise later and I think you will want some say in how those problems should be solved."

"Well, why don't you wait until the problems arise and then tell me?"

"I think the problems are practically here already."

"It appears you want to talk to me about some problems you're having."

"Okay, I want to talk to you about some problems we're facing but the confidentialiy issue remains the same. Will you keep what I tell you in the very strict confidence I told you about?"

"What if I told you I don't think I could do that?"

"Then I'll do the best I can to solve the problems myself."

"I think that would be best. I trust you to do what's right and I don't want to be burdened with secrets."

Well, I tell myself I tried to tell her about it. I was just as well pleased to handle it myself but I realized I needed her input about some aspects of disbursing the funds. After a few days I learned I would receive after taxes thirty-four million dollars. That is what I elected to take in one lump sum. That same day I spoke to my wife again.

"Kate, I want to talk to you about what's been going on that is not so strictly confidential. You must be aware I've been busy with some outside activities. The reason is I've unexpectedly come into some money and I've been consulting with a law firm."

"How much money?"

"That's confidential."

"Why must it be confidential?"

"Do you want to change your mind about maintaining strict confidentiality?"

"No, I won't change my mind about that. Can you tell me if it's a large amount?"

"It's large for me. Bill Gates wouldn't consider it worth a mention. Anyway, until I get some things settled I'm going to reduce the hours I spend in my workshop. Don't be worried if you find I'm not around so much, it's not another woman. It's just money. Also I would like you to make out a wish list, all the things you wished you had but felt we couldn't afford. I want to spend some of this money before it takes over my life. We'll go over the list and I'll tell you what will be doable."

I didn't want the money to take over my life but after a few weeks I found it was. I became consumed with decisions about what to do with so much money. Finally, I decided I would take out enough for the family and donate the rest to some Foundation. I decided I would set up a trust for Kate and each of the children but couldn't arrive at a figure. I wanted to give the kids enough but not so much that it would stifle their ambition. I thought Kate should have a say in this but if I mentioned I had in mind somewhere between one to three million for each trust she would go into shock. Everything on her wish list had been approved but that whole business came to less than a hundred thousand. She felt that was a fortune and I suspect she thought it represented the bulk of the money I had come into.

Without any good reason I decided on two million dollars for each child and Kate in the form of trusts, and two million for myself which I invested with the help of a financial advisor. Kate's trust was in her name but I had her sign a power of attorney for me to act in her name. I told her that was the rest of the money I had come into. She asked no questions. This left about 225 million to dispose of. I researched foundations over a couple of weeks but got so frustrated with all this money to dispose of that I arranged with my lawyers to divide it among three foundations as anonymous gifts.

When everything was done: the money all donated or invested, the lawyers paid, the financial advisors paid, and Carl offered a share, I figured it took three months out of my life and added three years to the sum total of my life's stresses. I'm not superstitious but if I were I thought that might satisfy the curse. Anyway I began to resume the life that had been so suddenly disrupted.

It didn't take a week before I realized I couldn't do it. I began turning down work that before I would have taken. It struck me like an epiphany that some of the work I had been doing was not for the love of the work but because I needed the income. I realized I truly loved working on the masterpiece violins and making violins de novo. All the rest was motivated not by love but by money.

I spent almost as much time in my workshop as before but it was all time spent on what I loved to do. I say, "almost" because I did take more time off to be with my kids and with my wife when they wanted me.

Other things slowly changed. We never lived extravagantly but enjoyed the details of comfortable living. Now we didn't deny ourselves anything that might appear on our wish list. Before Carl's voodoo such a wish would just stay on the list, usually after a while to die of neglect. Today we keep our wishes moderate and none ever die of apathy.

We lead a good life now, better than ever. I believe because of Carl's superstition his woman's voodoo curse worked for him, he gave away the winning ticket.

For me the curse was a blessing.

I'm mindful of an old proverb about an ill wind.

THE WILL

My answering machine had a message from a lawyer's office. Right away I didn't feel good. I never liked messages from lawyers and I don't think I ever will, I always feel threatened when I get one. I thought if I didn't return the call maybe he wouldn't call again, but I knew that wasn't realistic. Besides I was curious about it. So I called the office.

Surprise! I was mentioned in Ida's will and would I please come to the office on Wednesday, that was in two days, at 2:00 P.M. at which time the will would be read. Wow! I had wondered whether Ida would remember me but I never really expected anything.

Ida had died just a couple of weeks before. She was a lady whom I had known only for the six months before she died. It happened this way. I am a volunteer for hospice which is an organization which takes care of people who are terminally ill. Where possible we keep them at home but to do that there must be someone who will act as caretaker. Anyway, I had finished a case a couple of weeks before I got the call that they would like me to take another. Usually a longer hiatus between cases is preferred but this one was special, it was a woman who specifically asked for a man. I had never worked with a woman before but if that's what she wanted I was willing. I asked if her caretaker was her husband and was told she was a widow and her caretaker was her husband's niece who had come to take care of her.

I found the house in an exclusive neighborhood into which it fitted as the prototype. On my first visit Kate, the niece, let me in. She was an attractive young woman in her late twenties, and I noticed was wearing a wedding band. She led me into the living room and introduced me to Ida. Ida was a little woman in her early seventies. She was sitting in a big easy chair which seemed about to envelop her. She showed evidence of considerable weight loss and weakness but appeared relaxed and in no discomfort. From experience with many other hospice patients I estimated Ida had about four months left to her. It seemed to me that Kate and Ida genuinely liked each other. I explained what I could do as a volunteer: do the shopping, be a handyman for the house, act as a sitter to give Kate some respite, and whatever else they thought I might be helpful with. I told them they could call me anytime.

Ida said she was told I had been trained to take care of a woman's physical needs and wanted me to verify that. She said she preferred a man to talk to and thought that's what I would be doing mostly but she wanted to make sure that if she had a bowel or bladder "accident" that I could take care of it. I assured her I could and that it would be no problem for either of us. She smiled and said, "I like you already. I'm sure we'll get along famously."

Ida was right, we did get along well. I became fond of her and I believe she began to look upon me as a son. I spent five afternoons a week with her because that's the way she wanted it; she would send Kate out and tell her to get some respite. She insisted I tell her all about myself and then she began to tell me about herself. One Friday she started, "I have no children and I was an only child", she said, "so I have no nephews or nieces. I have some cousins somewhere but we've never been in touch with each other so I have no interest in them. I consider myself as having no family. My husband had one sister and Kate is her daughter. My sister-in-law married a bum who never made a living and eventually she divorced him. Kate spent a lot of time with us and we promised to pay for her education. My husband looked upon her as his own child.

Kate's mother died when she was a freshman in college so she came to live with us when school was not in session. In her sophomore year she eloped with a man whom we only met after the fact. It appeared to us he was an alcoholic, and we were devastated. My husband was so upset that he made a new will in which Kate, who eventually would have had everything, got nothing. Everything was left to me and I would dispose of it as I saw fit. My husband died the following year.

"I continued giving Kate money until she graduated college. She had no desire to go to graduate school and moved to another state where her husband had a job as a traveling salesman. She took a job in a law office.

"That was five years ago. We kept in contact by letter and phone. When she learned I had terminal cancer she said she wanted to come and take care of me. When I asked about her husband she said she would come alone and we would then talk about him.

"She came three months ago. I was able to take care of myself then but I knew I wouldn't be able to for long. I don't need Kate to take care of me and I don't need hospice. I'm a very wealthy woman, I can hire all the help I need. But I don't want hired help. I want people to care for me like you and Kate who are not doing it for the money—although I'm not sure about Kate. I like to believe she's here because she loves me so I don't want to consider other possibilities.

"She told me about her husband, Pete. He is an alcoholic, what is called a 'periodic alcoholic.' He will stay sober for weeks and then go out on a binge that may last from a long weekend to a week. During a binge he may not come home at all or if he does it will be to sleep and clean up then take off again. Kate has never seen him real drunk, just hungover and sullen. Those times he won't talk and won't listen to her talk, but he's never been abusive. When the binge is over he'll be full of remorse but claims he has no control over it. He says some people are homos and some are alcoholic, and neither can help it. He says it's a constitutional defect and refuses to take any treatment. He says nothing can help him. He told Kate she's going to have to accept him the way he is, but if she can't tolerate his behavior he won't stand in the way of a divorce.

"Kate isn't happy with him but so far has not wanted to divorce him. He's an excellent salesman and even with his binges has been able to make a modest living though not enough to save anything. Kate thinks if he got a fresh start someplace she might be able to persuade him to get some treatment. She wants me to let him come and live here. I'm thinking about it. I'll have the answer in a few days—I have to, time is short. Pete is coming tonight for the weekend so when I see you again on Monday I'll know what I have to do."

That Monday when Kate opened the door she was all dressed to go out. "Ida insisted that I leave as soon as you get here," she said, "she's anxious to talk to you alone and I think it's about me. If she gives you the chance please put in a good word for me." And she was gone.

Ida gave me a big smile when I walked into her room.

Her big chair was next to her bed now so she could make the transfer from bed to chair with just two steps. She no longer went into the living room. "I'm glad you're always prompt," she said, "I get so impatient whenever I have to wait. I feel my life ticking away with the clock. I made Kate shut off the chimes on my beautiful old grandfather clock, I couldn't stand to listen to the funeral music of the quarter hours."

She smiled again, "Down to business", she said with more enthusiasm than I had seen her display before. "Peter was here over the weekend, sober, and he and I reached an agreement. This was done between the two of us. Kate will learn about it later. I had made my decision Friday night and had made the arrangements necessary to implement it. I made a call to Australia to do it and that was fun. My husband had a very good friend in Sidney and he's the one I spoke to. We must have talked forty minutes, I can't wait to see my phone bill.

"When I met with Peter on Saturday everything was set in my mind. The only thing to settle was the price, I was confident Peter could be bought but I didn't know how much he thought he was worth. I had decided I would make him a generous offer: take it or leave it. If he decided to leave it he would not come here to live. I gave him my proposition and then took a nap for an hour. I told him he would have to give me his decision when I got up from my nap. He did. Sunday morning I had him write out my instructions and a check for himself. I signed the check and he took off. He told Kate I had given him a confidential mission and that he would be in touch with her. He was in very good spirits so Kate did not get upset. This morning I called my lawyer. He will be over this evening to put the agreement in legal terms and to make out a new will for me. I told Peter to come back next Friday to meet my lawyer and sign the papers. I want you to be here too, two o'clock, can you make it?"

I told her I could. She seemed relieved and very pleased with herself.

The next Friday, promptly at two, Ida, her lawyer, Peter, and I met in Ida's room. Kate was excluded. The lawyer read the contract that he had drawn up. It was a strange one. Peter was to institute divorce proceedings through Ida's lawyer and then immediately leave for Australia. He was to remain in Australia until the divorce was finalized. He was to receive $10,000 when he left and $5,000 each month until the final divorce decree at which time he would receive the balance of $100,000. If he remarried and stayed with his wife for five years he was to receive another $25,000. The $125,000 was put in escrow. All transactions in Australia were to be carried on through Ida's friend in Sidney or someone he designated. The terms of the contract were the same that Peter had already agreed to verbally.

While he was reading it over Ida asked me if I had any suggestions. I had none and Peter immediately signed it. He quickly read the divorce papers the lawyer had prepared and signed them. He said he was leaving it up to Kate to make any arrangements she pleased about their rented house and all its contents. He said he was flying out in two days and wanted nothing he was leaving behind. He said he was going to tell Kate that he was leaving on another confidential trip for Ida and would be in touch. He planned to say his good-byes by mail. Peter and I were then excused and Ida and her lawyer went to work on her will.

Even though the next day was a Saturday, Ida asked me to come and talk to her so I did. She said, "I've been thinking about how to tell Kate what has happened. The easiest way would be to tell her that the divorce was Peter's idea but that I did send him to Australia on some unfinished business with my husband's friend there. I will suggest to her to see my lawyer to expedite the divorce proceedings, and to move here with me permanently. I'm uneasy about not telling the truth but in this instance it seems to me it would not be a good idea. What do you think?"

I told her I shared her discomfort but at this point agreed there was no better way of doing it.

The next day Kate opened the door for me and immediately went out without saying a word. She was obviously upset but I couldn't tell what she was feeling. Ida said she had told her just what we had decided and that she had become very angry but had agreed to talk to the lawyer.

A few days later, as I was leaving, Kate cornered me. She was calm but somber, not her usual cheerful, smiling self. She said, "I know you were privy to what went on between Pete and Ida. I want you to tell me." I told her I considered what took place there was confidential and if she wanted to know what happened she should ask Ida. She said, "You're not going to tell me. Okay, but I'm going to ask you again after Ida is gone and I want an answer, I'm entitled."

Ida saw her lawyer on several occasions over the next two weeks. One day I came in just as he was leaving. Ida told me that the terms of the will had finally been settled the way she wanted it and that she had just signed it. "Now," she said, "I'm just waiting to hear from my friend in Sidney. My lawyer has written to him and everything is set. I had originally planned to wait for the divorce to be final but now I've decided that may take too long. I'm not going to wait for that."

It appeared she was right. She was growing weaker every day and I was getting concerned that I wouldn't be with her when she died. I thought she would want that and one day I asked her if she would like me to move in temporarily to spend more time with her. She said, "Thank you for the offer. You think I would like you to hold my hand when I die. That won't be necessary. My husband will be holding my hand."

I think it must have been that way, two days after she had heard from Sidney, Australia.

The counseling and supportive services of hospice are available to the family and significant others for a year following the death of the patient. Kate was well aware of this and at the funeral asked me if I would call on her the following day. I asked her where she was going after the funeral and she said she was being taken back home and expected she would have a houseful of old friends of Ida who would stock up her refrigerator and offer their help for any future problems. We settled for the following afternoon, the day before the will was to be read.

Kate let me in with a wan smile. "Thanks for coming," she said, "I'm going to need lots of support, I feel overwhelmed, and you're the only one in this city I can call on." We went into the living room and sat down. "I can cope with Ida's death," she went on, "it was expected and I had plenty of time to work through what grief I felt, but the divorce is something else. I'm crushed by that. I can only surmise that he thought he was freeing me of an albotross around my neck. He was carrying a heavy load of guilt about his drinking and he may have thought this would ease him of some of it. What I can't understand is that he never spoke to me about it. I suspect he thought I would talk him out of it. He knew I was crazy in love with him—tell me, did he really go to Australia?"

"Yes, he really did."

"Do you know where he is?"

"He was sent to Sidney but I don't know his address. I'm sure you'll hear from him."

"What makes you so sure?"

"He said he would write you and I believed him."

"He was sober when you met him. What did you think of him?"

"I thought he was an intelligent, personable young man. I would never have suspected he was an alcoholic."

"If he had stayed with me I think I could have helped him break his addiction. Do you think I should fight the divorce?"

"I don't know. I would want to wait to see what he writes you before I give an opinion."

"All right, now tell me what happened at that meeting between Ida and Pete. Ida's gone and doesn't care about confidentiality anymore."

"I'm sorry, Kate, Ida wanted it kept confidential even after she would no longer be here. Any information you get is going to have to come from Peter."

"I hope he writes, I'm not as confident as you are."

I spent the rest of the afternoon with Kate and then took her out to dinner. We learned something of each other. She asked how I happened to be a volunteer for hospice and I told her how much I appreciated the service my wife had got in her terminal illness and felt this was a way to repay the debt. I told her I had a son about her age a half a continent away. She told me what a miserable childhood she had had. She had never known affection from her father and though her uncle was generous with his money he was stingy with affection. Peter was the first man who showed real affection for her and she was so hungry for it she seduced him into marriage. It was not until a few years afterwords that she realized she had been attracted to him as the father she had never had. But that made no difference, the intensity of her love did not diminish. She didn't know if she could ever stop loving him.

At the reading of the will there were representatives of several charitable organizations including hospice, and Kate and I. As the will was read it quickly became evident that Ida had decided to be in charge even after she died. She had named me executor and I could see enough trouble ahead to last me the rest of my life. Ida left me outright $100,000 and I was to receive all the legal fees due an executor of an estate. Two trusts were set up: one for Kate and one for the various charities. Kate could live in the house for as long as she wished. All expenses, including any help she felt was necessary and which was approved by the executor, would be paid by the estate. Kate was to receive $5,000 per month until such time as she remarried. There were no exclusions as to the man she married except that the executor had to approve. After the approved marriage she would receive $10,000 per month for two years. After two years if the executor considered the marriage stable she would receive one million dollars and thereafter the income from both trusts after estate expenses had been paid. If Kate had children her trust would be distributed to the children upon her death. If there were no children it would be added to the charitable trust and distributed at the time of her death. If Kate divorced her second husband and there were no children she would revert to $5,000 per month and the process would start over. If she had children additional funds would be made available for them at the discretion of the executor until her death when the trust would be distributed to them.

There were many other provisions dealing with every possible circumstance that could be imagined, mainly concerning Kate. It was evident Ida didn't trust Kate's judgment and through her will intended to exert some control over her behavior.

The value of the estate was listed as, "in excess of ten million dollars." Other than that I had no idea of the real value.

After the reading was completed I arranged to meet with the lawyer on the following day to learn what my duties as executor were, and invited Kate out for dinner. Kate was in a state of shock and seething with anger; I was in shock and euphoric. I knew if I didn't want the responsibilities of executor I could resign and still receive more money than I had ever expected to accumulate.

When I asked Kate if she would go to dinner with me she said, "Yes, thank you." She didn't say another word until after she had gotten into my car and we had driven about three blocks. She turned to me and said, "Did you know anything about that will?"

"No, I didn't. Ida never confided in me about that. She spoke only with her lawyer. I had no idea she was so wealthy, and did not expect to be mentioned in it. I never dreamed she would want me to be executor."

"What do you think of it?"

"First, surprise that I'm in it; second, appreciation that Ida maintained her rigidity and determination to the end.— what do you think?"

"I assume you can see I'm boiling. I think I'm having a unique experience: a challenge from a dead woman. I'm convinced she had more than a little to do with Pete going away. If I don't hear from him, she will have won. If I do hear from him it's going to be a battle. Will you help me?"

"I'm committed to giving you support for a year."

"Thank you." She leaned over and gave me a kiss on the cheek as I was driving. I wondered if she were going to try to seduce me. I thought she wouldn't have any difficulty.

Both Kate and I saw the lawyer on several occasions and over a few weeks bank accounts were set up and the financial arrangements were functioning properly. Kate went back to the home she had shared with Peter and cleaned out everything. She had decided nothing was worth saving. When she returned from that trip she invited me to her home for dinner.

She had let her housekeeper go and had made the meal herself. It was delicious. I thought about her attachment to a father figure and wondered if I represented one. After dinner she told me she needed some advice.

"I've heard from Peter," she said, "and I don't know what to make of his letter. I felt angry enough after I got it to get rid of every last item in the home we had shared."

I said nothing so she went on, "He wrote that Ida had made him an offer that he couldn't refuse. He wrote that he thought I would be better off without him, that he had enjoyed the years we had together but that the time had come for each of us to start a new life. There was a return address on the envelope but he didn't invite me to write him.—Now, I want you to tell me, is Pete lying or did Ida lie?"

"You're going to have to get that information from Peter."

"Oviously, he'll say he told the truth."

"Let him send you a copy of the contract. You can make your own decision."

"I'll do that, and I'll also ask him if he still loves me. He told me many times he would love me 'til he died."

"And you told him you would love him 'til you died?"

"Yes."

"Is that still true?"

"I think so."

"Does that mean you won't marry again?"

"No. I want to talk to you about that. The man I marry has to meet with your approval. How about helping me find him."

"I don't think that will be difficult. You're an attractive woman and an heiress."

"I think it will be very difficult to find a man I would want and one who would want me after he knew why I wanted to get married.—Where will you look?"

"I have a wide circle of friends, I'll inquire. I'll also contact my son."

"Is he married?"

"No."

"Does he resemble you?"

"He's like me in many ways."

"Get him to propose. I'll marry him."

"I'll introduce him to you, but that's as far as I can go."

"That's far enough. Now tell me how to get acquainted in this town."

"The way for you to get acquainted is to give a party for charity and the charity to give it for is the local hospice. I will put you in touch with the right board member and you will soon become acquainted with some of the nicest people in town. Through them eligible young men will be found. You will also find that all the other charitable institutions in town will search you out for your support. After that one party you will be able to be a member of any charitable board you want. You will be a presence in the community, and suitors will flock to you. Such is the power of money."

"That's disgusting.—When do we start?"

"I'll call someone tomorrow."

"Good.—Now I must ask you something else, personal. Are you willing?"

"I'm willing to listen, and to oblige if I'm able." I could feel my heart begin to beat faster in anticipation.

"I hope you're able. It's been too many weeks since I had sex with Pete. I need you to make love to me. Are you able?—And willing?"

"Able, willing, and thrilled at the opportunity." I thought there could be complications but she was too enticing to turn down.

We stayed in bed late the next morning. She was more enthusiastic than I had expected. "This is the first time I made love with a man your age," she said, "I never realized there was so much to be said for experience.—I hope you'll be willing again from time to time." I assured her I would.

After I had introduced Kate to the right lady board member, events took off. Kate became a very busy young woman and was rapidly introduced to the younger generation of the society that Ida had moved in. She made no secret that she was in the midst of a divorce but that made no difference to how she was received except that everyone began looking for a suitable husband for her.

The charity party was the social event of the season, and shortly after that the divorce became final. Kate was having a wonderful time and dating frequently. Once in a while she would call me to spend a night with her. She had decided to remain chaste with her suitors until she found one she thought might make a good husband. I visited my son on a couple of occasions but he didn't come to visit me so I never introduced him to Kate. Besides, he had developed a live-in girl friend.

About a month after the divorce I got an urgent call from Kate that she needed some quick help. When I got there Kate opened the door herself. "I sent my housekeeper away," she said, "her ears are too sharp." She closed the door and before we even had a chance to sit down she said, "I got a call from Pete. He's on his way and will be here this evening. What will I do?"

"What do you want to do?"

"I don't know. Come in and sit down."

We went into the living room and sat.

"If you don't know, I can't help you."

"I really do know, but I'm afraid to hope and I'm afraid to ask."

"I'm listening."

"Okay, I hope he came here to ask me to marry him again."

"And what are you afraid to ask?"

"I'm afraid to ask you to give permission, and without your permission I'll lose everything. I don't want to lose everything."

"Are you saying that without my permission you won't marry him, even if he asks?"

"Yes, but that doesn't mean I won't live with him. You can't stop that. We can get along on five thousand a month and all expenses of the house paid.—It's even possible that someday if he gets treatment and beats his alcoholism you could give permission.—That is possible isn't it?"

"Yes, it is, Kate."

Kate jumped up, rushed over to me, kissed me, and sat in my lap. "You're a darling. I feel like making love to you right now but we don't have time."

She was right. Twenty minutes later the doorbell rang. Kate asked me to go with her to the door so the two of us opened it as a taxi drove away. Standing in the doorway was Pete and a pretty young woman. Kate was struck dumb so I invited them in and Pete introduced us to his wife. They were on their around-the-world honeymoon. The wife was the niece of Kate's uncle's friend in Sidney and a very wealthy young lady. They only stayed about forty minutes because they had a plane to catch. They both refused a drink, seems they met at an A.A. meeting.

After they left Kate said, "Dammit, dammit, dammit, Ida won. I couldn't compete with her when she was alive and I can't beat her even after she's dead.—Will you stay with me tonight?"

Of course, I did. I thought she needed some support.

COLONEL WRIGHT

I don't like reunions and I didn't plan on going to this one but my wife decided to visit her sister the same weekend this was scheduled for and I figured it would be worse to stay home alone than to go to the reunion of my wartime buddies. So I went.

Actually it didn't turn out so bad except that I kept wondering if I looked as old to them as they looked to me.

I suppose like in every reunion the ones who prospered are the ones who make a special effort to come. You rarely see any of life's failures at a reunion. So there we were, a bunch of successful old buddies reminiscing about our army days in the usual manner of selective memories.

There was one buddy I was particularly glad to see again; that was Captain Hosler, my roommate for a period of some months and the Flight Surgeon for our outfit. He came to the reunion as a practicing psychiatrist, highly successful of course.

Well, one evening we sat around the bar talking about some stupid career officers we had the misfortune to serve under at some time in our army airforce career. There were a couple of good stories and then one of the guys asked Hosler if he didn't have some experiences with career medical officers. "Yes, I did," he said and told us the following story.

"I enlisted in the Army Air Force expecting I would have no trouble becoming a Flight Surgeon. I was sent first to O.T.S., Officers Training School. My first assignment was to a Station Hospital at an airfield for Liberators, B24s. The C.O. of the hospital was a military career medical officer called Col Wright. His permanent rank was probably Major but for the duration of the war he had the temporary rank of Colonel. The work of the hospital was done by his Executive Officer. Wright apparently felt his job was to visit each ward and make sure everything was being done properly. All the medical officers in the hospital came from civilian life and all knew more medicine than Wright. I had heard from several of them that Wright was wrong most of the time. He would like to make rounds with them but after awhile they gave up trying to teach him. Sometimes he felt he had to make a suggestion and when he did the doctor he was with would turn to the nurse who was always present at rounds and tell her to make a note. That way everybody was satisfied and no harm was done. Unfortuately, I wasn't briefed about that system. One day, about two weeks after I got there and time enough to get acquainted with my patients Wright came to my ward to make rounds with me. The Executive Officer had noted my background and assigned me to the psychiatric ward. There I was, a lowly lieutenant new to the army, and the Commanding Officer came in and announced he was going to make rounds with me. When we came to Bert who was a big healthy looking guy Col Wright began to question him. Bert answered all his questions promptly and correctly and in true military fashion. Wright saw the diagnosis but probably didn't understand it, and none of the questions was medically directed . . . Of course that didn't stop Wright. He turned to me and said, "That man is a malingerer. Send him back to duty"

I said, "This man has a serious illness and cannot go back to duty."

The Colonel's face turned a deep purple. He said, "Lieutenant, I'm giving you an order.

Discharge this patient." Then he turned and marched out in a proper military manner. I did not discharge Bert. Later that day Major Gilmore came in to see me. He was the chief of the medical service and psychiatry came under the medical service. He said, "Lieutenant, you're in deep trouble and it's my fault. I didn't tell you what to do about Wright. Well, it's too late now." He looked at the chart and then spoke with Bert. He told me before he left the ward that as soon as Wright found a place to send me I would go. He apologized again for not preparing me for this. He also told me I could forget about going to school to become a Flight Surgeon, Wright tore up the application.

"Three days later I got my orders. I was sent to an aviation engineer outfit, about as far away as a doctor can get from being a flight surgeon. I got my orders in the morning. I cleared the post and got back to my ward shortly after lunch to say good-bye to the nurses. They told me Wright had been in and had sent Bert back to duty. Bert was very angry.

"Now let me tell you about Bert. He was an extremely bright guy. He went through M.I.T. on a scholarship then stayed there to teach and get his Ph.D. After he got his degree he decided teaching was not for him. He got interested in airplanes, learned to fly and stayed at the airport where he was taught to fly and worked as a mechanic, learning all the time. When war broke out he decided the place to be was in the aircorps where the advances in flying would be made. He ended up at the airfield which our station hospital served. He had figured out himself after extensive reading that he was a schizophrenic and suspected he would be classified as a paranoid schiz. He came to the hospital voluntarily because his hallucinations were becoming more troublesome than he could cope with. I think he also may have been afraid of what he might do. Before he put himself into the hospital he had worked for a lieutenant in the maintenance department. The men he worked with knew him as a quiet withdrawn· guy who was a super mechanic. Whenever anyone got stuck they would call Bert and he would quickly solve whatever problem they had. The lieutenant made him a Tech Sargent and left him pretty much alone as long as he was available to help when needed. Besides the big B24s there were a couple of A.T.s, Advanced Trainers, that were kept for the personal use of the V.I.P.s. Col. Wright was a V.I.P. and could use an A.T. when he wanted one. The other mechanics were trained for the B24s and weren't well equipped to maintain A.T.s. Bert had no problem with them so he was designated to do all the work on them. He would get a call that one of the V.I.P.s would want a plane and he would get it ready. He would know who wanted it and how far they wanted to go.

"I had kept in touch with one of the nurses who worked with me so I have a pretty good idea of what happened. Wright was in the habit of visiting a woman two hours away by air, one hour of which was over the ocean. About ten days after Bert returned to work he got a call that Wright wanted a plane for a four hour trip. He would be alone. Wright learned to fly while he was training to be a Flight Surgeon in the regular air force. He was no expert pilot but he could manage the trainer without any problems. Well, he took off with no problem—and was never heard from or seen again. The obvious conclusion was that he fell into the ocean.

"Of course there was an investigation. Bert testified that he had personally taken care of everything including putting in more than adequate fuel. The lieutenant testified he saw Bert taxi it out and fuel it up. He said Bert was the best mechanic he had. The investigating board had to conclude that Col. Wright crashed from unknown causes. I think I know the cause."

Printed in the United States
1409200006B/65